BLACK HOLE SUN

BLACK HOLE SUN

DAVID MACINNIS GILL

GREENWILLOW BOOKS

An Imprint of HarperCollinsPublishers

Black Hole Sun
Copyright © 2010 by David Macinnis Gill

The text of this book is set in 11-point Electra LH
Book design by Paul Zakris

Library of Congress Cataloging-in-Publication Data

Gill, David Macinnis, (date).
Black hole sun / by David Macinnis Gill.
p. cm.
"Greenwillow Books."
Summary: On the planet Mars, sixteen-year-old Durango and his crew of mercenaries are hired by the settlers of a mining community to protect their most valuable resource from a feral band of marauders.
ISBN 978-0-06-167304-7 (trade bdg.) — ISBN 978-0-06-167305-4 (lib. bdg.)
[1. Mars (Planet)—Fiction. 2. Science fiction.] I. Title.
PZ7.G39854Bl 2010   [Fic]—dc22   2009023050

10 11 12 13 14 CG/RRDB 10 9 8 7 6 5 4 3 2 1
First Edition

 Greenwillow Books

For Virginia, my editor

CHAPTER Ø

Outpost Fisher Four, South Pole, Mars
ANNOS MARTIS 238. 4. 5. 17:11

Now come the mousies nosing out their hole, thinks Kuhru as he wipes fresh bone marrow from his snout. Three pretty little mousies. Humans. Females. Ripe and soft and full of warm blood. He shudders. It will be ecstasy to hunt them down.

"Steady, you mongrels!" Kuhru growls at his snipers, both built like him, with gnarled manes of black hair, matted beards, their faces cratered with pox marks and battle scars. "Miss the shot, and I'll flay your miserable hides."

He tracks the girls as they scurry from the closed mine shaft onto the tundra. Ore buckets in hand, they fight the lacerating winds, oblivious to the snipers' red laser dots dancing on the backs of their heads.

A dozen meters from the shaft, they begin digging. One keeps watch.

Kuhru snarls when he sees pillars of their cold breath. Careless. Stupid. Soft. Such easy prey. "Fire, you dogs!"

Crack! Crack! Two girls drop.

Crack! The third girl falls writhing on the ice, a bullet hole in her calf.

"Not the leg!" Kuhru roars. He punishes the snipers with the bone he sucked dry, slamming the heavy knot of the hip joint against their skulls. "I said, not the leg!"

Then he bounds down the rise, his knuckles almost touching the ice. The wounded girl doesn't see Kuhru until he blots out the sun. She screams and tries to crawl away.

"Dræu!" she cries, her voice a rasping whisper. "No, no! God, please no."

Kuhru kicks her wounded leg. Laughs as she passes out, her head striking the tundra with a clack. An amusing sound. Lovely little mousie. How easily he could snap her soft neck and suck the life out of her body.

He squats and breathes her in, then notices something clutched to her chest. A shell? Here? He plucks it from her grip. It is as wide as his hands, the ridged back marked with a hexagonal pattern. He stuffs it in his belt.

"Wake up, mousie," he growls, spitting into her face. "Crawl back into your hole and tell the miners this," he says, when her eyes open. "My queen demands six for her table."

"No!" the girl screams, and pounds him with her fists. "You'll take no more from us."

"Dræu take what the Dræu want!" Kuhru backhands her,

and blood flies from her mouth. "Six children. The queen gives you ten days."

"What about . . ." she says, her voice fading, ". . . my friends?"

He stands and slings the dead little mousies over his shoulder. "The Dræu don't waste good meat."

CHAPTER 1

Above the Fossiker Line, Mars
ANNOS MARTIS 238. 4. 7. 06:01

Mars stinks. From the depths of its rock quarries to the iron-laden dirt that covers the planet's crust, it has a pungent, metallic tang that you can taste in your mouth. And it isn't just the soil. Our polluted air is poisoned with the stink of human waste and burning fuel. The terraformed oceans stink; the newborn rivers reek; as do the lakes, which spew a perpetual efflux of sulfur. The whole planet is a compost heap, intentionally designed to rot and burn endlessly so that one day, its air will be completely breathable, and its waters capable of supporting life. But tonight the stink is so powerful, I can smell it up here. Ten kilometers above the surface. Where I'm standing on a small square platform. Looking straight down.

About to wet myself.

"Oh, quit whining, Durango," Mimi tells me. "You are such a melodramatist."

"That's not even a word." I flip up the visor of my helmet.

Take a healthy sip of oxygen from a tank I brought along for the job. This high up, the atmosphere is as thin as a layer of old lady skin, and I'm seeing black spots dance before my eyes. It's bitter cold, too. Ice crystals have formed on the metal platform like it's sprayed with quartz, and my exhaled breath stretches out like a frozen rope. Forget the poetry— it's cold enough to make pashing an icicle feel like puckering up to a hot capstove.

"*Melodramatist* isn't listed in my thesaurus data bank," she says. "But I *am* capable of adaptive self-programming."

Bugger. It's bad enough having an artificial intelligence flash-cloned to my brain, now said AI tells me she's spawning new words.

"I heard that," she says.

Which comes as no surprise. Mimi hears everything. "I meant for you to hear me," I say.

"Did not."

"Did so."

"Are you arguing inanely for a reason? Or just stalling?"

"Just stalling." I peek over the edge of the elevator platform. No railing. No lifeline. One missed step, and you're a human meteoroid. My knees start shaking. Vertigo hits, and I almost pitch headlong over the edge.

"Speaking of my thesaurus data bank," Mimi pipes up. "Would you like me to look up the meaning of *chicken* as well?"

I drop to hands and knees. "I'm about to die, to cark it,

to shuffle off this mortal coil. Your talking is only going to make it happen faster."

"'Wee, sleekit, cow'rin, tim'rous beastie,'" Mimi quotes from her favorite—and my most despised—poem, written by some fossilized Earther. "'O, what a panic's in thy breastie!'"

"Why did I ever agree to this job, anyway? What kind of idiot takes a space elevator ten kilometers into the atmosphere just to jump off it? That's a rhetorical question," I forewarn Mimi. "Don't answer it."

"You're so cute when you're terrified."

I lean over the edge again. A few meters below hangs an escape pod. Beanstalk operators use them when the space elevator gets stuck. All I have to do is hop from here to the pod.

From here to the pod. Here. To the pod.

Might as well ask me to jump from here to Earth.

"You are wasting time," Mimi says. "Your acrophobia is simply a manifestation of your desire to control every aspect of your life. To defeat it, all you have to do is adjust your heart rate and breathing. And then, let go."

"Easy for you to say, Madame Freud. You don't have any hands."

"Also? You should use the mask again. My sensors are reporting a drop in blood gas levels."

"Are you accusing me of passing gas?"

"No, of being full of hot air. Now shut up and get on with it."

"Fine."

I suck down enough oxygen to saturate my lungs. Set the tank aside on the platform. Cinch the strap holding the assault rifle to my back. Then check that the small fortune hidden inside my body armor is safe. The fortune is to pay a ransom, and the rifle is for the criminal I'm hired to kill—if the fall from space doesn't kill me first.

"Cowboy," Mimi says, "you have less than one minute to begin descent protocols. Move."

"*Miststück!*" I swear. "I'm too young to die." But I flip my visor shut. Clench my eyes tight. And drop into nothing. A second later my boots hit the top of the escape pod. My stomach keeps going.

"That was very anticlimatic," Mimi says.

"Tell that to my stomach."

"Is it too young to die, too?"

"No, but it's good at passing gas."

I slide the pod's air lock open. Then drop inside. On the floor, I peek through the porthole of the second lock and get another eyeful of atmosphere. The plan calls for me to drop through the lock. Then slide down the chute. It's a bad plan. A bad, bad plan. And I'm the whacker who thought of it.

"I'm an idiot," I say aloud.

"Some truths are self-evident."

"Ha-ha."

I stare at the clear polymer tube that extends *almost* the length of the space elevator's elephantine cable. *Almost.*

Right. The *almost* part of the equation really bothers me. *Almost* can land you several kilometers from the drop zone. Maybe in a nice, quiet sand field. Or maybe in the middle of an acid-rain retention pond. Both mean a quick funeral, and I can't afford a funeral right now. The squad I command, my davos, is so flat-busted broke, we've eaten nothing but red dust in two days. It's my job to make sure we get fed, and I'm doing a lousy job of it. Which is what brought me to this.

After pausing to do a final systems check on the nano-bots that regulate my body armor, I search the night sky for a fixed point of reference. Phobos and Deimos, the twin moons, are potato-shaped lights on the horizon. In the distance is Earth, pretending to be a star, taunting us with its arrogant blue oceans. I fix my eyes on the false star, a technique for reducing nausea. If it works, I won't puke in my helmet this time.

"Mimi," I say. "Engage all communication and tracking frequencies. I'm ready for drop. On my mark, in thr—"

"Your mark calculations are incorrect," she says, then makes my foot hit the switch to activate the lock. The hatch's irises open. The bottom drops out.

"Buh-bye," Mimi says.

"Not carking funny!" I yell as I fall like a ton of ore dropping through the tube—just before the air gets sucked out of my lungs.

"Hold your breath, cowboy," Mimi says. "It's a long way to the surface."

"Gah!" My eyes flutter. Feel consciousness slipping away.

"Speed of descent is nine hundred sixty-one kilometers per hour," Mimi says. "Terminal velocity reached. Isn't this fun?"

"No!"

As strong as my symbiarmor is, it can never protect me from a terminal velocity fall. The impact will liquefy my internal organs and turn my brain to gray matter soup. I try to give a command to Mimi, instructing her to control my descent. But the g-force is too great. Throat can't form a sound. Head lolls back. Hits the tube with a thump.

That's when Mimi zaps my brain stem with a jolt of static electricity. "Wake up. One horrible, disfiguring death was enough. I do not need a repeat performance. Wake up!"

"Ouch!" Reflexively, I slam both forearms against the sides of the tube. My descent rate slows.

"Deceleration maneuver in progress," Mimi says. "Good recovery, cowboy."

My teeth chatter. "Th-thanks. F-for no-no-thing." The fabric that coats my symbiarmor sops up the friction from the tube walls, but it can't do anything about a jolt of electricity to the brain stem. My limbs jerk, and I make embarrassing grunting noises. Never again, I promise myself. No matter how much a job pays, I'm never doing a space elevator jump again.

"That's what you said last time," Mimi reminds me.

"This time," I say with absolute conviction, "I mean it."

"You said that last time, too."

I look at the bustling twin cities of Valles Martis and Nuevo Madrid, two clusters of brilliance that overpower the dim lights of their smaller neighbor, New Eden, our crumbling old capital city. Where the man I'm to kill is hiding out.

"Six seconds to impact," Mimi says. "Drop zone on the roof of New Eden Waterworks targeted and confirmed."

"I'm still going too fast!" I yell as the tube ends and I fall through low-lying clouds. Reddish gray wisps shoot by. Precip condenses on my visor. Where's a squeegee when you need one?

"Four seconds."

I tuck into dive position.

"Prepare for impact. Three. . . two. . ."

Whomp. I slam into the roof feetfirst. Instantly my symbiarmor solidifies. My body is a projectile, and I tear through the steel roof like it's foil. Cut through the iron trusses. The heavy gauge wire catwalk. The thick ductwork. And land hard on a concrete platform.

"Landing successful," Mimi says. "Symbiarmor now in normal operational mode."

"Landing successful? Says you," I subvocalize so that only she can hear me. "I hit so hard, I cracked my butt."

"I believe you had a butt crack before you landed."

"Har. Har." Bad poetry and bad jokes? I thought she was an artificial *intelligence.*

"I heard that."

"Good!" Slowly I climb out of the impact crater I made in the concrete. Dust and debris tumble from the hole in the roof. "Think anybody heard me fall?"

"There are dead people on Earth who heard you fall."

"You're exaggerating again."

"I am not programmed for exaggeration."

"You're not programmed for sarcasm, either, but that hasn't slowed you down." I catch a whiff of air and gag. "Why does it stink like a sewer in here?"

"Because it *is* a sewer in here."

"See what I mean about sarcasm?" I unholster my armalite assault weapon. Pull the half-moon–shaped clip and blow dust out of it. "Where are they?"

"Which *they* do you mean precisely?"

"The kids I came to rescue? And the man I'm supposed to kill?"

"Thank you for using nouns," she says. "That *they* is on the opposite end of the waterworks, four hundred meters to the south." Then her tone changes. "However, I am reading nine biorhythm signatures in close proximity. You need to move, cowboy. This *they* is coming fast."

She doesn't have to tell me twice.

"Move, cowboy!"

Maybe she does.

I run past a huge supply pipe and slide into the shadows as nine CorpCom shock troops slam through the doors. They carry needle cannons and wear heavy metal-plated armor that makes their movements slow and mechanical. My sym- biarmor's technology is light years ahead of theirs. But they have me outnumbered, so I don't do anything stupid—like trying to take them all out at once.

Been there. Done that. Have the head wound to show for it. "Did they see me?" I ask Mimi. Using the circuitry in my suit, she can monitor telemetry communications in the vicinity. Very helpful. It almost makes up for her smart mouth.

"No," she answers. "But they have noticed the hole."

"You think?"

"The leader just said, 'Look at that carking big hole.'"

Their leader orders two troopers to do recon on the crater. The rest fan out to search the perimeter. A pair of troopers heads toward my hiding place. Silently I click the safety off and raise my armalite. Ready to fire.

"Would you like me to signal your backup?" Mimi asks.

The pair is in my sights. Too busy chatting to spot me. Sloppy. "I can handle a couple of shock troops."

"The two approaching soldiers, yes," she says. "Statistically, however, the odds don't favor engaging all nine at once."

The troopers move like they're in slow motion, and their needle cannons can't pierce symbiarmor. Easy targets.

"May I remind you that the objective is to rescue and recover, not to engage shock troops?" Mimi pauses. "Even if you have a sixty-five percent chance of success."

"Ha. More like ninety-eight percent."

"Eighty percent."

"Ninety."

"Eighty-five is my final calculation," she says. "Take it or leave it."

"What if I leave it?"

"Then there is a fifteen percent chance your handsome face will have a third eye socket."

Ouch. "I only see one alternative." I slide my weapon into its holster. Then stand, hands raised. Walk toward the approaching squad. One of the troopers stops. His eyes widen, and his arms drop flaccidly to his sides.

"I surrender," I say, then wink. "Take me to your leader."

So what happens? Instead of just accepting a willing prisoner, the trooper's partner opens fire and sprays a round of needles into my belly.

"Whoop!" he yells. "Look at that! We caught ourselves a Regulator."

I look down at the mass of metal needles sticking out of my chest. That confounded rooter. When this is over, I'm kicking his big, fat ass.

The shock troopers surround me. The leader barks, "Come with us."

"Mimi," I say, walking slowly. "We're going to need that backup."

CHAPTER 2

New Eden, Pangea, Mars
ANNOS MARTIS 238. 4. 7. 06:26

"One of these brats is going to die," the fat man screeches at me, his tremolo voice echoing off the waterworks' concrete walls. "You have thirty seconds to choose which."

"Which what?" I ask.

"Which one is to die!"

"Oh. I wasn't sure. Your sentence structure made it a little unclear."

"Imbecile!" he roars, face turning purple. "Choose!"

I love it when the villains pitch a hissy. The fat man's name is Postule, and he's standing on a concrete peninsula that juts out over the sludge-filled retention pools. He waves a meaty hand at two children behind him. Both are in shackles, dangling by a chain over the churning cesspool of the New Eden Waterworks.

All I need is a good running start, and I can knock him straight into the vile, greenish water that fills the building with its sickeningly sweet odor.

"Not a good idea," Mimi reminds me.

Because the children are wired with C-42 explosives, and the fat man holds a tension kill switch. If he lets go, they both are dead. And I get paid nothing for the job. This is not how I planned the mission.

"'The best-laid schemes o' mice an' men gang aft a-gley,'" Mimi says.

"No literary references when I'm working." I canvass the perimeter for a landing zone. After my surrender, the troopers brought me to this room, a concrete box with walls twenty meters high and a glass skylight in the roof.

"There's a good spot for entry," I tell Mimi.

"Beat you to it," she says. "Drop coordinates transmitted to the rescue team."

"You mean *backup* team. I don't need rescuing."

"Acrophobia *and* grandiose delusions?" she says. "With your plethora of psychoses, it's a wonder I fit into your brain at all."

"Then maybe you should lose some weight."

Postule starts shouting. "I don't think you are taking me seriously, *puer.*" Once upon a time, he worked for the Bramimonde clan, one of the richest, most powerful families in the old Orthocracy. Now he kidnaps wealthy children and ransoms them back to their families. And insults his betters by calling them "little boy" in the bishop's Latin.

"He is not bluffing," Mimi urges me. "There are a number of outstanding warrants on his records. Kidnapping. Assault. Murder. Cowboy, he will kill them."

"Thanks for the clarification." I have one card up my sleeve: Postule thinks I'm alone. That's his mistake.

So I grin at the fat man, who can't figure out why I would be smiling. Then I tap my temple twice. Wince at the tingling behind my synthetic eyeball. In my field of vision, a small screen pops up. I expect to see the eager face of my partner. There's only blue-green static.

"Mimi," I ask. "Where's my backup?"

"Indeterminable," she says. "I have lost the signature."

"I hate when you say that."

"Which is it going to be?" Postule barks, losing patience. "The boy or the girl? My mood is turning foul, so be quick about it."

I yawn.

"Remove his helmet!" Postule orders one of the troopers. "I want to see his eyes when he kills the brats."

One of the troopers yanks the helmet off my head, and my dark hair falls into my face. The leader of the shock troopers reaches for my holstered armalite. "Give me that fancy gun, boy."

"Stop!" Postule bellows. "Idiot! Don't touch it. Those pistols are booby-trapped. Just leave it where it is. If he moves, rearrange that handsome face."

I grin. "Thanks for the compliment. But you're not my type."

Postule snarls. Yanks the helmet from the trooper, who brings it to him. He shines the visor with the sleeve of his red velvet robe. "Top-shelf equipment. It will fetch a fair coin on the black market." Then he gives me the up-and-down look. "Look at that—you still have acne. How old are you, boy?"

"I'm an age-eight point five," I snarl. "Old enough to do the job."

"What a coincidence." Postule laughs. Spits into my helmet. "The last Regulator I killed said the very same thing. Your helmet will sit next to his on my trophy case."

"Mimi, I take back what I said about kicking the shock trooper's ass—I'm going to kick Postule's instead."

"I will be sure to annotate your to-do list," she says.

Postule shakes the kill switch at me. "Make your choice. Or be prepared to pick up the pieces."

Where's my backup? "Mimi?"

"Indeterminable."

So I have to stall some more. Slowly I pull the purse of coin out of my symbiarmor. I toss it to Postule. "There's a bishop's ransom in there."

He picks the purse up. Presses it against his face and shudders like he's caressing a lover. "I've always wanted to be as rich as the bishop."

"You've got your coin." Which I can't let him keep. "So how about letting the children go, and I won't have to."

"Your sentence structure made it a little unclear." He smirks. "You won't have to *what*, boy?"

"To kill you. And all of your men."

Postule throws back his head. Laughs. "Kill me? Kill them?

How do you plan to do that?" He waddles forward, the deck creaking with his weight. Then he notices my left hand—the pinkie finger is missing the top two knuckles. "Look at that! You're nothing but a garbage Regulator, a *dalit.*"

I snort. Like calling me *dalit* is supposed to offend me. Ha. I've been called so many things—coward, failure, deserter, traitor, bad son—that *dalit* doesn't cause a blip on my pulse.

"You think that's funny?" Postule bellows, his jowls shaking. "Bring him here!"

The troopers drag me forward. Postule jams the kill switch against my face. Its sharp metal edges cut into my jaw. I can smell the acid from the batteries used to power the switch. I can also smell the stink of breakfast on Postule's breath, some kind of sausage spiced heavily with sage and peppers. Probably to hide the flavor of rat.

"In all," I say, "I prefer the stink of raw sewage to your halitosis."

Postule spits in my face. "I am going to teach you manners, *puer.*"

"Who taught you yours?" As the warm spittle trails down my cheeks, I resolve again that yes, I am definitely kicking his ass.

"You know what we used to do to *dalit* in New Eden?" the fat man huffs. "We gutted them. Then we strung them up on the city gates as a warning to all the Regulators who failed to make the ultimate sacrifice for their masters."

"That's not very nice of you," I say. "But kidnapping your

former master's children isn't exactly a noble occupation, is it?"

He roars, more spittle flying from the gaping maw of his mouth. Several teeth are missing. His molars are rotted shells. Though he can pinch fancy robes, he can't steal a proper dentist.

"Mimi, tell me some good news."

"The drop team is in position," Mimi says. "I'm opening a multivid link to her headset. Telemetry contact is confirmed . . . now."

Postule pushes the switch harder, cutting my lip. "I am not a nice man."

"Then we won't have any problem getting rid of you."

"We?" The fat man mocks me, looking to his right, then left. "Who's *we*?"

"Go!" I shout. Then grab the kill switch, my left hand clasped hard over Postule's paw.

With my free hand, I fire a burst of hollow point bullets at the line of shock troops. The charges explode. Four of the troopers blow back off their feet and land in the cesspool with a splash. The fifth trooper swings his needle cannon around. Takes aim at my head.

"Kill him!" Postule shouts.

I duck, using Postule as a shield. I keep one hand over the switch and press it to his fleshy throat. Then back us away from the trooper as needles sink *thwick-thwick-thwick* into the metal deck.

"Idiot!" Postule gurgles. "Don't shoot *me*! Shoot the brats instead!"

Before the shock trooper can react, the skylight above us explodes. Shards of glass cascade down, landing on the platform with a crescendo of noise.

"Ho, chief!" A Regulator in black symbiarmor looks down at me, her rappelling rig ready for descent. It's Vienne. My backup has arrived. "Permission to engage?"

"Are you kidding me? Engage! Engage!"

From the edge of the skylight, she opens fire. Four troopers fall to her armalite, which pumps out twenty rounds in the time it takes for their bodies to face plant the concrete.

"Save some for me, Vienne!" I call to her.

"Keep up, chief!" She raises the hot muzzle at the last remaining shock trooper, who starts running. Check that. Tries to run. His heavy armor keeps him from getting far.

"Stand still and let her shoot you!" I yell.

"No worries, chief," Vienne calls down. She rappels from the roof, her lithe body moving like a vennel spider on the end of its line. Midway down, she stops. Raises the armalite. Fires one round. The shock trooper goes down.

She lands and quickly shucks the rappelling harness.

Vienne is the dream soldier. Wicked sniper. Machinelike precision. Built like a ballerina and as strong as high-carbon steel. Beautiful in a way that intimidates men instead of attracting them. And she follows my orders to the letter.

She surveys the situation. Downed shock troopers. Check.

Children trussed up to a winch. Check. Her chief wrestling for a kill switch with a morbidly obese man. Check. Like it's all in a day's work. "Next order, chief?"

"We've got to free the hostages," I say, "before our chubby friend can drown them."

Postule lets a gurgle escape from his lips. His massive body begins to sag against me. "Methinks you've defeated me, Regulator," he says. His weight forces me to change my center of balance.

"Methinks you better keep a grip on that switch, fat man. Vienne! Unchain the kids."

"Affirmative!" Vienne answers.

"Stand up," I tell Postule. "Or I'll slit your throat."

He laughs. "A Regulator kill a helpless man? I think not. It's forbidden by the Tenets."

"He has got you there," Mimi says.

"But the Tenets don't say anything about not *hurting* a helpless man," I reply to Mimi, and then tell Postule, "A slit throat is more than you deserve."

"I offer you a trade," Postule says as he grunts. "I keep the ransom. You keep the brats."

"You're not in any position to negotiate."

"Then I shall have to change my position." Postule exhales, and his body goes limp. All of his weight is dead against me. I step aside and let him fall. His carcass slams onto the deck, and his hand eases open, his grip loosening.

"Cowboy!" Mimi warns me. "The switch!"

"Got it!" I grab the kill switch. The kids are safe.

"That was close," Mimi says. I'm too busy inspecting the switch to respond, so she continues. "I thought you should know—your transport will arrive in thirty-seven seconds."

"Vienne! Get the children loose. Our ride is on the way." I pick up the ransom coin and can't resist patting myself on the back. "That's what I call a job well done."

My old chief taught me three lessons: Never believe anything you hear and only half of what you see. Never go into debt because you will never get out. And never pat yourself on the back because karma will bite you in the ass.

"Job well done? Think so?" Postule says as he suddenly rolls to the edge of the platform, where he grabs another switch. A switch that I overlooked. "Say farewell to your coin, *dalit*."

Karma, I think, meet ass. I turn toward Vienne, who is unchaining the girl. "Look out!"

Too late. A trapdoor swings open. A second later a small explosive charge splits a link on the heavy chain. The force of the blast hits Vienne full in the face, and the girl slips from her grasp. The chain snaps. The girl plunges headfirst into the water, hands still shackled behind her back, and sinks like a ton of ore.

CHAPTER 3

New Eden, Pangea, Mars
ANNOS MARTIS 238. 4. 7. 06:41

"No!" I shout, as water fills the hole the girl's body made. Behind me, Postule laughs as he tries to run, his prodigious belly bouncing. There's no way to stop his escape. Vienne is still down, but I can't worry about her now—the girl comes first.

I sprint to the platform edge. "Mimi," I say. "Delay the transport."

"Beat you to it."

I rip off my boots. Then dive straight into the murk. Momentum carries me a few meters, but I know the weight of the shackles will drag the girl straight to the bottom of the cesspool. If I'm a lucky blighter, the bottom won't be very far. I swim down, down, down.

No girl. No bottom. Nothing. I am not a lucky blighter.

How many meters to the bottom? Five? Ten? The early Mars cities like New Eden were built by slave labor with no consistent planning, so the sewer system could be open or closed. Shallow or as deep as a black hole.

"A little help here, Mimi." I kick hard to propel myself deeper. "Where is the girl?"

"Indeterminable."

"I hate when you say that."

"Yes, you have told me that—"

"A thousand times."

"Eight hundred forty-three times, to be precise. But who's counting?"

"You are! Eight hundred forty-three times!"

"Well, *someone* has to remember these things."

My lungs burn. I've been below the surface maybe thirty seconds now. Visibility's zero. My only hope of saving the girl is to find the bottom fast.

"Vienne is trying to make contact," Mimi says. "Would you like me to display her feed on your aural vid?"

"I'm busy!"

"I will take that as a *no*."

I kick again, propelled by frustration. When I reach out for the next stroke, my fingers hit concrete and the thick layer of slime that covers it. The gunk burns my skin, even in the water. I blow the remaining air out of my lungs. Bubbles shoot past my face, and I immediately feel the sting of the absence of oxygen. A few more seconds of this, and I won't even be able to save myself. Where *is* she?

"Cowboy," Mimi says. "I am sensing an unusual frequency."

"What kind of—"

Then I hear it. A low, deep hum. To the right. My head snaps toward the noise. My hands comb through the slime, reaching, recoiling, searching and finding nothing, nothing, nothing. Golden spots dance before my eyes. Sound crackles in my ears. In a matter of seconds, the world is going to turn black, and my life is going to end in a massive tub of recycled excrement—it's not what Regulators would call a beautiful death.

Wait! My hand brushes something solid. The chain!

Reflexively, I grab a handful of links. Pull until the shackles are firmly in my grasp. The girl is thin, and underwater, her weight is minimal. In the murk, I can see nothing. Her limbs feel limp. I hope she's only unconscious.

"Mimi," I say, "scan her vitals."

"No heartbeat or respiration," Mimi replies. "She has expired."

Not on my watch. I slip my head between her arms. Her body drapes over my back like a human cape. The extra weight pushes us to the mucky floor, where I bend at the knees and launch upward.

Air! We break the surface, and I suck in a long breath of stinky-sweet, canned Martian air. Then flip to a sidestroke, holding the girl's head above the surface. There! A couple meters away—a ladder within reach. I grab a rung. Her weight increases as I pull her from the water. When I finally half crawl onto the platform, I lay her gently onto the concrete.

Her face is caked in crap, and her lips have a scary blue tinge. Greenish liquid pools under her body. Her black hair is matted to her face. I push it back and notice that hers is not a child's face. The girl is older—maybe two years older—than her mother claimed. Which means she's of age, not a kid. I've been lied to. Why?

"Mimi," I say, still short on breath, "scan for vitals."

"None detected," she replies after a few seconds.

"Don't even think of dying now, girl." I wipe her face clean. Clear her airway. Begin to resuscitate. The first chest compressions push only a jigger of water out of her lungs, and I switch to mouth-to-mouth. Her skin is cold. Lifeless. The only breath in her lungs is mine.

"Mimi?"

"Nothing yet, cowboy."

"Am I doing this right?" I ask.

"According to the available data, yes."

"Come on. Breathe!" I switch to CPR and count off the compressions. My shoulders ache, and my forearms burn. But I'm not going to stop. "Give me something. A pulse, a blip. Something!"

"It's been two minutes," Mimi says after my arms are numb from effort and I'm almost hyperventilating. "I still have not detected any vital signs."

"I am not. Giving up." The girl's skin is colder than ever. I count off chest compressions and scan the perimeter. Postule is long gone. So is the ransom. The whole job is fragged.

I've failed this girl and my davos. Even my father.

"Mimi," I ask reluctantly because I don't want to hear the truth—CPR isn't going to work. "Anything?"

"Nothing."

"Chief," Vienne says, coming up behind me. "May I assist?" She kneels to check the girl's pulse.

"Save your breath," I say, knowing we're defeated. "She's sucked in too much liquid."

"How much is too much?"

"A few ounces."

"That's not enough to kill her." Vienne pulls off her helmet. Runs a hand through her blond hair. "Something's not right, chief. Her color is wrong for a drowning, and her mouth smells metallic. She's been drugged."

"Drugged?" I say aloud. Then say, "Mimi?"

"The sensors in your symbiarmor aren't capable of medical diagnosis." She adds with a sniff, "I'm not a medibot."

"There's no way to tell," I say to Vienne. "Let's give her a dose of epinephrine to kick-start her heart." I unzip a pouch on my belt. I press the tube syringe against the girl's chest. Fire a button. "Five, four, three—"

"Heewack!" the girl shouts. Her eyes fly open, and she swings with both shackled hands, a punch that connects with my chin.

I land on my butt. Try to scramble to my feet, but the girl is on me too quickly. She straddles my back and swings a thin forearm across my neck. It's obvious she intends to crush my trachea.

"Geroff meh," I gasp, my face reddening. "I hepping . . . you."

The girl's answer is to squeeze tighter. Her technique is textbook. Straight out of battle school training. This is no little society girl—she's a soldier. Her mother has got a lot of explaining to do.

Vienne draws her armalite from its holster. "We're the rescue party, Miss Bramimonde. That Regulator is my chief, and he just risked his life to save yours."

She grunts. Keeps squeezing. My mouth opens like a fish that's jumped from its holding tank. "Hep . . . nee."

Vienne puts the barrel to the girl's head. "This gun is loaded with explosive bullets that leave big, nasty, infectious holes, not little pinpricks like a needle cannon. Stand down, soldier."

Something clicks. "Oh," the girl says. After untangling herself from my neck, she stands. Salutes me. "Regulator Odori-Ebi reporting for duty."

Then her knees buckle, and her eyes roll back into her head. When she pitches forward, I catch her in the crook of arm.

"Excellent grab, chief," Vienne says as I lay the girl down on the platform once again.

I'd like to think the catch is due to my prodigious strength, but it's probably because she hasn't eaten much during her weeks of captivity. "I notice you weren't in any hurry to pull her off me."

"You know the adage—what doesn't kill us makes us stronger."

Gingerly I touch my neck, where a bruise is already rising. "Funny, I don't feel stronger."

"That's because," Vienne says, patting my shoulder, her touch causing me to twitch spontaneously, "she wasn't that close to killing you."

I carry a second epi syringe to the boy and then ask Mimi to call in the transport. "Would you happen to have a fix on the fat man?"

"Postule's signature is no longer within range."

I'm not surprised. I kneel down over the boy, who has wispy black hair and a pixie face turned bluish by the pharmies. How the mighty have fallen, I think. At least we've been able to salvage something from the job. We'll take the boy and Ebi home to their mother, collect our fee, and finally get something to eat.

How old is he? An age-five? An age-six if he's petite like his sister. An age-six would be old enough to be conscripted into the CorpCom military. But this is a child of privilege. His fate will take him Offworld to a private school on the Rings, where he'll train to become management. The same fate would have awaited me. If I hadn't been trained from the day I was born to become the lord and sovereign of Mars.

"Wake up, kid," I say, and push the button on the syringe. "Destiny is waiting for you."

CHAPTER 4

Western Valles Marineris Gorge
ANNOS MARTIS 238. 4. 7. 08:08

Outpost Fisher One, formerly known as Heaven, was once the hub of Martian commerce and space travel. Before the population left the subterranean outposts to build gleaming habidome towns closer to the equator, towns that became cities that left the outposts behind. But now, Heaven is a forgotten storage bin. The Orthocracy converted its space into thousands of dusty storage bunkers full of packaged foodstuffs, bolts of unused fabric, crates of machine parts, and an infinite number of quarantined shipping containers riveted shut and welded tight to prevent the escape of the plague. The disease decimated Earth. Because of Orthocracy controls on commerce. Mars fared much better.

Today the bunkers are almost empty. The woman who emptied them takes an elevator from the surface to the bottom level. Here is where the food is kept. So are the quarantined containers. Her scavengers have already stripped the upper levels of their treasure. Fabric and spare parts for her connections with the black market. Raw materials to be bartered for transport and good favor. And now, food.

Food can buy anything. It is the rarest commodity, and even better, her crew has no use for packaged, dehydrated meals. Only blood can whet their appetites.

"Start with the last bunker," she commands a group of twenty raiders as the elevator stops and she twirls out. "Leave nothing behind. Not a scrap. Not a crumb."

She is a sliver of a young woman sporting jet black tresses that almost reach her tailbone. Ringlet curls frame a delicate, heart-shaped face with alabaster skin so fine that it seems translucent. She lifts the hem of her dress as she exits the elevator, keeping the gossamer fabric from dipping in the dusty floor. Her feet are those of a child. They are bare. As she sweeps toward the raiders, the air fills with the smell of her musky perfume, and underneath it, like a murmur, the unmistakable scent of blood.

Slowly bowing low, their long, matted hair drooping to the floor, they supplicate themselves in response and chant, "Yes, my queen."

"Dræu make such good pets," she says, watching them scamper down the long rows of padlocked bunkers. Children were born here. Grew to adulthood. Lived and died and were cremated here, their ashes strewn on the surface to aid the terraforming. They are gone now—as worthless as the dust that drifts from the decaying walls.

"Every little bit helps," the queen whispers, recalling

the mantra of the original settlers. A whole life lived in a hole in the ground. Rubbish. Sacrifice for future generations. Rubbish. The Orthocracy? Rubbish. The CorpComs? Rubbishier rubbish.

She is going to change all of that. A little more time. A few more raids.

In a few hours, she thinks, this last level will be empty. Then the true treasure hunt begins. The Dræu are hungry. A fortnight has passed since fresh meat was on the menu, and the lack of food has made them surly. Difficult to control. Dræu are splendid warriors, beautiful in their anger and drive to devour everything in their path. Wild. Furious. But like any animal kept on a tight leash, they begin to chafe and soon turn that ferocity on one another. Twice in the past two days, fights have broken out among them. One bad boy even gnawed the meat from his own fingers. He had to be punished to understand the errors of his actions.

Lost in thought, she taps her palm with an electrified prod. It is almost a meter in length when fully extended. Made of titanium. On the tip is a hard steel ball the size of an eyeball. She smiles ironically. Funny, the bad boy's punishment was to lose an eyeball. She removed it herself. With the prod. Then ate it. It was disgusting, but the lesson had to be learned. Pain is such a gifted clarifier.

Down the corridor, a group of Dræu reaches a bunker marked with a large red X.

"Leave those be," she calls. "Your queen has no interest

in spreading the plague." Unless it becomes necessary, she thinks. When one is planning to overthrow the government, one must never exclude possibilities just because they lead to a global pandemic.

Behind her, an elevator door opens. The occupant's scent is well known to her. "Kuhru," she says without turning around. "You have delicious news for your queen, no?"

"Yes, my queen," he growls, a sound that sets her nerves on end.

For a woman reared listening to the splendid melodies of Chopin, the florid operas of Mozart, and the sanguine ecstasies of Masahiro, the steel-on-glass screech of Kuhru's voice is an affront to the ears.

"Yes what?" she says, back still turned. "Details, please, Kuhru. Did you deliver my message to the occupants of Fisher Four?"

Fisher Four is the only other outpost left standing. A volcanic eruption destroyed Fisher Two a decade after it was built, and Fisher Three was closed due to flooding. However, if the Orthocracy filled Fisher One with forgotten treasure, then ipso facto, Fisher Four should be a trove as well. The only complication was the miners, a pesky group of humans who would not desert the mines, even under the threat of death.

"Yes, my queen," he says. "I delivered your message."

The queen notes a change in his voice, a higher pitch that indicates he is lying by omission. "How many did you kill? Kuhru, don't lie to me."

"Two."

"Just two?"

"There were only three humans, my queen."

"And if you had killed all three, there would be no one to deliver my message? Very good, Kuhru. Your reasoning skills are improving. Now, did you bring the leftovers to me like I commanded?"

Kuhru says nothing. She turns. Her face is calm, the alabaster skin showing no blush of anger, no signs of emotion. "You didn't!"

"The journey was long," he growls, trying to soften his voice to evoke sympathy. "My Dræu were hungry."

Her voice rises, taking on a singsong quality that almost hides the ferocity of her anger. "Your Dræu? *Your* Dræu?"

Kuhru falls to one knee. He bows so low, his broad, thick nose touches the floor. "Forgive me, my queen. I misspoke. All Dræu belong to you."

She taps the electric prod against her thigh. "Do not think a little bowing and scraping will incur my sympathies. Your queen gave you very explicit orders. One: Give the message to the miners. Two: Bring any kills back to me."

He fawns before her. "Please, my queen. Do not punish your faithful servant. I—I brought you this." From the inside of his coat he pulls a small, flat shell. The outside is dappled brown, and the pattern looks like rows of interlocked triangles. He holds it at arm's length. "Kuhru thought you would like it. It is pretty. The queen likes pretty things."

"Idiot!" she screams, and swats the shell from his hands.

It hits the concrete floor. For several seconds it spins in the dust. When it stops, the queen sees a pattern on the shell—one that should no longer exist on the planet.

She gasps and snatches it up. Takes a closer look and lays a palm on the outside of the shell. Her eyes roll into her head.

Ecstasy.

"It's fresh," she says, and smiles as if intoxicated. Inside, she *feels* intoxicated. "Kuhru, darling. Where did you find this carapace?"

"Cara—?"

"This shell! Where did you find it?"

"Took it. From the human girl that was left."

"Impossible." She cradles the empty shell to her breast, fondling it like a stuffed toy. "They are all dead. Exterminated. But this shell is fresh. And it's small. A hatchling! That can mean only one thing."

She shoves the tip of the prod into Kuhru's nostril. He squeals in pain, although he is half a meter taller and out weighs her by a hundred kilos. "Gather the raiders. You must travel to Fisher Four."

"Because of a shell?"

"No, you imbecile," she says, and twitches the prod to pull him most painfully to his feet. "Because the miners have more treasure than I ever dared dream."

CHAPTER 5

Temple District, New Eden
ANNOS MARTIS 238. 4. 7. 08:48

Returning the hostages takes us the better part of the morning. Because of the pharmies, they sleep all the way to the temple quadrant on the edge of New Eden, where we reach the Bramimonde estate.

The main house is a cruciform of metal and concrete with high windows. A bank of terraces juts out over the gardens. I grew up in a house like this. Until the CorpComs burned it to the ground as punishment for my father's crimes.

We meet three servants at the rear entrance. Two of them sweep the children away, while the third servant—a silver-haired man in a brown, plain tunic—leads us to Dame Bramimonde's inner sanctum.

"I'll collect our fee," I tell Vienne.

"Affirmative," she says. "We will rendezvous at Ares's pub afterward, no?"

"See you soon. And Vienne?"

"Yes?"

"Thanks. I couldn't have done—"

"No, chief, I failed you. I should've grabbed the girl before she fell."

"No. I missed the switch."

She raises a hand, then puts it down. Awkward movement. Awkward silence. Didn't know she had an awkward bone in her body. She moves with the kind of grace that takes your breath away if you let it. Me, I never let it, because I'm the chief, and the way a soldier in your command moves isn't something you get to notice. Our relationship is purely professional. Not that we have a *relationship* relationship. Just a professional one. That's purely professional.

"It is never the chief's fault," Vienne says.

It's *always* the chief's fault. Mimi taught me that. But arguing will only embarrass her more.

"Meet you at the pub."

"Are you sure, chief?" she asks. "Would you like backup?"

"I think I can handle an aged Orthocrat," I say, and wink.

"You incompetent idiot!" Dame Bramimonde screeches as I enter. The air in here is stuffy, and it smells of silk flowers and dust. Same for the Dame. On both counts. "How could you have made such a mess of a simple mission?"

"Nice to see you again, too, Dame," I say. Then ask Mimi to scan the room. Dame Bramimonde isn't the most trustworthy client we've had.

The Dame sits in a high-backed chair. Her face is a white

mask of powder, azurite lips, eyebrows a thin line of indigo, straightened and dyed cobalt bangs, and dozens of strings of cerulean beads woven into her hair. She is Orthocracy aristocracy, meaning that she's fluent in several languages, has exquisite taste in art, and will slit your throat if given half a chance.

"Scan is copacetic," Mimi says. "Unlike this woman's manners."

I answer the Dame's question. "The mission wasn't that simple. You left out a few facts that complicated the whole operation."

"Complicated? Ridiculous." Dame Bramimonde strokes a flat-faced cat in her lap. Its purr sounds like a series of hiccups. "I sent you to rescue my daughter and return with the ransom. Instead, you bring me that . . . that *boy*. I suppose it's my own fault, hiring *dalit* instead of professionals."

Bile rises in my throat. Right now the Dame's children are getting scrubbed clean, every nook and cranny hosed with water—real water, not the ChemAqua we commoners use. Meanwhile, I'm still covered in dried sewage. My body a walking pile of stink. Having to beg for a contracted commission. I despise Orthocrats.

"What's wrong, Regulator?" She pinches the animal on her lap. It cries out but doesn't dare move. "Cat got your tongue?"

"Nothing has my tongue."

"Then why are you still here? The stench from your person is destroying the olfactory feng shui of my home. Oh, forgive me—you don't know the definition of *olfactory*."

"You do so!" Mimi pipes in before I shush her.

"I'm waiting for the commission," I say flatly.

"We established," the Dame says, "that you didn't complete the job as directed."

"We brought back your daughter. Who, by the way, is not a kid. Why didn't you tell me she was a Regulator?"

She curls her lip. "You lost the ransom and you did not kill Postule. To think he once was my trustee."

"Postule was protected by shock troops—another minor detail you left out. He got the ransom, but we returned your son. That makes us even."

"I don't want the boy!" Her voice pitches an octave higher. "If you had returned instead with a sack full of the excrement you've wallowed in, I would be more pleased with the result."

I smile through clenched teeth. "You know, CorpCom military would be interested in a Dame who hires Regulators to do her dirty work."

"Sharing that information would be stupid."

"I've done lots of stupid things."

"That is painfully obvious." She sniffs. "What would CorpCom think of a *dalit* who does mercenary work?"

"Unattached Regulators are outside CorpCom military authority."

"Unattached? Is that what you call working for handouts? Better you had performed self-immolation when your father was disgraced."

"He wasn't disgraced—he—" I say, and instantly regret it.

Dame Bramimonde's smirk twists into a macabre grin. "Failure is its own disgrace."

"Pay me."

"Half. Or nothing."

"You're a thief."

"I'm a businesswoman." She removes a small metal case from a drawer on her console. Tosses it to me. "Here is your coin."

I feel the weight of the coin. It's not enough. She's shorted me, and I'm not going quietly. "Why just the girl? Why save her?"

"She's my heir, of course. The woman who will take over as CEO when I retire."

"She's also a battle school–trained Regulator. Why would your heiress become a Regulator?"

"A necessary evil, I assure you. The clichéd warrior CEO is *en vogue*. My daughter will make that sacrifice for the good of her family. Surely you know that as well as anyone, don't you, Durango? Or should I use your real name, Jacob Stringfellow?"

I turn my back on her. Head for the door.

"How dare you insult me in my own home! Better men have seen the gallows for less!"

In the before days, you could be put to death for disrespecting an Orthocrat. "Times have changed, Dame. Deal with it."

"Come back here!" Her screamed is followed a second later by the crash of pottery smashing against the wall. "*Dalit!*"

I'm slamming the door behind me, ready escape this mausoleum, when the Dame's servant blocks my path, darting from behind a silk azalea bush. He gestures for me to follow him to the main entry lock.

He places a finger to his lips and peeks around the corner. Crooks a finger, calling someone to join us.

"Mimi? Scan please."

"One other heartbeat, cowboy. It's Ebi."

"Ebi?" I say.

The girl we rescued is gone. In her place stands a regal young woman. Freshly scrubbed, her broad cheekbones emit a warm, cosmetic glow. She dismisses the servant and pulls me into an alcove.

"I wanted to thank you," she says. "Your davos risked your life to save us."

"All in a day's work."

She takes my hand. "If you had only rescued me, I might believe that. However, you saved my brother as well, and I know—I know that his life was not part of the contract."

I rub my head. "Any Regulator would've done the same thing in my place."

"But Mother would not have. You saved my brother's life," Ebi says, bowing. "The House of Bramimonde owes you, Regulator. I swear to repay you one day—in full measure."

CHAPTER 6

Maris Valloris, Pangea
ANNOS MARTIS 238. 4. 7. 09:01

When Postule finishes climbing the stairs to the bell tower that looks over the port city of Maris Valloris, he is wheezing, his face as red as the sun setting on the horizon. He's clutching his chest with one hand and holding the ransom to his bosom with the other. The queen waits for him. She has waited for one hour and seventeen minutes and is feeling, well, cranky. And the queen hates feeling cranky.

"You're late," she tells the fat man.

The room is lit by a high skylight. The sun's fading rays fall on the queen's robes, and she is pleased with the way the watermarking accentuates the light, highlighting the fleur du lis pattern embedded in the cloth. The walls and floor of the room are bare, examples of the clean lines the architects of Maris Valloris used throughout the whole of the city. Light and concrete. CorpCom architecture. Some like it. Most just tolerate it. The queen doesn't give a fig either way.

"Please—huff—forgive me," Postule says between gasping breaths. "There is no elevator—huff—and there are many stairs."

"Eleven thousand six hundred and seventy-five. One more step than the longest stairway on Earth. If you had read the placards along the way, you would know that. Of course, you would have kept me waiting even longer." She removes a small dagger and a boiled egg from the pockets sewn into her purple velvet robes. With the tip of the blade, she peels the shell, leaving the white untouched. "Didn't I warn you how impatient I am?"

"Yes . . . my queen. Please . . . forgive me. I have the . . . ransom." He tries to bow on one knee.

Effortlessly, she skips forward and kicks his leg out from under him. He sags to his side, then rolls onto his back.

"Breathe, you imbecile." She pulls the money from his grasp, then counts it. Carelessly, she tosses the coin aside. The loose coins scatter, making a racket that she pauses to appreciate.

She straddles the fat man and plops down on his belly.

"Oof!" he exhales.

"Oof? I'm light as a feather. You're in such terrible shape, Postule. If your connections weren't so useful to me, I would gut you and feed your entrails to the Dræu. How would you like that?"

"My queen," he groans, "I would not."

She bites the boiled egg in half. The other half, she places on Postule's lips. "Open up."

He complies, and the egg falls into his mouth.

"Chew." He does. The queen sets the razor-sharp edge of the dagger against his gullet. "Now swallow."

"Swallow?" the fat man whines. "But the knife—"

"If you love me as your queen"—she smiles mischievously—"you'll do as I ask without question. You do love me, don't you?"

"My love for you is as wide and deep as the Hellenic Sea, my queen."

Liar. "Then swallow. And don't make a peep if you feel a little prick."

With a look of wide-eyed panic, he swallows the egg. His Adam's apple bobs beneath a coating of flabby skin, and the edge of the knife opens a four-centimeter cut. Postule sucks in a breath. But doesn't cry out.

"Good boy," she says, bouncing off him. "Now I know that I can trust your loyalty. Even if I can't trust your judgment."

"My queen?"

"Your task was simple. Receive the ransom. I said nothing about trying to drown the Bramimonde children. Killing your hostages is bad for business. We have a simple formula. Take the children. Collect the ransom. Let the children go unharmed. Everyone knows this, so they pay. If we deviate from the formula, that's when doubt creeps in. Why should parents pay if their heirs are going to die anyway?"

"But, my queen, Dame Bramimonde is the one who deviated from the formula. She sent Regulators to rescue her daughter."

"Do you think I'm so stupid?" the queen snarls. "That I wouldn't know that? But they weren't real Regulators, were they? They were *dalit*, and there were only two of them. How did a squad of shock troopers fall to two *dalit*?"

"They were not damned ordinary *dalit*! One of them crashed through the roof!"

"First, don't dare curse in my presence again. Second, who would be stupid enough to crash through a roof when they could walk through the doors?"

"His name was Durango."

Of course, it was Durango. It had to be him. Fate, that foul hussy, wouldn't have it any other way. "Nevertheless, you did try to drown the hostages, so I must give you another job. Postule, my bloody friend, I think that it's time you met the Dræu."

"My queen! Please!" He clasps his hands together in prayer and crawls to her on his knees.

"Stop begging. I'll tell you when to beg. Now get up." She hooks a finger in the corner of his mouth and draws him, thrashing and moaning, to his feet. "Oh, please, Postule, do learn to tolerate a little pain. You have a very long and difficult journey ahead, and we don't want you dying from sheer terror along the way."

CHAPTER 7

East New Eden is a crowded, loud, fetid part of the city where a smart man travels with one hand on a knife and the other on his purse. Which makes it the perfect place for unattached Regulators like us to find work.

I cut through the bazaar on the way to Ares's pub. The bazaar is held in one of the oldest covered streets in New Eden, an avenue with an arched metal roof that keeps the rain off. Though most of the core city is under habidomes, the domes leak like a sieve when it rains, and in New Eden it's always raining. But at there's least something to do. Hundreds of small shops and booths line both sides of the streets. Anything you want, you can get here—clothing, linens, pots, weapons, even meat, as long as you don't mind rat on a stick.

At Ares's pub, I find Vienne outside, sitting at a table. Loitering nearby are a couple of fellow *dalit* Regulators who helped arrange my drop from the space elevator—Jenkins and Fuse.

Shorter than most, Fuse is a bit of a liar. Brash. Buzzed ash hair, thin sideburns, ears a skosh too long, one bicuspid missing, scarred lip, pointed chin, girlish hands. He's waiting for the coin I promised and chatting up Vienne to pass time.

"Come on, love. Throw a blighter a bone," he says while sliding into the chair next to her. Then slides a hand onto her knee.

"Silly boy," Mimi says.

Fuse is wearing symbiarmor. That's the only reason his elbow doesn't break when Vienne hammers it. And why his ribs don't snap when she punches them three times before he can blink.

"Hoof." He gasps for breath.

"You did ask for a bone." I pull up a chair. "Next time specify whether you want it broken or not."

"Got it." His face turns from purple back to red. Then he grins. "I like a female with spunk. Especially one with mad dinkum tai bo skill. So, love, how about I spring for your meal? Once your boss here pays me the coin he owes, that is."

"He's my chief." She cuts him a look that could ignite thermite. "Nobody is my *boss*."

"I'll take that as a *yes*." He grins wide enough to show off his missing tooth.

"Your heart rate is rising," Mimi interrupts. "Stress hormones releasing. You seem irritated."

"Your point?"

"Are you irritated?"

"Ha." Mind your business, Mimi. I'll mind mine. I set the coin on the table. "Is that how you lost that tooth? Chatting up female Regulators?"

"Not exactly." He gives me a conspiratorial wink. "Listen, if I'm treading on your flag, so to speak, fess up now and I'll give it a rest. Me and my cobber, Jenkins, we've got places to go. Right, Jenks?"

"Right. I reckon," says his friend, who is built like a transport container with legs and sports a shaved head and a mug so spotted with ancient acne scars, it looks like the surface of Deimos. "Uh. Fuse? What's it that I'm saying *right* to?"

"Don't fuss your pretty noggin about it," Fuse says.

Jenkins leans against the side of the building. His symbiarmor shirt is tied around his waist, and the sleeves of his undershirt are rolled up to reveal his pulpy biceps. He's got a square nose and a boxy chin punctuated with a goatee. Left ear pierced multiple times. Broad shoulders and chest and wears a leather jacket over his armor.

Vienne frowns at him. "It's against the Tenets to bare yourself in public. Cover up."

"If I do that"—Jenkins pulls the shirt over his bald head— "the ladies won't be able to admire my guns."

"If those are guns," Fuse teases, "then you're shooting blanks."

"Best stop vexing me before I get upset. You know what

happened last time I went feral." He opens his mouth. Taps a bicuspid corresponding with Fuse's missing one.

Fuse rolls his eyes. "One lucky punch, and the great gob thinks he's a regular pugilist. What he's not telling you duckies is that it took the blighter sixteen roundhouses to make contact, and even then, I had to do a spill over a—"

"Look," I say, exasperated, "if she lets you buy the meal, would you shut your carking yap?"

"Affirmative, chief."

"Vienne, accept his offer."

"Is that an order?"

"Yes! Accept before I have to gag him."

"That would be fun to watch."

"Vienne!"

"I accept. Reluctantly."

Fuse whoops. "Works every time."

"There's a fib," Jenkins snorts. "It's never worked before."

"Wanker!"

"Fossiker!"

"Shut up now," I warn them both. "Or the deal's off."

Fuse pantomimes a zip sealing his lips. "Sutting upth nowm."

"Thanks be to the bishop!" I pile the coin on the table. Half I give to Vienne and the other half to Fuse for hacking into the system that controls the space elevators. Annoying he may be, but when it comes to machines, he's a right clever jack. He's also a great demolitionist, from what I hear.

"Where's your cut, chief?" Fuse asks as I slide his pile across the table.

My share of the coin is already encumbered. "I spent it."

"Free with the financials, no?" Fuse says. "Spent it all on the ladies, no doubt. And a man with your looks, too. You'd think they'd be swarming about you like flies. It's the pinkie, I expect. Not many ladies have got interest in a *dalit*— Ow! My ear!"

Vienne has it folded between her thumb and index finger. I count to sixty before ordering her to let go. She gives the ear a twist for good measure and smacks him on the make of the head.

I flip an extra coin onto the table. "Vienne, get these hardworking Regulators a liter of *aqua pura*. My treat."

"Heewack!" Jenkins shouts. "Let's hit the cantina!"

"Don't hit it too hard," I call as he bounds up the steps to the cantina's front door.

"You, also. Go!" Vienne orders Fuse to follow Jenkins. He runs up the stairs, too, his heavy boots clanging on the metal treads. When he's out of earshot, she leans closer to me and puts her hands on the table. For some reason, my palms start to sweat.

"*I* know the reason your palms are sweating," Mimi chimes in.

"Stow it." I spin a coin on the table. It keeps my hands busy. "No comments from the peanut gallery."

Vienne tilts her head toward me. Her brow knits and her

lips rub together in thought, then she snatches the spinning coin. "You're not joining me? I would enjoy—"

My company?

"—not having to listen to those two idiots alone."

"Not exactly the answer you were hoping for," Mimi says.

"Hush!" I say aloud, hissing, and then clap a hand over my mouth when I realize my mistake. Vienne draws away. Damn. "Sorry, I didn't mean you! I was just . . . just thinking out loud."

"I'll go." She pushes back her chair and starts to rise.

"No!" I snag her by the wrist. "I mean, um, sorry I offended you. Didn't mean to. It's not that I wouldn't like to—" You're blowing it, Durango. "It's just that." Stop! "Think I'll stay here and enjoy the sunshine."

The sky overhead is blanketed with clouds. No sun in sight. "Sunshine. Got it. Listen, if you want to be alone, just say so." She tugs on her arm, and I realize that I'm still holding onto her, my fingers pressed against her wrist. Then I notice that I can feel her pulse, and it's beating fast.

"One hundred and two beats per minute," Mimi says. "Vienne's baseline resting heart rate is forty-nine beats per minute."

"Hush." This time, I don't say it aloud, but I do have sense enough to let go of her wrist. "Vienne, it's not that. I—"

"You don't have to lie to me, chief."

"I'm not—"

"I'm not stupid. I know what you're doing." She slaps the

coin on the table. "How much longer are you going to starve yourself? You've not eaten a full meal in weeks."

"Until I'm not hungry?" Whew, that was close. Relieved, I sigh loudly and rub my temple, which is sore. Since the AI implant surgery, it's always sore.

"Have it your way," Vienne says with a hint of frustration. "But being chief doesn't mean you've got to do everything yourself."

Not knowing how to answer that, I watch in silence as she climbs the stairs and enters Ares's pub. I spin the coin again. What was I thinking, grabbing Vienne that way? You're such an idiot, I tell myself, and when Mimi doesn't pipe in, I can tell she agrees.

I drag my chair over to the side of the building and lean back. Pull the cowling over my head and pretend to nap. It's only a couple hours since dawn, but it's been a long day already. That happens when your day starts off on a space elevator. A jump from atmosphere to surface. I still can't believe I screwed up the courage to do it.

"Me, either," Mimi says.

For once I ignore her. I'm too tired and too unsettled to bother arguing.

I'm still visualizing the tube drop when I drift off to sleep, where like always, the nightmares are waiting for me. Images of wounded troopers, disfigured bodies, my own soldiers at my feet, dying.

"Regulator," a young voice calls from outside the dream.

I awake panicked, my hands pawing the searing pain on my face. My skull is melting away, I'm sure of it, and I catch the indelible stench of digestive enzymes.

"Excuse me, Regulator," the young voice says again, and someone pushes my chair.

"What in the f—," I say, standing up with a raised fist. Then I notice a familiar aristocratic face staring up at me.

"Jean-Paul Bramimonde." The boy reaches up, offering his hand. "I have a business proposition."

Like his sister, he cleans up well. The young jack looks entirely different in a plain gray jumpsuit. His hair is coiffed, too, slicked close to the scalp, and he's had a manicure. "What're you doing in the core city, kid? Looking to get snatched again? Because there are a hundred cutthroats who'd gladly do it."

My warning doesn't even faze him. "I am here to hire you." He opens a small purse full of coin. More than his mother paid me. "I want to train to be a Regulator like you and my sister."

"Put that coin away. Now!" I clap a hand over the purse. "Anybody sees it, they won't bother with kidnapping. Just slit your throat and leave your corpse rotting in an aqueduct."

"You do not want it?" He withdraws, taken aback. "But Mother said *dalit* will do anything for money."

"Your mother doesn't know squat." My temper almost erupts before I remember that he's a kid—his mother's snotty manners aren't his fault. I put a heavy hand on his shoulder.

Turn him around and walk him to the street. "Even if I was willing to take your coin, I can't teach you. I trained to be a Regulator in battle school. Not with a master, which means I'm not allowed an acolyte."

"But—"

"It's writ in the Tenets, and a Regulator never breaks the Tenets. Now go home. Before the Dræu get you."

But he's not giving in that easily. "I do not believe in the Dræu. Nor the boogeyman." He locks his heels and glares defiantly. "Tomorrow I will return with two purses full. Then you will change your mind."

The desire to take the boy's offer is worse than my hunger. That much coin would pay off Father's guards for a whole year. Maybe two. But I can't accept. Vienne would flay me if I broke the Tenets.

I shake my head. "Don't count on it, kid. Money doesn't buy everything."

"Of course it does." He bows gracefully. Then glides back into the bazaar, acting like he owns it. For all I know, he does.

"Mimi, track his biorhythm signature until he's out of range. Make sure he's safe."

"How sweet," she says. "I thought your gruff demeanor was just an act."

"He's a self-centered, spoiled rotten little git."

"Yes," she says. "He reminds you of yourself."

"At that age, maybe."

"At *this* age, too."

Now I'm the one who wants to make obscene gestures. "Go to sleep, Mimi."

"I do not need rest."

"I need a rest from you. Take a break. I'll call you when I need you."

"Rest order received," she says. Then goes silent.

I'm settling back in the chair when I spot the three miners. They meander through the bazaar, their patched coveralls making them look out of place and, at the same time, too poor to interest even the brassiest vendors. Their hair is powdered orange-red with iron dust. Their faces smudged and desperate. It's obvious they're looking for help.

Look somewhere else, I think. Quickly, I close my eyes. But it's a wasted effort. Trouble always finds me. People like this, their desperation is inversely proportional to the amount of money in their pockets. The more they need a Regulator, the less they've got to pay for one. Not this time. Not me. No more charity work. I need paying clients. It's the curiosity that kills me. Miners? What are miners doing in New Eden?

I sneak a peek.

They catch me.

The tallest of the three, a female with ruddy cheeks and matching hair, points me out. Though she's about my age, the worry lines on her forehead are deep. She's thin, but tall for a miner, with shoulder-length brown hair and a long neck.

There's a heart-shaped, delicate face under all that dirt.

She says something, probably about me. In unison, the men shake their heads. Good choice, I think. I don't work for miners. And if they knew who my father was, they wouldn't want me, either.

The female, exasperated, rubs her fingers together. They're talking money now. She thinks I'll work cheap. The two men are wary—I swear one of them says *dalit*. After a few more seconds, she throws up her hands, disgusted.

Limping slightly, she walks past two booths, one selling spare duster parts and another hawking amino gruel that is only marginally more appetizing than the duster parts.

Keep walking, sister. I close my eyes and let my head roll to my chest.

"Regulator," she says. Her voice is raspy and sharp.

I let out a deep breath. Snore.

"We're wanting to hire a Regulator." When I don't respond, she pokes my shoulder. "Where I come from, ignoring somebody is reason for whipping."

"Where I come from," I say, eyes still shut, "waking a Regulator from a sound sleep is reason for killing."

"Good thing," she says, "you've not been asleep, right? Folk said this cantina was the place to go for hiring help."

"Got money?"

"Some. Not much."

"That's my answer about wanting work—some, not much."

She pulls away abruptly. "Suit yourself."

"Always do," I say.

She waves for the two men to follow her, which they do, giving me a wide berth, as if *dalit* is a disease you can catch. I watch them scoot inside the pub. Miners in Ares's—could they possibly make a more stupid, dangerous choice?

Yes, as it turns out, they could.

CHAPTER 8

Jaisalmer District, New Eden
ANNOS MARTIS 238. 4. 7. 09:43

Sighing, I follow them to the second floor. Inside, Ares's pub is a sauna of body odor, pipe smoke, and the ubiquitous red dust. There's a U-shaped bar in the middle of the room, a half ton of polished steel and iron that was once the wing manifold of a Manchester, a mining rig that stands three stories high and can process a ton of ore in a minute. All of the Manchesters were decommissioned once Mars reached Phase Blue. Their parts show up in all sorts of interesting places. Like a smoky pub in the armpit of Jaisalmer District.

Seated around the bar is a ragtag collection of mercenaries. Most of them are freelance Regulators, like Jenkins and Fuse, who are sitting in the back corner. Their table is a steel cable roll turned on its side.

Vienne leans against the back wall, a metal cup in hand. Her focus, though, is on the room. Always vigilant. I catch her eye. Then move to the opposite end of the bar, near where the miners are talking to a decommissioned Regulator turned freelancer named Ockham. He looks to be an age-twenty-five, maybe older, with graying temples, a balding pate, and a diagonal pink scar that runs across his nose and empty left eye socket.

"You want me to do *what?*" Ockham roars with laughter. "For how much? You miners, I never knew you derelicts had such a sense of humor. Always got your heads stuck in the ground. Thought of you as a dour lot, I did. But no, you say with a straight face that you want a Regulator to travel a thousand kilometers south to protect a worked-out mine. Ha!"

He pounds one of the men on the back. The miner's knees bend, and he absorbs the blow by falling to the floor. No wonder the miners need help, if this is the best they have to offer.

"We're serious," the man says, getting up from the floor. "Sorry you've decided not to be."

Ockham shakes a fist. "You've got a lot of nerve waltzing into a pub and insulting your betters."

Idiots. Absolute *piru vieköön* idiots. I can see the next steps in this dance: The girl miner insults the soldier. Said soldier chooses one piece of his arsenal and kills all three of them. No tribunal will convict him. He's a Regulator, and they're just miners.

"Damn," I curse under my breath. "Mimi, any advice?" But there's no answer—she's in sleep mode. Then, because I can't help myself, I do something predictable. Yet stupid.

Predictably stupid. "Ockham! You old son of a moon dog! Let me buy you a drink! No, two!"

Elbowing my way to the bar, I wedge myself between the girl and Ockham. As I ask the owner to set this fine soldier up for another round, I touch the side of my nose to let Vienne know that trouble's coming. She nods, then smiles.

"There's a fair suck of the salve!" the miner girl complains at me for butting in. "Aren't you the rude one?"

I turn my back on her and raise a glass in salute to Ockham. "To the Corporation!"

Ockham looks befuddled for a second, but a free drink gets his attention. "To the Command!" He clicks my glass. "Smooth, that was. How about another?"

"Another!" I shout.

"Another!" he echoes.

Then Vienne is beside me. "Get the miners out of the pub," I whisper to her. "I'll meet them outside."

"Yes, chief." She crooks a finger, signaling the miners to follow her. "Not a word. Let's go."

But the girl shakes her head petulantly, refusing to leave, and the two men can't figure out which one to listen to. So they do nothing. What a bunch of stubborn fossickers. They'll ruin everything.

The next round of drinks comes up. I raise a glass. "*Sláinte!*"

"*Sláinte!*" Ockham's remaining eye blinks twice. "Do I know you, boy?"

"We've met a few times. Here, you know. And there. Mostly there. Some heres. A couple of theres. But mostly— mostly heres?"

Ockham squints. Leans closer. Takes a long look at the hand wrapped around my glass, concentrating on my pinkie finger. Then his eyes widen. "*Dalit!*" He slams the full glass on the bar. "Never thought I'd take a drink with the likes of you."

"Me neither, Ockham." I down my *aqua pura* and pay the tab. "But times are hard, and you do what you have to."

"You pimple-faced brat." Ockham slaps a thick, calloused hand on mine. "Don't think you're walking that easy."

I slip my hand from under his. Grab his thumb and twist it. He grunts. His face reddens.

"Actually, Ockham," I say with a pretend grin. "It's going to be real easy. Or messy. Take your pick."

Fuse stands. "If there's to be a ruckus, chief, me and my cobber here have got your back. Innit right, Jenks?"

"Huh?" Jenkins scratches his head. "What's right?"

"That you and me have got the chief's back." He winks at Vienne. "Just say yes, Jenks."

"Yes, Jenks."

"There you have it, chief."

Vienne rolls her eyes. Ignores them and puts a hand on the butt of her armalite.

Ockham acknowledges her with a wink of his missing eye. "There was a day," he says, trying to ignore the death grip I have on his thumb, "when you all'd be nothing but a pool of piddle under my boot." He cracks his neck and works his shoulders. "Now, you boys still would be. But you, young lady, you move like you know which end of the armalite to shoot, which is more than I can say for the big man there."

"Huh?" Jenkins says. He peers into the barrel of his gun. "It shoots from this end. Right? Oy, Fuse. Right?"

"You made my point, big man." Ockham laughs. With his free hand, he downs another drink. Slams it on the bar, shattering the glass. Moving like a blur, he presses the jagged edge against my jugular. "Here's a lesson for you, boy. A smart Regulator doesn't have to beat a whole davos to win a fight."

Vienne draws. Drops to one knee. Firing position. "Say the word, chief."

Damned miners. Right now, I'm wishing I hadn't put Mimi into sleep mode.

"Mimi, wake mode, please."

Thirty seconds. That's all it takes to wake her. But thirty seconds is about twenty too many.

"You're wondering," Ockham says, "if I'll do it. That's not the question you ought to be asking. What I do doesn't matter, young chief. It's what you do that counts."

"Actually," I say, "I'm wondering what."

"What *what*?"

"What to do with your thumb when I break it off."

I give the thumb a twist as I yank his hand off the counter.

He swings the glass again. I duck and sweep his legs. Then jump back and watch him hit the deck.

He's not down long. With a quick kip up, he's back on his feet, showing great flexibility for an oldie. I drop into a defensive stance, ready.

Instead, Ockham pops his neck. Rolls his shoulders. Drops the broken glass on the counter. "Nice move, boy. Next time it won't be so easy. I owe you one." He pats me on the cheek. Walks past the others, laughing loudly. "Drink up, piddlers."

Without looking back, he hits the door.

Good riddance.

"You're bleeding," Vienne says.

I touch my neck. Find a red stain on my fingertips. *Der scheißkerl!* The old fossicker cut me.

"Look what you've gone and done." The miner girl gets chummy with my personal space. "Chased off the only Regulator who'd talk to us. How're you going to make amends?"

"Amends?" Vienne spins the girl around and sticks a gun barrel up her nose. "That little brain of yours needs more oxygen. How about I open an airhole?"

"You'd not dare!" the girl gasps.

"Yes, she would," I say, and start walking toward the back of the pub. "Vienne, stand down and follow me."

"Yes, chief."

"You, miners. Let's talk." Seconds pass. The miners don't move. "Last chance, people."

The two old men look to the girl. She strikes a pose, hands on hips, trying to sashay in a pair of grungy overalls. She grabs the rest of my drink and downs it.

"Blech!" She wipes her mouth her sleeve. "What is that rot?"

"Water," I say. "The real stuff. Coming or not?"

She stamps the floor. "Yes, damn it!"

The three of them file past me. I rub my forehead with the heel of my hand, trying to block the radioactive glare Vienne's giving me.

"Good morning, cowboy," Mimi says, and makes a sound like a yawn as I close the door behind us. "What did I miss?"

CHAPTER 9

Jaisalmer District, New Eden
ANNOS MARTIS 238. 4. 7. 10:11

The miner girl slaps her coin on the table. "That's our price. One hundred coin," she says. "We need a Regulator to show us how to fight the Dræu. We'll want you as soon as you can book passage to Hell's Cross."

I pull up a chair. Lean back and put my boots on the table. "You're getting ahead of yourself here. I never agreed to take the job. I'm just trying to save your stubborn hides from getting flayed. This is New Eden, not the mines. You can't go about insulting people of rank."

The girl puts hands on hips. She blows a sprig of hair from her face, frustrated. "Didn't know the oldie had got the full boot on."

"She means," one of the other miners cuts in, "we meant no offense. We ain't used to the way of surfies."

"I know what she meant," I say.

The girl pouts. Then she shifts her weight to favor her

good leg. I can see why. Bloodstains on her coveralls. She's been wounded.

"Damn the surfies," the other man says. "They don't care a whit about miners. Why should miners care about them?"

Miners are the poorest of the poor. It wasn't always that way. Once upon a time, the mines were invaluable. On Earth, they learned how to heat up—and destroy—a planet with pollution. On Mars, our grandparents' grandparents put those lessons into effect, purposely creating a greenhouse effect that sped up terraforming by decades. As the colonies grew, Fisher Four, which rested under a perpetual cloud of dust, was the most crucial part of the second phase of terraforming. But to the residents of the outpost, Fisher Four was Hell, even before it became obsolete, because their lives were short and painful. If the Manchester machines or a chance encounter with a Big Daddy didn't kill them, rust lung disease would.

"You've got a point there," I say. "Except you happened to pick a surfie who was armed."

"You're headed down a bad road, cowboy," Mimi warns me.

"It's not like we haven't been there before." I sit up. Take my boots off the table. "Tell us why you good miners have gone looking for Regulators."

The girl flashes a satisfied smile. "Like I said. To teach us how to fight the Dræu so we can defend ourselves next time."

Next time? "The Dræu attacked you before?"

They all bow. If the Dræu really did do half of what rumor says, it's no wonder the miners are looking for help. I catch Vienne's eye. She shakes her head. We're thinking the same thing—as fighters, the miners aren't up to snuff.

"The mines aren't worth anything," I say. "Why would the Dræu be sniffing around?"

"They demanded," she answers, "six children. You've heard of the Dræu. You know what they do with children."

Eat them, I say to myself, because it's too heinous to say out loud. The exploits of the Dræu may be exaggerated, but there's one thing that's true: They are cannibals.

Vienne catches my eye this time. As far as the Tenets are concerned, I have no choice but to accept. When a lesser people are in mortal danger, a Regulator is honor bound to help them. We must serve with one eye, one hand, one heart. If *dalit* don't uphold the oath, what good are we?

"We'll take the job," I say, looking at Vienne, who smiles. "But you're going to need more than a two-Regulator crew to fight the Dræu."

"Fight?" the girl says. "We said nothing about fighting. Training is what—"

"Will get you killed. Every last *chùsheng* one of you. No, what you need is a whole davos of well-trained Regulators to defend you."

"How many Regulators in a davos?"

"Ten," Vienne says.

The first man blanches. "Ten?"

"At full strength," I say. "We can make do with eight. Maybe fewer, if they're good."

The girl picks up the coin from the table. Shoves it into my hands. "Hire all you want. If you can get them for a hundred coin."

"A davos of Regulators can't work for so little," I say.

"That's all we've got," the girl says.

Of course it is. Trouble always finds me, and it's always dirt-poor. I sigh. "It's a contract." Then we shake hands to seal the deal. "I'm Durango. That's Vienne, my second."

"My name is Áine Phelan," she says, holding onto my hand a few seconds longer than she should. "He's Spiner, and the other one's Jurm."

"When will you be leaving for Fisher Four?" Spiner adds, "We need to catch the next TransPort."

"Tomorrow morning," I say. "At the earliest. I've some personal business, and it'll take time for us to round up more Regulators." Then I suggest they catch their TransPort as scheduled. Vienne and I will follow with the recruits. If we can get any recruits.

"How'd we know that you'll do as promised?" Jurm asks. "A pretty boy like you'd be prone to fickleness."

"Care to repeat that?" Vienne snarls.

Jurm does just that. "A pretty boy—"

"Jurm," Spiner says. "No need to be so ornery."

"Don't blame me," Jurm grumbles. "She the one who asked."

Áine offers her hand to me. "See you soon, chief. Spiner, Jurm, let's go."

As the miners leave the room, taking a wide berth around Vienne, Áine hands me a slim metal case.

"Here's directions to Outpost Fisher Four," she says. "And half the coin. You get paid the rest when the job's done."

"What, exactly, does *done* mean?" I ask.

"It means either that the Dræu pledge to leave us be or that the Dræu are all dead."

I shake my head. "The likelihood of either of those things happening is minuscule."

"Then," Áine says, her voice breathy, "minuscule is what you've got to look forward to for payment. Chief, pleasure doing business with you."

When they've gone and the door is shut, I ask Vienne, "What do you think?"

"Clumsy."

"She's been wounded."

"I meant her attempts to flirt with you."

My ears start to burn. "Oh. Yeah. Well. Except when I asked *what do you think*, I meant, what kind of davos do you think we can get together?"

"No Regulator worth a lick is going to work a hundred-coin job."

"We are," I say.

"We're different."

By different, she means better. "Well," I say. "If worse

comes to worse, I already have a couple of Regulators in mind."

She glares at me. "I said, *good* Regulators."

"One's a carking good demolitionist, and the other one's. . . well, he must be good for something."

"No, not them, chief. Please."

I flash a cheesy grin. "Come on, Vienne. It'll be fun."

"You and I," she says, hands on hips, "have completely different definitions of *fun*."

CHAPTER 10

Jaisalmer District, New Eden
ANNOS MARTIS 238. 4. 7. 18:21

"No farging way. Not if they paid me a bishop's wage,"
Jenkins says when I make him the offer of a job. "They're
miners. I don't want nothing to do with their kind."

As promised, we spent the bulk of the day hitting the
pubs in search of good Regulators who'd work for piddle-
squat. Like Vienne said, we found good Regulators, and we
found a few *dalit* ready to work for their next meal. But we
didn't find what we were looking for, except a couple of
tussles that Vienne ended fast.

"Worse has come to worse," I told Vienne after we found
ourselves empty-handed and hungry from missing dinner.
"We've run out of options."

An hour later we find Fuse and Jenkins deep in the bazaar.
They're milling around at a coppersmith's booth, checking
out a collection of used spittoons and nose rings. Not buying,
just looking, since they spent their payday in the pub.

After Jenkins's refusal, Fuse grabs his forearm. "Buck up

now, Jenks. I never took you for a bigot. At least listen to what the chief has got to say. You never know. His offer might be attractive. Right, love?"

"I've killed eleven people in tai bo combat," Vienne tells him.

"So?"

"So if you call me *love* again, there's a good chance I'll make it an even dozen."

"Rowr! Saucy." Fuse makes a clawing motion. "Like I said, I enjoy a suzy with a chunk of spunk in the old trunk, if you know what I mean."

"The only chunks you need worry about," she says, and pulls her weapon, "are the ones I'm going to blow off if you don't shut that yap."

"Then I'm shutting up. Not another word." He winks like he's got a tic. "See? Zipping so no sound—"

"You used that line already," Vienne says.

"I'm recycling for the betterment of Mars."

"Enough!" I bark, feeling a bit more put out than necessary. When I've got their attention, I lay out the terms of the contract.

"A hundred each?" Jenkins roars. "That's all you're offering?"

"No," I say.

"Glad to hear it. What else you got?"

"No, you don't understand: one hundred split among the whole davos."

"You're out of your mind." Jenkins spits into a spittoon. When the merchant cries out in complaint, Jenkins raises his open palms. "What? I'm not allowed to test-drive them?"

I stick to the subject. "I'll take *you're out of your mind* to mean you're declining the job."

"They're cannibals. That means they eat people. Find yourself another sucker, chief. Leroy Jenkins ain't going to be cannisnack."

"Cannisnack?" I ask, confused. "What's that?"

"You know. Cannibal. Snack. Cannisnack."

"R*iii*ght." Strike Jenkins from the list. I turn to Fuse. "How about it? You're a demolitionist. The miners used to stockpile explosives for the mining operations. I bet they still have some of it. They might share."

Fuse licks his lips. Pulls me aside for a quiet word. "You and me, we're men of the world. Right, chief?"

"Of the world, yes. Of the same world, probably not."

He shrugs my comment off. "The Vienne of yours, is she attached?"

"You mean, like, to a male?"

He winks. "That'd be the one."

"No, she's not. Vienne is only interested in her duty, her davos, and her chief."

"But she could be, no? If the right jack come along at the right time."

Not on your life, I think, and almost tell him that before I get an interesting idea. A very interesting, useful idea.

"That's sneaky, cowboy," Mimi says.

"I've not said anything," I tell her.

"But you thought it."

I put a big brotherly arm around Fuse's shoulders. He's a good twenty centimeters shorter than me, with narrow shoulders. A year older, too. Not that it matters. Regulators don't care about age. "If the right jack did appear, I suppose she would be—"

His ears perk up. "Open to the idea?"

"Less likely to shoot him than normal."

"That's not very reassuring."

"Well—"

"But I'm a risk taker." He punches me playfully in the gut. "I'm willing to give it a go. When do we leave?"

"Tomorrow morning. If we can round up a few more Regulators. I'd like to have at least six, so that leaves us needing three."

"How so? I count you two, me, and Jenkins. That leaves you needing two."

"Jenkins declined the offer."

Fuse clicks his tongue. "Let me handle Jenkins, and you two go about your business. Meet us at the TransPort tomorrow at dawn. East End Station, no?"

"Right."

"See you then." He winks at Vienne. "Bright and early, love. Don't bother with the face paint. You're dead sexy just the way you are." He skips out of the tent as Vienne draws her weapon.

"There's no killing him now, " I say, grabbing her arm. "The Tenets expressly forbid shooting a member of your own davos, especially in the back."

"Chief!" She jams the armalite into its holster. "Tell me you didn't!"

"Had to."

"But that fossiker's just going to blow himself up!"

"Let's just hope," I say, grinning, "that he takes a few Dræu along with him."

CHAPTER 11

My father is a fallen angel. I tell myself that as Vienne and I climb the icy steps that lead from the TransPort station up to the surface. I tell myself that every time I make the trip to Norilsk, a gulag that swallows up prisoners like a black hole swallows light. It helps me choke down the anger in my belly.

"Is this the right place?" Vienne asks, strands of hair whipping across her face as we reach the surface.

Diesel exhaust fills the air with a burnt haze. Transport trucks rumble by on the avenue. Lined up, bumper to bumper. The chain is endless and moving fast. Their engines run loud. Their drivers even louder. Laying on their horns. Spitting cuss words in English, Japanese, French, Spanish, and Farsi. I can speak three languages. I know how to cuss in seven.

"It's the right place," I yell over the noise. The station exit leaves us between two hulking gray buildings coated with rust dust. Government buildings erected by the CorpComs. Great slabs of concrete stacked atop one another. No design. No ornament. No heart. No soul. They remind me of my father.

"We cross there." I point to a circus traffic signal that's about to change. "Go."

In unison, we jog to a checkpoint fifty meters ahead. This is the visitors entrance to the Norilsk Gulag. Father is expecting me.

"He is a fallen angel," I repeat, subvocalizing.

"Is that a new mantra?" Mimi says. "Or are you trying to keep from chundering your lunch again?"

"I've not had any lunch," I tell her.

Vienne walks in silence beside me. I like silence. Especially in constant companions.

"Is that a knock at me?" Mimi says.

"Yes." I steal a glance at Vienne. Shoulders erect. Chin high. Eyes fixed straight ahead. A body that moves with such grace, it makes me want to swing her into my arms, press her body against mine, and . . . and . . . get ideas. Ideas that a chief is forbidden to have for another Regulator. Especially his second. At the checkpoint, a gate blocks the way. Two guards man the guardhouse, a female sergeant and her partner. They look bored. Until they notice the armor.

I stop. Turn my back to the guardhouse. "Here's enough to book the TransPort to Fisher Four," I say, slipping some coins to Vienne.

"The rest is for?"

"To pay off guards."

"And you will save enough for your dinner."

"Yes," I say, although it's a lie. Every bit of money in my possession will go to paying off somebody.

She places a fist in an open palm, then bows slightly. The Regulator greeting. I do the same. Except when she rises, our eyes meet. Her eyes are hazel. Since when?

"Since forever," Mimi interrupts. "Are you the most unobservant Regulator in the history of the order? Yes, hazel eyes, blond hair. Height, one point nine meters. Weight—"

"I got the picture," I growl silently at her. "No reason to belabor the point."

"Apparently, there is, o observant one. A Regulator notices everything, cowboy. I certainly do."

"What's that supposed to mean? Well?" Mimi doesn't answer me.

"Chief," Vienne says. "Please don't dawdle. If you miss the TransPort, I will be stuck riding to Hell with those two."

"Come on, Vienne. It wouldn't be that bad."

"Yes," she says. "It would."

After we part company, I walk to the guardhouse. The male guard stares at me through a wire mesh screen. "Dr. Jacob Smith to see a prisoner. Medical prerogative." I give him Father's prisoner number.

"Sorry," he says. "Didn't catch that number."

I set six bits on the sill on my side of the screen. Slide

them through an open slot in the mesh. I repeat Father's number.

"Ah, that prisoner. Come inside the guardhouse for inspection." He winks. "Doc."

Graft and corruption. Hallmarks of the CorpCom era. Inside the house, the guard slides a lockbox across the desk while his partner, a sergeant, scans me with a wand.

"Fancy," Sarge says, admiring my symbiarmor and giving it a flick. "Can't even tell it's armor. You've had an upgrade. Is this the newest line?"

The other guard doesn't give a rat's petard. Just the business at hand. "Place your weapon inside the box."

I pull my armalite out of its holster. Set it in the box. Gently. Then start to close the lid.

"I'll handle it from here, Regulator," he says, then reaches for the grip.

"No!" I grab his wrist. Feel the soft flesh give as I pinch too hard and catch a nerve.

He grunts, his eyes widening. With his free hand, he fumbles for his sidearm as I slam the lid shut. Then release him.

"On the floor!" He's found his pistol, which is now in his shaking hands. "On your knees!"

The woman laughs. "Quick one, innit he? Like a ruddy viper. Had you dead to rights before your beady eyes could blink."

"Sarge!" the guard says. "He assaulted me!"

"Saved your worthless life is more like it." She takes his pistol away from him. The safety is still on. "About to grab an armalite. Don't you know what happens if you do that? The things are rigged with explosives. One touch from you, and we're both dead."

"Really?" he says.

"Really," I say. "The armalite's coded with my biorhythmic signature. Standard Regulator stuff. Can I go in now?"

"Five minutes. No more." She opens a door leading to a long corridor. As soon as I step inside, the door clangs shut behind me.

At the end of the corridor, there's a chair and a window. Nothing else.

"Mimi, could you give me a few minutes of radio silence."

"Anything for you, cowboy. Tap when you want my attention."

I take a seat. A sheet of Plexi separates me from a man. He's sitting in a chair like mine, his chin resting on his chest, eyes closed. I tap on the window, and he looks up.

He's lost weight. His cheeks are hollow, the wrinkles on his forehead too loose, and his skin is blotched red. There's no sign of physical abuse, though. No bruising. No wounds. No scars, either, except the old ones under his right eye and the crooked nose, trophies from the beatings he took from the mob that dragged him from the stand during the trial. It's the cancer that's shrinking him. The treatments I'm paying for are enough to extend his life but not to cure him.

There's not enough money on Mars to do that.

He's sixteen centimeters shorter than me, and the years in solitary confinement have bent him. Still, he feels taller.

"You need a haircut."

"Hello, Father."

"Jacob." His voice is monotone.

"It's been a while, sir."

"Six months. One week. Four days."

He forgot hours.

"Seventeen hours."

Or not.

"But who's counting?" I say, trying to lighten the mood.

"I am," he says. "All I have to do is count. Bunch of derelicts won't even let me have a book to read except the Bible, and I can quote it chapter and verse."

It cost me the payday from a primo job to buy the Bible for him. "You're looking tosh. The food must be—"

"Awful. Didn't you say something about bribing the trusties in the kitchen? About time you did something about that, if you have the means."

The bribes I pay puts extra in his bowl. Otherwise, he'd be living off gruel. "I'll see if I can find the means, Father. Good commissions are more difficult to find than—"

"You disappoint me, Jacob."

Here it comes.

"Your biological mother was chosen for her intelligence and physical prowess. A PhD in molecular biology who was an Olympic swimmer. The surrogate who birthed you was the finest available. Your birth was without event. Your education demanding, your training flawless. This is not your destiny, Jacob. It is your destiny to become the leader of Mars, not a common *dalit* mercenary."

For a moment I say nothing. Look down and away from his relentless gaze, the way I did as a child. "You made me a *dalit*, Father."

At the end of his trial, he was forced to spend a day and a night in stocks. The Regulators commissioned to Stringfellow gathered in the temple square, all three hundred of them. When the clock struck signaling the end of his time in the stocks, they all committed suicide, an act that showed true sacrifice. Only two Regulators refused to join the ritual. Me. Because my father forbade me to kill myself. And Vienne, who had sworn her life in service to my own. That's how we became *dalit*. Masterless. Outcast. Pariah.

"What? What did you say, Jacob?"

"I said, Father, that if I'd had my wish, I'd have died horribly alongside your other Regulators."

"And wasted a lifetime of planning and hard work. They need you, Jacob. How could I deny this planet its savior because of a senseless, antiquated ritual?"

"Regulators live by those rituals. The Tenets—"

"Spare me the cant about the Tenets. They're as useless as the old fools who wrote them generations ago. We live in modern times, Jacob. They call for modern men. The

Orthocracy is dead. The CorpCom government is a passing phase, a transition to a new government that will rise from the ashes of both! That government needs you."

I signal for him to keep his voice down. "Father, your words are a thin line from treason."

"It is the thinnest lines that define us, Jacob."

"Define you. Not me."

"If you cared about your father, you would stop this foolish charade!" Flecks of spit splatter the Plexi. "And become the man I designed you to be!"

I shake my head slowly. Rub the thick, rubbery scar on my temple. Every time, the same conversation. Yes, he calculated every possible variable, added every ingredient he could control. Maybe I should've become more than I am. Maybe he should've thought of that before he released the deadliest beasts on Mars on his own troops. Troops that included me.

"Answer me!" he bellows.

Above us, a tone sounds. A guard appears behind Father. I stand. Make the fist in palm sign of the Regulator and bow low to show my respect.

My father is a fallen angel, I tell myself, but when I rise, he's gone.

When I leave the prison, I see two shadows on either side of the catwalk, and I know something's amiss.

"Mimi," I say after tapping my temple. "Don't even

bother with a scan. I recognize the stink of collectors when I smell it."

"Too late," she says. "I pinpointed them while you were still at the guardhouse."

"Thanks, by the way," I say. "For giving a few minutes alone with Father."

"Believe me when I say, cowboy, it was my pleasure."

Mimi hates Father. Can't blame her. He's the one, after all, who caused her death.

It takes a few seconds for the collectors to appear. Two males. Age-tens. When I head for the traffic signal, they sidle up. Both wear light gray suits with high, black tab collars. Pretending to be men of the cloth. The disguise is a good one, and most citizens of New Eden keep their distance. During the Orthocracy, priests were dangerous men. No one has forgotten that.

"Oy, Durango," the taller one says. "Heard you pulled a job. Impressive. Except the kidnapper you hit has connections. Unhappy connections, if you know what I mean."

"Mimi?" I say as we reach the far side of the street. I turn for the entrance to the Tube. "They're packing, right?"

"Service revolvers," she says. "CorpCom shock trooper standard issue. Be careful."

"Aren't I always?"

"No."

"Oy!" the tall man says. Punches me in the back, and the armor absorbs the blow. Hope he skinned his knuckles.

I turn on him. Grab his fist, which is ready for another punch. Give it a squeeze, which he feels through his glove. "Save the chitchat, messenger boy. What does Mr. Lyme want?"

The second jack—the standover man—moves to step in. I draw the armalite with my free hand. Aim at his nether regions. "Don't think. Don't blink."

He freezes.

"Good man," I say. "Now back up, messenger boy. Tell me—Mr. Lyme sent you because?"

He squints. Tries to pretend the bones I'm grinding together don't hurt. "Your last payment wasn't enough. It's costing Mr. Lyme more and more to give your poor papa the same level of protection, no?"

"I hold up my end of the bargain," I tell the collector, and let go the fist. The armalite I keep aimed. It's the quiet ones you've got to worry about. "Mr. Lyme gets half my take of every job in return for keeping the predators and the recidivists off my father. Your boss made a righteous bargain."

"That means what to me?" He flexes his fist. Grins. Takes my act of kindness as weakness. Smug rooter.

"It doesn't mean much to you," I say. "But when I cut this deal with Mr. Lyme, I made him a promise."

"What kind of promise, Durango?"

"That I'd put a hole through his head if he broke our deal."

Collector laughs. So does his associate. "That's a good one. You're one funny kid."

"Not when my father's concerned."

"You're a bit slow on the uptake, though," he says. "I told you, the deal's changed. The price of protection's tripled."

"Tripled?" I say. "You're out of your skull."

"Can't afford the hay?" Collector picks his teeth with a flint match. "Mr. Lyme says he can cut you in on a side trade. There's good money in it for a fine strapping lad like yourself. A bloke of your abilities and looks who can transport merchandise."

"Like what?"

He leans in, tries to whisper over the ferocious winds. "Rapture."

"You want a Regulator chief to run contraband?"

"Not contraband! Don't call it that." He winks conspiratorially. "Think of it as freelance pharmaceuticals."

"Not happening." I drop low. Sweep their legs with a quick roundhouse. Cut them off at the knees.

Collector falls hard on his tailbone. The standover man follows suit. They roll backward, moaning onto the icy asphalt, dust staining their light gray robes with streaks of rust. It looks like blood. Part of me wishes it were.

In an instant the barrel of my gun is lodged in one of Collector's flaring nostrils.

"Give Mr. Lyme a message," I say calmly, although my heart is racing. "Tell him if anything happens to my father, I'll take my business to his competitor. *After* I've kept my promise."

"Yeah," Collector says. "Got that."

His partner lifts him to his feet after I step away.

"This isn't over, kid. Mr. Lyme? You'll never even see him coming, but he'll come all right."

"Go on, messenger boy." I wave the armalite at him. "Walk fast."

Collector makes an obscene gesture as they stumble away. "If you didn't have that weapon."

"But I do. And it's legal for me to use it. Remember that next time, before the thought of me trafficking pharmies even enters that microbe you call a brain."

A second later I'm bounding down the stairs, headed for the Tube. My train is arriving, and I'm just in time to catch it.

CHAPTER 12

East End, New Eden
ANNOS MARTIS 238. 4. 8. 08:13

The TransPort monorail station at the east end of New Eden reminds me of a toilet. It's the miasmatic, pent-up odor of thousands of humans passing through every day, with only a creaking ventilation system to move the air around. In the surface cities near the equator like Valles Martis, the air is clean and breathable. Once or twice Vienne and I tried to find work there, but *dalit* are shunned in those cities, like our presence is a form of pollution.

"Stupid damned miners. Stupid damned South Pole," Jenkins curses as he throws his bags into the luggage berth above our seats. Packed away in a duffle, his fifty-caliber machine gun clanks as it lands on the rack.

"Excuse me? There are children present," says a pucker-faced woman a few rows ahead. Her daughter is seated beside her, earbuds on, bouncing to music. The woman covers the girl's ears anyway. "Watch your language, sir!"

"Who you calling *sir?*" he says. "I work for a living, you lemon-faced fingringhoe."

"Well, I never!" she says, horrified.

"You did at least once!" He makes a rude hand gesture. "Unless that's somebody else's kid sitting in the next seat."

Seeing Jenkins's amputated pinkie, the woman puckers up so much, her mouth almost flips inside out. She presses the call button. Now he's done it. A conductor will be coming soon.

"Sit down!" I hiss at him. "Stop being a jackass and act like a Regulator for once."

"Me? She's the one got all huffy." Jenkins plops down beside the porthole, pulls his armalite from its holster, and lays it on his lap.

"That is not safe," Vienne says as we slide into the row behind him. "Follow travel protocol."

Jenkins growls, "Mind your own business."

"He's just compensating," Fuse turns to tell Vienne.

"You're the one with the short fuse, Fuse," Jenkins says. "Get it? Short *fuse.* 'Cause you're short."

Vienne elbows me in the ribs, then mouths, *Told you so.*

I throw up my hands, as if to say, *Like I had any other choice.* "Okay, pipe down, you two." I push my own bag into the overhead compartment. "You know the rules, Jenks. Holster your weapon or pack it away."

"Aw."

"You heard me."

He jams it into the holster. Stows it. "Nobody ever lets me have any fun."

After he's finished, I call the three of them together. "We need to establish a comm link for the duration of the job."

The boys start pulling the earbuds from their suits—the old-fashioned way of synching. I shake my head. "Not that way. My telemetry functions can do it automatically. Just spin your seats around." They unlock their section and turn it so that we're facing one another. "Now, join hands."

"Yes, sir!" Fuse grins. He takes hold of Vienne's hand and interlaces his fingers with hers. "Your methods are unorthodox, chief, but I like them. How about you, suzy? Doesn't sharing flesh with the Fuse make your blood turn all ho—ow!"

"No, it doesn't."

"Vienne, don't break his fingers. He'll need them later."

"Why?" she says as she complies. "Like I said, he's just going to blow them off."

Fuse sticks his freed fingers in his mouth. "That's was harsh, lo—I mean, Vienne. *Vienne!*"

"Hands, Regulators," I say.

"You take hers this time, Jenks," Fuse says, grimacing.

Jenkins tilts his head to the side. "Ain't held hands with suzies too much. Not sure I'm keen on it."

"For the love of—!" I bark. "Take her carking hand! She won't bite!"

All their heads turn to me like synchronized artillery.

"Well," I say, "maybe she will, but not if I tell her not to. Hands!" Finally we manage the maneuver without anyone else getting hurt. "Mimi, synch them to my aural frequency. On my mark. One. Two."

"Done."

"Already?"

"I had," she says with a lilt to her voice, "plenty of time to prepare."

When the synch is finished and we all find our seats, Jenkins says, "Holding hands is fun. It tickles."

Fuse shakes his hand. "The pox it does!"

Jenkins turns back to Vienne. "Now I know why Durango's the chief and you're not—he's got the prettiest suit."

I hear Mimi titter in my head. "Out of the mouth of babes . . ."

Then Vienne turns to me and fake smiles. "Don't even think of ordering me to babysit him."

"Wouldn't dream of it."

"I've heard that before."

I start to argue when the conductor enters the car. She goes to the puckered woman, who turns and points at Jenkins, then at me. The conductor nods, and her face puckers up, too.

Uh-oh. I know what's coming. Vienne and I've been down this road many times before.

The conductor straightens her hat. Walks purposefully past Jenkins and Fuse. And stops beside me. "Fare card."

She forgets to say *please.* I pass her the card using my bad hand. Let her take a good, long look. She freezes, lip quivering, then pinches the card between thumb and forefinger like it's covered in pox germs.

"Party of four traveling to Outpost Fisher Four," she says after swiping the card through the reader belted to her hip.

"That's right," I say through a forced smile.

"For what purpose?"

"Work."

"Does your work involve weapons?"

"Usually. We're Regulators."

"I know what you *are,*" she says, and keeps the card. "There have been complaints from the other passengers."

"About what?"

She glances at my pinkie. "You'll have to vacate this car."

"What?" Vienne says, her voice rising. "We've paid for our seats like—"

She leans over us, pretending to keep her voice low, but making sure other riders hear her. "Passengers are seated at the discretion of the conductor. And I want you out of these seats now. *Dalit* aren't fit to ride in the same car as decent citizens."

Fuse turns and starts to argue. I shake my head no. Even if we once risked our lives to defend people like this officious rotter, we have to remember that we're still Regulators. They think we're trash, but that doesn't mean we have to act it. "If you say so. We'll move. Fuse, Jenkins. Grab your gear. We're moving out."

"Huh?" Jenkins says. "Moving out where?"

"To the baggage compartment," the conductor says loudly.

"But I just got situated," Jenkins complains.

Fuse tugs their bags from the rack. "Let it go, Jenks. You know the drill. We've been shown the door before, right?"

A few rows ahead, the puckered-up woman starts to hiss. The other passengers join in, and in a few seconds, the cabin sounds like a bucket of snakes. The conductor flounces to the back door, obviously enjoying the heads turning our way, and opens the hatch. There's a metallic click, and wind and noise rush inside.

I stand to the side as first Vienne and then Fuse and Jenkins file out.

When it's my turn, I look the conductor hard in the eye. "You don't happen to speak Chinese, do you?"

"No, I do not," the conductor says. "Why do you want to know?"

"Oh, no reason." I clap my hands together and bow. "*Jiào nǐ shēng háizi zhǎng zhì chuāng*. And have a nice day."

After a long walk through a couple dozen cars and a litany of complaints from Jenkins, we reach the baggage car. The few seats are stained and torn, surrounded by stacks of luggage locked behind security doors. The conductor makes sure we know about the security cameras, then hustles away in a rush, like she's suddenly aware that she's pissed off a very big man with a very big gun.

"It's not first class," I say as we stow our gear again. "But at least we've got it all to ourselves."

"Huh," Jenkins says, which sums up pretty much what all of us are feeling.

I take my own seat. Settle in for a nap. The trip to Fisher Four will take a full day's travel. Might as well get some sleep.

"So," Fuse says, swinging around in his seat. "You two been together long, davos wise, I mean? Me and Jenks has been best cobbers since the day we became Regulators. We're both conscripts. My parentals are first-generation immigrants from Earth. Worked as conscript servants before marrying and having seven children—six of us boys, of which I'm the baby—plus taking care of a few of my cousins off and on. Jenks, he comes from miners. His parentals carked it during a cave-in, and he got stuck among the Orphan Workers Program till they conscripted him. Did I tell you how we got decorated at the Battle of Noachis Terra? It's quite the tale, if I say so myself."

And he does say so himself. Rambles on for several more minutes. By the time he takes a breath, my ears feel scorched and Vienne looks like she wants to claw her way through the side of the rail car.

"Vienne," I groan, "I take it back. You can shoot him."

"How many times?" she says.

Fuse throws both hands up in a defensive gesture. "Oy! I get the message. What a couple of grumpies you two are."

He slides into his seat. "Oy, Jenks. Got anything choice in that nosh bag of yours?"

Vienne and I exchange looks. She starts to speak, and I put a finger to her lips to shush her. For a few seconds it's as if time is frozen. I let out a short breath, and Vienne blinks, then pulls back. Slowly she takes my hand in hers and lowers it. Almost imperceptibly, she shakes her head no, and I'm not sure which of us she's talking to. I take a deeper breath, my mind a swirl of emotions as she makes a fist and turns her face to the window.

Damn.

"Mimi," I rub my fingers together, thinking about the touch of her lips. "Keep an eye on things."

"Which eye?" she says. "Your real one or the synthetic bionic one?"

"It's figure of speech."

"I was being ironic."

"Or sarcastic."

Slowly at first, almost as if the platform instead of the train is moving, the station passes by the window. A moment later an air horn blasts as the engine winds over the ribbon of rail, the city growing smaller as the TransPort blows out of New Eden. Soon the biodome of the settlement seems far away and unreal, a shrinking dot on the Mars landscape. The picture in the window melts into a liquid of color and sound so that only the distant peak of Olympus Mons remains. The horizon is gone—not melted, just gone—and the world I know becomes flat and red and dusty.

I close my eyes, and the dream comes quickly: I'm back in the hospital, the reconstructive surgery ward. Father stands over my bed.

"This is the third rejection," the surgeon says. "His brain waves simply are not a match for any donor that we have on record. Alas, the experiment is a failure."

A faceless bureaucrat in a lavender CorpCom suit suggests, "Perhaps his mind is too weak to host an artificial intelligence."

Father disagrees. "Too strong is more likely. My son's DNA is of the highest quality. His surrogate was chosen from hundreds of thousands of women, all of them strong, intelligent, brave. No, it must be the donors that are inferior."

"Or incompatible," the surgeon says. "We can keep trying."

"No," Father says, patting my hand with all the affection of a piece of meat. "I cannot risk Operation MUSE. You'll need to seek more suitable subjects."

From the haze of sedation, I grope for his arm and somehow find it. "Mimi," I say, my voice slurry and sounding very far away. "Use Mimi."

"Who is this Mimi?" Father asks.

"His former chief," the suit says. "She was KIA in Tunnel Two-E."

"Do it," Father tells the surgeon.

"But sir," the suit protests. "We are already in violation of ethic protocol, as well as legal—"

"Damn your ethics," Father bellows. "And bugger the law. That didn't stop our last project, and it won't stop this one. My son is destined for greatness. This experiment will help him reach it." He mechanically pats my hand again. "Doctor, you may proceed. And give him a higher dose of anesthesia. I do not want him to remember this conversation."

But I do remember it, and the memory jars me awake. I rub my eyes, not knowing how long I've been asleep.

"Only a minute or two," Mimi says. "But do try to get some shut-eye, cowboy. It's a long ride to Hell."

CHAPTER 13

Bishop TransPort Station,
Outpost Fisher Four
ANNOS MARTIS 238. 4. 9. 15:22

By the time the TransPort train reaches the end of the line, we are the only things left in the baggage car. Despite Mimi's repeated reminders, I've gotten little to no sleep. Par for the course these days.

Vienne is first out of her seat. "Ready, chief."

Fuse and Jenkins are still asleep in the seat in front of us. Jenkins's snores sound like he's sucking his soft palate through his nose.

I grab my bag from the rack. "Hop to, Regulators!"

"He's awful bossy," Jenkins says, yawning and stretching.

"Because he's the chief," Vienne replies.

Jenkins pauses to cogitate that one. His eyes glaze over.

"Aw, look what you've gone and done." Fuse snaps his fingers in Jenkins's face. "His brain's overloaded. You can't push a terabyte of data through a transistor, lov—duck—Suz—Vienne! Yes, Vienne."

"File out!" I say. "Don't make me say it again."

"Bossy britches," Jenkins grumbles.

Fuse pops him in the head. "Sorry, chief. He's a might peevish after a long haul. He'll be more pleasant once he's had a walkabout."

On the landing area, the first thing I notice—the whistle of an arctic wind outside the dilapidated station, followed by the slap of frigid air on my face. The second thing I notice— no greeting party.

Just an empty station that's seen better days. The way an ancient ruin has seen better days. Tiles fallen from the ceiling. Platform covered in rat droppings. Paint peeling from the walls and handrails. It's a disgrace the way the TransPort company has let the station go downhill from neglect.

"It's carking cold here," Jenkins complains, obviously still peevish. He drops his duffel and begins hopping around. "Where's our ride? I'm freezing my ass off."

"I'd be your ride." A miner steps out of the shadows as the TransPort train pulls away. It's Spiner, part of the crew that hired us. Never thought I'd be happy to see such an ugly face.

"Welcome to Hell's Cross, Regulators. My name's Spiner."

I offer a hand in greeting. He looks at it like it's infected with plague. "Nice to see you, too. Mimi," I say, "scan the area. Find out what he's up to."

"Attempting scan, cowboy," she replies. "Acoustic resonances here are complex. Give me thirty seconds."

"Fifteen."

"I'm an AI, not a time machine."

Jenkins raises his hand in greeting, a gesture that Spiner also ignores. "When do we eat, Ruster?"

"When you get hungry, I s'pose," Spiner says.

"No, I mean," Jenkins huffs, temper rising, "when're you going to get us some grub? And a bed, while you're at it."

Spiner scratches his concave belly. "I'd not known *dalit* was allowed to sleep in beds like decent folk."

"Decent folk? I've had about enough of that rot!" Jenkins grabs the miner by the straps of his overalls and lifts him up like a scruffy puppet. "Don't no mud puppy talk to me like that!"

"Put 'im down, Jenks!" Fuse barks. "How many times'd I tell you about that?"

Jenkins plops the man, who is swinging and kicking wildly, on the ground. "Ah, it don't hurt him none."

Fuse steps between them. "What Jenkins means in his own imbecilic way is that it's been a long time since we bugged out of New Eden, and we'd like a chance to tuck in and have a lie down."

Spiner looks as if someone asked him to solve integrals in three dimensions.

"Stand down," I say. "Jenkins, put away the knife—I'll handle this. Spiner, what's the next step here? We've been in the open too long."

Spiner nods, oblivious. "The old woman says I'm to carry the six of you to the Cross."

"Six?" I say. There are only four of us. "Mimi, where's my scan?"

"Completed," Mimi responds. "I detect a total seven bio-rhythmic signatures. All human."

"Yes, six," Spiner says to me. "You four and the Regulators behind you."

I do a double take. Regu—

"Very interesting," Mimi says. "The other two signatures are in my data banks. You're not going to like this: One is Ockham—"

"Ockham!" I say. "I know you're here. Show yourself!"

The old Regulator steps out from the shadows. Now I know why Spiner was so out of sorts. Ockham is the last Regulator he ever expected to get off that train. Me, too.

"You messed up my little game," Ockham chuckles, leaning against a support column and cleaning his nails with a survival knife. "How'd you know it was me?"

"X-ray vision," I say. "Why are you here?"

"Doing the same job that you're doing. Thought you and your three little Regulators could use a hand. Even up the odds, you might say."

"What about your fee?"

Ockham winks with his one eye. "Found a private investor. You can split up that little pie. I'll keep the big all to myself."

On cue, a boy dressed in the collarless uniform of a CorpCom inductee steps from behind a concrete column.

"Jean-Paul Bramimonde," I say.

"Regulator?" Jenkins says to Spiner. "You said two more Regulators. That boy ain't no Regulator. He ain't big enough to pick up a—"

"What game are you two running?" I interrupt.

Jean-Paul squares his shoulder. Lifts a proud chin. "You refused to be my master, so I hired Ockham instead."

"You took money to be this boy's master?" I ask Ockham.

"Which is my right," Ockham says. "According to the Tenets."

"We're on a job!" I yell at him. "You didn't ask permission to do any training."

"That's just it," Ockham says as he grabs his gear and leads Jean-Paul away. "I don't need your permission to do nothing. Do I, *dalit*? Come on, young Bramimonde. Let's take a look at this famous South Pole they gab so much about on the nets."

"Chief?" It's Vienne's way of asking if I'm going to allow this to happen.

"Let it be. For now," Five Regulators is infinitely better than four. Even if Ockham is a presumptuous gasbag. "Regulators! Roll out! We've got work to do."

Vienne wrinkles her brow but falls in line. Fuse, taking his cue from her, does the same.

"I don't like it," Jenkins huffs. "An old man like that horning in on a job. I saw Regulators like him in my old CorpCom. Two years I spent taking their guff. Do this, boy, do that, boy. I'm almost a nine-year. I ain't taking orders from no walking fossil."

"If you're fobbed about it," I say as we follow Spiner down a path that cuts through the permafrost, "think how the miners are going to feel."

CHAPTER 14

Outside the station, the continental divide of the Prometheus Basin rises into the steel blue sky. The wind whipping down from the basin rim almost freezes us before we can take ten steps. Behind me, Jenkins complains about the cold and Fuse complains about Jenkins complaining. I swear, they're like an old married couple.

"More walking," I bark at them. "And less talking. Regulators! Double-time!"

We start jogging down the narrow, icy road, and a dozen meters later, we pass through an open wrought-iron gate that acts as the mine entrance.

A sign above the gate reads TO KNOW WORK IS TO KNOW GOD. They might as well have written THE ORTHOCRACY WAS HERE.

Ahead of us stands a steel tower that controls a lift mechanism. That's the main shaft, I'm guessing. A tipple, which was used to bring the ore to the surface, marks a second shaft. Both the tower and tipple are coated in thick rust, an indication that they've seen no use in years. To my left are several giant mounds of heavy guanite, the leftover product of the mines. Before, guanite was a valuable resource, but now it, like the miners, is considered worthless.

"Monitor everyone's vitals," I tell Mimi. Then call to Spiner, "We have to get out of this cold fast. I don't want my crew dying of hypothermia before the fun starts."

He points to a corrugated metal structure a hundred meters ahead. "That's the tram house. It takes us underground. Where it's warmer. Not warm. But warmer."

The tram house is ten by ten, with one door and four Plexi windows. The ground around it is streaked with snow, the soil furrowed and warped, as if cut by a massive scythe.

"In the before days," Spiner says as he leads us inside, "all this ground was permafrost, and the foundation for the tram house had to be jackhammered out of it. That was before Phase Blue come and living got easy. Well, get on the lift. It takes us down to the tracks."

No wonder the Dræu think the miners are easy pickings—the lift door stands wide open, and the only elevator is an open hydraulic lift. It's an open invitation for the cannibals to waltz right in and take whatever they want.

"Mimi," I say. "Start a list for me. First item, close down this lift."

"Check."

"And keep sweeping for human signatures. Make

sure there's no ugly surprises waiting for us."

"Beat you to it," she says. "Nobody here but us ducks."

"That's chickens."

"Yes," she says, "I know my poultry."

"You're telling jokes now? Since when do you have a sense of humor?"

"I told you," she says. "I'm evolving."

"And that's supposed to reassure me?"

We reach the tram. It is an open ore car modified to carry people. The driver sits in a jump seat, controlling the vehicle with a joystick. The passengers sit on benches and hold on for dear life.

As soon as we start, wind and dust whip through the tram. The air is tepid and stinks of sulfur. Even though there are rows of dim lights on both sides of the tunnels, entering the black hole of a mine means leaving the rest of the world behind. Day and night no longer matter. Time itself seems to stop.

"You're very quiet," Vienne says as she sits beside me. She lowers her voice. "Something's troubling you. Is it Ockham?"

She locks eyes with me, and I feel a sensation of fluttering behind my belly button, like my legs are being unscrewed, when she turns her head so that her hair falls behind her neck. Her chin lifts, and my eyes trace the curve of her lips.

Stop. Don't think of her like this. Don't think like this at all. I force my eyes closed. Push the air out of my lungs until they shake like my hands are shaking, then let the air out in

controlled segments. When I open my eyes, I can breathe
normally, and the rush is gone. For now.

"It's Ockham," I agree. "And the boy. And this job. We
need all the Regulators we can get, but Ockham's taking on
an acolyte here, now, in this place? That's stupid."

"Poor judgment," she says, nodding in agreement.

My voice is hushed. "It's against the Tenets to shoot
another Regulator, right?"

"This is why I will never be chief," she says. "I would've
shot him by now."

"Ha!" I laugh, and she fails to remain stone-faced. For
a moment I lean close to her. Despite of everything else,
there's something about Vienne that makes me stronger,
even though she turns my insides into jelly.

Soon we reach warmer air, which is infused with guanite dust. It blows around like powder, and we can't help but
inhale it. Soon all of us have brown nostrils, and our lips are
caked. We already look like miners.

Ahead, the trail widens to accommodate rows of squat
concrete houses. Ugly. Utilitarian. This place reminds me of
the Norilsk Gulag.

"Is this Hell's Cross?" I ask.

"No! The Cross is more swanky than this. It's called
Crazy Town," Spiner says. "Used to be where the slave labor
lived. They got left behind when the mines closed, then
went crazy and torched the place."

We leave the tram and walk in silence through Crazy

Town. It smells like dried, musty plaster. All around us, the boulevard is jammed with debris. Burned-out fuel barrels scattered among the skeletons of trucks. A bulldozer. A small bus. The buildings are sagging hulks with crumbling archways, dried-up gardens and fountains, broken-out windows, and swaying walls held together by rusted-out rebar.

"Spiner," I ask, "what's our destination?"

"Hereabouts," he says, and makes a hard right into pitch darkness. A few seconds later he flicks on a headlamp. The beam sweeps across our faces. "Come on, now. You're not afraid of the dark, are you?"

I wait long enough for Mimi to do a sweep. Then give the order: "Regulators! Helmet lights on. Follow him."

"Yes, chief," Vienne and Fuse reply in unison.

"See, love?" Fuse says. "We're already two peas in a pod."

"Get your own pod." Vienne punches him so hard, his armor seizes up. "Next time I draw blood."

"Nice right cross you've got there." Laughing, Fuse shakes his arm, relaxing the hardened sleeve. "If ever there's a friendly row among the troops, remind me to choose your side."

At least he's good-tempered about getting his ass kicked, I think.

"His suit doesn't think so," Mimi says. "The nanobots controlling the bioadaptive fabric are responding slowly to the aversive stimulus. They aren't used to forceful blows. Apparently Fuse isn't a battle-hardened soldier."

"That was something," I say, "I didn't need an AI to figure out."

Over the next few minutes, Spiner guides us quickly through a cavernous room. Then Jenkins yawns and leans against a wall, knocking loose a shower of dust that coats him from head to waist. He jumps up and starts slapping himself. "Damn this farging guanite!"

"What kind of dance is that?" Fuse says, laughing.

Jenkins stops mid-slap. "Huh? Dance?" Then his eyes narrow. "Stop having a laugh at me!" He makes a dive at Fuse, and they both end up tussling on the ground.

"Boys!" I shout, and they stop, but not before exchanging a couple more shoves. "Fuse, stop baiting him. Jenkins, behave yourself."

Then I notice Ockham watching, arms folded, like he's judging them. And judging me. He steers Jean-Paul toward Spiner and then slows down. Waiting for me.

All right, I think. You want to have words, let's have words. "Some place, no?" I say after catching up with him.

"It's no place for Regulators," he says.

My helmet beam highlights his face. In the narrow light, his scar and missing eye give me the feeling that he's wearing a grotesque mask.

"So I was cogitating," he says, "how was it that you got to be chief of this little davos of yours?"

"Circumstances dictated it."

"Did circumstances give you only one Regulator, too?"

"She's worth five."

"A davos is to have ten." He blows his nose into his hand. "The Orthocrats, they knew the right way to train a Regulator. Not some assembly line of mass-produced piddle-poor knockoffs. No offense."

"None taken."

"Fibber," Mimi says. "You're very offended."

"That's where the word *davos* come from," Ockham continues. "A master would take on nine followers at the same time. The acolytes learned how to fight single-handedly, but they learned how to fight as a group, to defend their brothers, too. They lived together, ate together, fought together, and when it had to be, died together."

"Pompous windbag," Mimi says. "Every Regulator knows this."

"Shh. Let him talk. Let's see what his angle is."

"That's why when a master died," he continues, "the acolytes all joined him in death or became *dalit*. It was a beautiful death. It was the Tenets. All that changed when the Orthocracy fell apart. Regulators went from being peace-keepers to soldiers."

"Common knowledge, Ockham," I say, thinking of Vienne. She's devoted her life to serving the Tenets, her davos, her chief. Her greatest ambition is to die a Beautiful Death. My ambition is to keep her alive.

Ockham knocks the dust off my shoulder, revealing the double chevron symbol of chief sergeant. "The old masters never needed stripes to be leaders."

"The old masters are dead," I say. "Times change."

"Maybe. Maybe not, no?" Ockham says, lifting his head, showing the stubble on his chin and jowls. For a glimpse of time, he isn't an over-the-hill, burnout mercenary, but a young soldier, strong and confident. "Something else I wanted to get off my chest. You and that Vienne?"

"What about us?"

"I've seen the way you look at her. You think you love that girl, and you probably do. But feelings have got you blinded to something. Want to know what?"

"No," I say, resisting the urge to throttle him, "and I'm not all that interested in you telling me."

He does anyway. "Because the thing about her that makes your head spin like a busted gyro is the very thing that will keep you apart."

"You're pretty poetic," I say, "for a crusty oldie."

"How'd you think I got this crust, sonny?" He laughs deeply, and his face takes on its weary caste again. "War ain't the only battles I've lived through. There's worse wounds than them what bullets leave in you."

Let it go, I tell myself as Ockham moves up to be with Jean-Paul. It's not worth the trouble to give him the smack he deserves.

"Do it anyway," Mimi says.

"Quit kibitzing," I tell her.

"It's my job to kibitz."

"I thought it was to keep me alive."

"I'm an AI of many talents," she says. "Plus, there are less obvious ways to keep you alive."

Up ahead, Spiner switches on a light, and the group takes a left turn. Vienne waves us forward.

"Double-time," I say.

We begin jogging, crouched low to avoid an encounter with the ceiling, and catch up at the end of the tunnel. We stop in front of an air lock, a circular iron door with a porthole in the center.

Here the tunnel is almost perfectly round. The surface is as smooth as glass. "You miners do good work," I say, running a hand along the wall.

Jenkins scoffs. "Good work, nothing. The rusters didn't dig this tunnel."

"Good eye," Spiner says. "Big Daddies did the work. No man can match them chigoes for tunneling. Not even the best guanite miners on this planet."

"Who would that be?" I ask.

"Us, of course."

"Poor but proud," Vienne says quietly.

In the glow of the lights, I can make out a brick wall to the left and a broad steel gate to the right, wide enough to drive a power sled through.

"No multivids for security?" I ask Mimi. "No retinal scanners?"

"Nothing," she says.

"No surveillance equipment at all? I don't believe it."
Fisher Four really is a hundred years behind the rest of Mars.

"Stop exaggerating," Mimi says. "You're just used to very
sophisticated technology."

"You're alluding to yourself?"

"It goes without saying."

"But you said it."

"Au contraire," she says, "you did."

A few seconds later white light floods the tunnel as Spiner
rolls open the air lock. "Home sweet home," he says, and
steps inside.

CHAPTER 15

Hell's Cross, Outpost Fisher Four
ANNOS MARTIS 238. 4. 0. 00:00

"What's so sweet about this dump?" Jenkins grumbles.

After taking a quick look, I'm wondering the same thing. We wind our way through an area littered with junk, then reach a series of arches shaped like onions. Torn and faded, flags hang from the arches, and you can still make out the red Cross and Circle of the Orthocracy. Rusted razor wire covers all but one of the arches, the one we pass through onto a stone masonry circle. Ventilated wind blows guanite dust across the circle, piling up on the relic of a mining truck, a couple of garbage dumpers, and a hodgepodge of rotted baskets.

In the distance I hear the sound of grinding machinery. Like the echo of some kind of hammer. Something hinky's going on here. Are the miners still working the mine?

Ahead is a two-story square building, maize in color, with two octagonal towers. There are gun slits in the towers, which rise at least thirty meters into the air. I keep thinking sky, instead of air, but when I look up, there's that soupy blackness, reminding me that we're a half click, maybe a whole kilometer, underground.

The towers do mean one thing: the square building was built to be defended. Finally, something we can sink our Regulator teeth into. There are three doors—two narrow ones to the left and right secured with iron bars, the third, the middle entrance, is twice as wide, with two doors made of heavy steel strapped together. The doors stand open, leading down a flat-roofed corridor littered with small crates.

"Welcome to the Cross," Spiner says.

The ground is paved with girih tiles that form an intricate quasicrystal pattern. The tiles lead your eye to middle of the courtyard and a statue of Bishop Lyme, the first leader of the Orthocracy. The Great Poxer himself. Dressed in a frock, he holds a pickax in one hand and the *Book of Common Prayer* in the other. I've seen the statue in a dozen different places. It's always the same, except for him holding the pick. In New Eden, it's a pipe wrench. In the greenhouses at Tan Hauser Gates, it's a trowel. And in battle school, it's an armalite.

"The old zealot sure got around," I say.

"'Look on my Works, ye Mighty,'" Mimi says, "'and despair.'"

"Byron?"

"Shelley."

"Always get those two confused."

"Byron had the clubbed foot."

"Thought Oedipus had the clubbed foot."

"I despair for you, cowboy." Mimi makes a noise like a sigh. "It's a good thing you can shoot straight."

Behind the statue alongside a high crane, I point out two minarets, tall spires with crowns shaped like onions to match the arches. I'm thinking there are two galleries at the top of the tower shafts. In the before days they probably were part of the temple. Now they'll make excellent nests for a sniper.

The rest of the building is nothing to cheer about. There are four entrances to the courtyard—one opposite this one, and two at the right and left. All of them lead to corridors like the one we entered from. A series of columns and onion-shaped arches create an arcade that runs the courtyard interior. I can see two dozen or so doors—the miners' quarters, I'm guessing—which means the rooms would be vulnerable if the enemy breached the courtyard.

The air smells stale and fecund. Like an old boot. With fungus growing in it. Wind whips left to right across the stone. More *chùsheng* dust. Funny, I thought being in a cave would make it less windy, but it's as bad as the surface. There's not much here otherwise. A few scaffoldings where the miners are making repairs on the masonry. More faded flags. These marked with the slogan of the revolution: LIBERTY, EQUALITY, JUSTICE. None of that here. Sad to think— the miners helped overthrow the Orthocracy, and this place holds no evidence that they'd gotten anything in return.

"Show me upstairs," I tell Spiner.

"This way." He leads us up two short flights. "Here's where we sleep and eat."

"What about the latrine?" Jenkins says.

"We dig a new one every month."

"No plumbing?" I ask.

Spiner laughs. "The Orthocrats blew the sewer lines when they left. For drinking water we channel runoff from the tundra."

"No plumbing!" Jenkins shouts. "Next thing you'll be saying you've got no toilet wipes."

"Orthocracy took those with them, too," Spiner says, scratching his stubble.

"Those bluey-blowing budgie smugglers!" he roars.

Fuse pats his shoulder. "That would be right, Jenks. Don't fret so. We'll find a lord high substitute. Or we can pack our bellies with amino gruel, and there'll be no problem needing the stuff, right?"

While Fuse consoles him, I do a quick bit of recon to confirm my assumptions. The arcade is about three meters wide, lit by a series of gas lamps. The structure could give us a good firing position, but there's only a string of arches and short columns and a rail for cover. Not a place for a firefight, that's for sure.

"Mimi," I ask, "got this mapped out?"

"Does the bishop crap in the woods?"

"Anything I missed?"

"If you didn't see it, I didn't see it."

"What about the eyes in the back of my head?"

"Your suit doesn't have that upgrade," she teases.

"Okay," I say to my davos. "Let's go meet the people we're rescuing."

CHAPTER 16

Hell's Cross, Outpost Fisher Four

When the door swings open, the room is dark. Spiner clicks on his headlamp and sweeps the chamber, searching the four corners but only finding empty tables and benches. "The room's empty," he says, confused, rubbing his neck. "There's nobody here."

"Astute observation. Regulators, secure the area." While they move to defensive positions, I quickly scan the arcade and the courtyard for signs of life. Hell's Cross is hushed as a graveyard. The hammering I noticed earlier has stopped.

Taking the stairs back down to the courtyard, I check for tracks on the tiled floors. None. But there should be, unless someone covered them. No other signs of an attack, either. The miners left willingly or they were never in the meeting room in the first place. For whatever reason, the people we've traveled a thousand kilometers to save are hiding from us.

"Mimi?" Then I check the entrances. Even though it's quiet, it could still be an ambush. "Any signatures?"

"None within a thirty-meter radius. That's as far as I can extend the telemetry in this space."

Damn it. Where are they? Did the Dræu get to the miners before we did?

"Regulators! Expand the perimeter," I call out, my voice echoing too much. "Mouths shut. Eyes and ears open."

Ockham leaves his post to join me, Jean-Paul in tow. He points his armalite at the statue in the middle of the courtyard. "Maybe the bishop is hiding them."

"It's not a time for jokes," I snap, and step up on the dais. From this vantage point, I have clear line of sight on all the entrances, as well as the second-floor stairwells, which are lit with iridescent glow lights. It's going to take a while before my eyes adjust to the darkness that blankets the Cross.

"Vienne," I say, "search the arcade. Use the right stairs. Jenkins, start searching from the left. Ockham, check out the corridor at twelve o'clock. Fuse at three o'clock. I'll take the one at nine." They all acknowledge the order, although Ockham takes his time about it.

"What about me?" Jean-Paul asks, grabbing my empty holster.

Stay out of the way, kid. "You can guard Spiner."

"But I have no weapon, chief."

"Improvise." And don't call me chief, I think. You're not a Regulator yet. I move into position. Kneel down and sweep the dimly lit corridor.

"Anything?" I ask Mimi.

"Not yet."

"Open a vid link with the crew." Vienne, Jenkins, and Fuse have found no hostiles. "Ockham? What's your status?" Then I realize that we're not communicating with Ockham. "Mimi, remind me to synch with the old fart at the next opportunity."

"I'll put *old fart synching* on your to-do list."

"Ha-ha."

Vienne is the first to reply. Fuse is next, followed by Jenkins. All clear. So far. After a quick glance back at the statue—Jean-Paul is guarding Spiner with a length of rebar, and Spiner is scratching his head, befuddled by the whole production—I move deeper into the corridor. The light dims as I walk. My eyes take a few seconds to adjust because I don't want to use the helmet lamp and alert anyone.

Wish my bionic eye had heat vision.

"Me, too," Mimi says.

No doors here. No windows or portals. Just a long stretch of corridor that leads into God knows what. If any of the fossickers are hiding here, they don't have a pulse, because Mimi would pick up their signatures.

"Regulators—" I say into the vid. But before anyone can respond, a siren sounds, and I clap my hands over my ears. "*Wŏkào!* What the hell?"

"A raid siren, cowboy," Mimi says. "It's coming from the courtyard."

I race back down the corridor and hit the courtyard at

full speed. Spiner is bent over, hands clasped over his ears. Jean-Paul is still guarding him.

"Vienne! Report!" I shout into the aural link.

Static. A quick visual of the arcade. It's Vienne, signaling okay from the left corner. She heads down the stairs. Fuse and Ockham reach the courtyard.

Without Jenkins.

Where is he? "Jenks, report!" I say, upset at the thought of losing a soldier. "Before I shoot you for desertion!"

With a laugh, Jenkins swings down from the arcade. Lands like an artillery shell on the paved stone ground. The sound of the siren begins to fade, and I realize by the self-satisfied grin on his face, he's the one who set it off.

"What is wrong with you, Regulator?" I ask as Jenkins swats the dust from his knees. "Why'd you pull that stunt?"

"Didn't feel like taking the stairs." He shrugs. "What? It didn't hurt. Honest. My suit took the hit for me."

"No, no, no." I pinch the bridge of my nose. A lecture about the shortsightedness of abusing your symbiarmor isn't what I had in mind. "Why. Did. You. Soundtheairraidsiren?"

He grins. "To make them come running."

"Who's *them*?"

"The mud puppies, chief," he says, like it all makes perfect sense. Does he expect me to read his mind? Yes, as a matter of fact, he probably does.

"Cowboy," Mimi interrupts, "my sweep is showing multiple signatures bearing down on this location."

"Is it the miners?"

"Probably. They're human."

"Probably human is better than probably Dræu." So, Jenkins was making sense after all. Then I say aloud, "At ease, Regulators. Jenkins's little stunt might just work, and we don't want to accidentally shoot our hosts." So the miners were hiding after all. Why would they do that? We're here to help them.

As they move out of the shadows and into the courtyard, I count heads. There are thirty to forty miners, almost sixty percent of them male, although the females wear the same brown coveralls and are streaked with just as much soot and grease. They eye us with a mix of contempt and fear and keep their heads half bowed, as if shielding their eyes. I recognize a familiar face among the men—Jurm, the other man with Áine and Spiner.

They begin forming a circle around us. We take position around the dais.

"These rusters ain't used to civilized folk," Jenkins tells Fuse. "They act all proud about squatting in their black holes, like it makes them holy or something. They're always whining about how they got abandoned and how everybody hates them, but when a helping hand gets offered, they run and hide like babies."

"Settle down," I tell him.

Ockham steps forward. "Is it me, or are they giving us the stink eye?"

"It's just you," I reply. But maybe it isn't. Something's missing from the equation here, and one quick look gives me the answer. There are maybe fifteen children, all under age-five. The rest of the miners are oldies, all of them well past age-twenty.

Vienne notices the same thing. "There are no young adults. How can we train children and oldies to fight the Dræu?"

Nodding, I bite my lip. "We'll get by. We always find a way to make it work."

"More company," Vienne says, pointing to the arcade. It's the area that Fuse searched. "Mimi, new item for my list: Speak to Fuse about doing a more thorough search next time."

Two women stand at the railing, looking down on us. The younger of the two is Áine. I don't recognize the older woman, who has long silver hair and a face that looks as if it's been chiseled from sandstone. She's wearing a tan frock and robes the color of mud.

I glance at the circle of miners, who are carrying wrenches as long and heavy as their arms. They're squeezing us, drawing the circle tighter, dragging the wrenches on the ground so that they squeal. Fuse and Jenkins stand back-to-back, eyes darting around, looking to me for guidance. I shake my head no, even as their hands inch compulsively toward their armalites.

"Welcome, Regulators," the older woman's voice rings out.

"Funny, I ain't feeling too damned welcome right now," Ockham says, and draws his weapon, and my heart almost stops.

The miners all swing their wrenches up to their shoulders. Ockham responds by aiming the red dot from his laser sight right between the old woman's eyes. His finger's resting on the trigger. His free hand is hovering near the three light-mass grenades clipped to his belt. "How'd you want to play it, rusters?"

The circle closes like a noose tightening.

"Ockham," I say, moving close to him. "Stand down. This isn't the way to start a job."

"Tell that to the lynch mob," Ockham says.

"I'm telling you!" I bark as the oldie moves the sights from the old woman to Áine and back again. He could be Vienne's twin, technique wise, but that's where the comparison ends. "Now stand down! I'm giving the orders here."

He's about to argue when Spiner jumps up on the statue dais. "Hold on, Regulators. We don't get many visitors down under, except them that wants to rob us of our little bits of nothing, so our people ain't much on courtesy and the like. If they meant to do you harm, you'd be wandering the tunnels instead of standing here, I'd warrant you that."

"That," Vienne says, moving next to me, "was oddly reassuring."

"I'm not sure *reassuring* is the word I'd use." But still, I feel the tension drop a few decibels. Time to put this situation to bed. Staring at the old woman, I hold my arms wide to show that I'm bearing no arms—other than my armalite, a sidearm, a combat knife in either boot, and a shiv tucked up a sleeve. "Me and mine came here in good faith for a fee that frankly isn't normal rate. But when we get here, you treat us like plague carriers. Where I come from, that's not copacetic."

"My sincerest apology, Regulator," the old woman says, her voice like the sound of a soft metal bell. "When we saw the man who threatened to kill Áine, we were worried."

"Fair enough," I say.

The old woman comes down to join us. She sticks out a boney hand. Her skin's so thin, the veins underneath look like bloodworms. When we shake, my own hand engulfs hers, and it feels like a gentle squeeze would crush her bones.

"Come upstairs," she says.

We follow her and Áine through a metal door. It's supported by iron straps, and there's a heavy throw bolt on the inside. It's strong enough to keep out your average thief, but against a trained, determined enemy, it wouldn't last more than a minute. Maybe that's why the miners are so good at hiding. It's the only defense they've got.

"Where's the grub?" Jenkins asks. He takes a seat on a long bench next to a stone table.

"Give it a rest, right?" Fuse sits between him and Jean-Paul, with Ockham at the end. Vienne stands behind the bench, ostensibly waiting for me to sit, but she's actually sweeping the room for threats.

"Mimi?" I ask, just to make sure that Vienne hasn't missed anything. "All clear?"

"No new biosignatures," she says. "And no boogeymen hiding in the closet."

"Thanks, but I think *we're* the boogeymen in this room."

"Excellent point," Mimi says.

"About that grub," Jenkins says, his mind still on the same track.

"We've some food to share later," the old woman says.

"Not much," Áine says quickly. "We miners ain't used to eating like you rich folk."

"We understand," I say, trying to keep to the subject at hand.

"Understand like blazes," Jenkins blusters. "Them rusters out there, they looked fat enough to me. We come thousands of kilometers on TransPort, walk an hour through tunnels, and you ain't even decent enough to feed us? Don't cry poor to me. You got food hid, I know you do. Ain't like miners not to have something set back."

"Poor thing," Ockham interrupts. "His belly's empty, and he's at nobs end about it. Shame, no? Tell me, chief, do you have to change this boy when you're done feeding him? Or is wiping his own ass something he's capable of?"

Jenkins whips a combat knife out of his boot. "How's I wipe your ass with this, oldie?"

Ockham yawns.

"Stop it," I say in a low voice that echoes off the rock walls. "Both of you."

"You'll not be giving me orders, chief," Ockham says. "It's not you paying my freight."

"I'm in charge of this job," I snap. "And I say no bickering. You don't like that? Find yourself different work. I don't care a whit who's paying your damned freight."

"Is there a problem?" the woman asks. Beside her, Áine smiles coyly. Plays with a strand of brown hair.

"We're just cranky from the TransPort," I say. "It's been a long ride." I clear my throat and introduce my davos.

"Welcome, all of you," she says. "You met Spiner, Jurm, and Áine before. I'm named Maeve, but the miners call me old woman."

"It fits," Jenkins says.

Fuse slaps him.

"Ow! Oy, I'm just speaking the truth."

"Yes," Maeve says, "he's right. It does fit. But we got off to a bad start. My apologies for the greeting you got. As I said, miners are wary folk by nature."

Jenkins huffs. Fuse elbows him. Maeve ignores them both.

"Now to business," she says. "These past months, we were raided by the Dræu again and again. They attack out of nowhere, take what children they can carry, then disappear. We all know what the Dræu do to children. CorpCom law is useless out here, and we've got no weapons nor training in defending ourselves, so I sent Áine to hire a Regulator to train us. Blessedly, you all came instead, but we know that if we rise against the Dræu, they will try to kill us all."

"Which is why you need us to force them to move on," I say.

"Move on? Tch." Áine clicks her tongue softly. "Not likely, handsome."

Maeve pats Áine's hand, a loving gesture that I interpret to mean *Enough with the flirting*. "What Áine is trying to say is, the Dræu are not reasonable folk, so them moving on would not be achievable." Maeve goes on to state the terms of the contract and what will bring the final payout. "Either the Dræu are defeated, or they agree to sign a blood oath to never attack this outpost again."

"The Dræu sign a blood oath?" Mimi says. "Not likely, *handsome*."

I can't help but smile. But across the table, Áine smiles in return. Oh no. What have I done?

"Stepped in it," Mimi says.

Maeve unrolls a sheath of electrostat. The contract is imprinted on it, and there's a box for my thumbprint. I scan the document to make sure it's all kosher, but I pause with my thumb hovering over the signature line.

"Before I endorse this. Once I'm in charge, I'm in charge of everything: fortifying defenses, training your folk in the use of weaponry, defeating the enemy in battle. You provide the support, the materials, and the food."

"We've not," Áine says, "promised to just turn ourselves

for you to use any way you'd like, Regulator."

"But if that is what needs done, then we'll do it," the old woman says. "We agree to your terms. Our lives are in your hands."

"You can count on us," I say.

"Let's see if you can still say that," Áine murmurs, shifting the weight off her wounded leg, "after you've had a taste of the Dræu."

In battle school, our masters drilled this mantra into our heads: *All warfare is based on deception.* From the recon we could pry out of the miners, the Dræu have a hundred fighters. We have five Regulators, a pint-sized acolyte, and about forty ornery miners. So my first job is to deceive the Dræu into thinking we've got *beaucoups* more personnel than that and the personnel is well-trained.

My other job is to make use of the skills the miners have to build defensive structures to control the enemy's route into the mines. If the Dræu can't reach the Cross, then they can't attack. The problem is, there are dozens of tunnels, and we can't defend them all.

"There are forty-two tunnels, to be exact," Mimi says.

Vienne, Áine, and I stand in the dim light of Hell's Cross. Our faces are illuminated by the glow of a open electrostat, which displays a cross-section map of the Fisher Four mine. From this angle, it looks like an ant colony. The tipple and ore houses are on the surface. Six different lifts lead to the tramway. Twelve different exit stations lead to elevators connected to the maze of underground stations. Most of the active mine shafts and worker settlements are a kilometer south and four hundred meters below us.

Vienne looks over my shoulder, pointing out the route that we took to reach the Cross via Crazy Town, and Áine stands close, pointing out landmarks.

"So we have forty-two tunnels of varying sizes," I say, tracing the lines with my finger. "All of them lead either directly or indirectly to the four main corridors that lead to the Cross. There are only a handful of paths the Dræu can use to attack with a large force, like the way we came in. But there are too many spots where they can send in a skirmish line to harass us."

"'You can ensure the safety of your defense if you only hold positions that cannot be attacked,'" Vienne says, quoting from *The Art of War* and glaring at Áine.

"Right," I say. "So we're going to do this in two phases. First, we'll close all but one of the corridors."

"Why not close them all?" Áine asks. Then sticks her tongue out at Vienne.

"Because we want the Dræu to attack," I explain.

"What?" Áine squeaks. "That's madness!"

"No, it's plumbing. We know the water is going to flow. We just decide where it's shunted to. Which brings us to the second phase." I tap the map. Sweep my fingers across it. "This corridor leads to a bridge, which leads to where?"

"The surface," Áine says. "And we call that the Zhao Zhou Bridge. You'd never heard of it? We use it when we go foraging. But it's full of junked-up machines."

"Which makes it perfect," I say. "The debris will slow down any rush attacks, and the Zhao Zhou Bridge will funnel them into our redoubt."

"Our what?"

"Redoubt," Vienne says, smirking. "A defensive structure designed to fight against sieges."

Áine sticks out her chin, letting Vienne know that she doesn't appreciate her little lecture. "Well, Miss Know-it-all, we don't have one of those here."

"No problem," I say. If I don't do something about their bickering now, there will never be an end to it, and it might jeopardize the job. Then I hit on a plan. "No problem at all. In fact, you're going to build us one."

Áine chokes. "Excuse me? You're having a laugh, right? We don't know about building redoubts or whatever you call them."

It's my time to smirk. "Vienne is going to show you."

"Chief!"

"Not her!" Áine snarls. "There's a fair suck of salve!"

"Tough." I roll up the electrostat. "I've got to talk to Fuse. There's some blasting to do, and he's the right one for the job. You two enjoy yourselves. And oh, you've got twenty-four hours to get the job done."

"Twenty-four hours?" they chime together.

"But how?" Áine says.

"With what?" Vienne asks.

"You're both smart girls," I say. "I'm sure you'll think of something."

As I walk away, a silent argument rages. I grin and ask Mimi to locate Fuse for me.

"Fuse is on the Zhao Zhou Bridge," Mimi says. She shows me his coordinates on the aural vid. "You know what was going on back there, don't you?"

"Yep. I decided to let them hash it out."

"Hash what out, precisely?"

"Their little turf war. We've got to be one unified force against the Dræu, so the sooner they learn to cooperate, the better."

Mimi is silent, but I have the unnerving feeling that if she still had a head, she would be shaking it.

"What?" I say.

"Sometimes, cowboy," she says, "I wonder if you are as dense and impenetrable as symbiarmor."

"I am who I am," I say, and head out to check out the bridge.

When the corridor ends, I step out into an open cavern. All around me, there are high cliffs. Check that. Not really cliffs. Cuts. Most of the walls of the massive cavern were cut by machines. Cut from the walls in large chunks so that the walls look like steps to a giant's house. It's like an open pit mine underground. The walls are dark brown but look black where the overhead array of lights doesn't touch them. It feels like there's no end to the cavern, but the lack of a sky overhead leaves me feeling claustrophobic. It doesn't help that a deep gorge splits the cavern in half, and that the gorge is supposed to be bottomless.

As casually as I can, I walk to the edge of the gorge and toss a chunk of rock into its black maw. I count off seconds, waiting for the sound of it hitting bottom. When I get to one hundred, I quit.

Thank God for bridges, I think, and start walking toward Fuse.

The Zhao Zhou Bridge measures about one hundred fifty meters in length and is twelve meters wide. Built of slabs jointed with dovetails, the main semicircle arch rises high above the gorge that separates the corridor leading to Hell's Cross from a wide cliff on the opposite end. There are ornamental railings on either side and an arched swing gate on each end.

The deck of the bridge is littered with the carcasses of broken machines and tools. Which will have to be cleared. Off to the right, I count six heavy cranes. Rust covers the cockpits where operators once sat, and the massive cables that hang from their booms lay in heaps beside the treads. Farther away, near the side tunnels, I see an endless supply of shipping containers stacked ten high. In the before days, they were used to transport ore via the beanstalks. Now they're scattered like a gigantic child's building blocks. Building blocks. There's a thought.

"Mimi," I say, "keep scanning the area. Let me know if you pick up anything."

"Will do," she says. "But cowboy, these repetitive scans are putting a strain on your suit's capacity and therefore, you. Your body needs to sleep."

"I'll sleep when I'm dead."

"Which will happen sooner than later if you do not rest."

"In the meantime, give me a pinch if I start nodding off."

When I reach Fuse, he's holding a piece of electrostat. But it's turned upside down, and he's scratching his head like the map's an impossible puzzle. Clearly, cartography is not this soldier's forte.

Fuse jumps when I sneak up behind him. "Oy! Chief!" He pats his chest. "You almost gave me a coronary. Let a jack know you're coming, right?"

"Sorry, Fuse," I say, turning his map to the correct direction. "First order of business is for you to close up every secondary and tertiary tunnel connected to this corridor. We're going to funnel the Dræu from that main tunnel over there and across this bridge to a redoubt that Vienne and Áine are designing."

"So that's a bridge?" He points at the map.

"As in, the one you're standing on?"

"Oh, right. I see now. That's more like it. So, I'm to shut down a bunch of tunnels. Right. What've I got to work with?"

"Anything you can scavenge to do the job. If it's not nailed down, use it."

Fuse surveys the area, pointing out the small mountains of discarded machinery and mining equipment. "I dunno, chief. Not much here that's not falling apart. What about the cranes? They might be handy for moving some junk around. Think they still work?"

"Fix them if they don't," I say. "Also, the old woman Maeve says there's some C-forty-two in storage if you need it for closing down the tunnels. In the before days, miners used it for blowing tunnels."

"Explosives?" Fuse's eyes light up. "This changes everything."

I give his shoulder a shake. "Thought it might." I turn to leave but find Jenkins at my elbow.

"Fuse is going to blow things up?" he asks.

"He is."

Jenkins's eyes sparkle. "Can I help?"

"No carking way!" Fuse says. "Remember the last time you *helped*? I lost both my eyebrows."

"Aw. They grew back."

"The miners are collecting scrap in the back," I say, cutting their argument short. "How about you lend a hand?" I steer Jenkins away from Fuse and toward the archway that leads to the Cross. "Gives you a chance to show off your muscles."

Jenkins grumbles. Looks longingly at Fuse, who has

already climbed into the cockpit of a crane. He tries to crank the motor, but all we hear is the clicking of a solenoid. He's got his work cut out for him.

"Come on, Jenkins." I've got no idea what job to give him to occupy his hands, but I breathe easy knowing he won't be near the explosives.

"Cowboy," Mimi interrupts. "I have an urgent message from Maeve."

"Hold up a second, Jenkins," I say. Then tell Mimi to route Maeve through. "Put it on aural."

"Durango," she says, her voice popping with the bad connection. "We have a situation with you and yours. It's Ockham. He's causing a ruckus."

That *scheißkerl*. I've had about all I can swallow of him. "What kind of ruckus?"

"It's better you see it in person," she says. "Please come to the Cross. Before somebody gets killed."

"The scrap collection will have to wait," I tell Jenkins. Then signal Vienne and Fuse to join us in the Cross. "Seems there's a patch of trouble with Ockham."

"There's always trouble with that oldie," Jenkins says, almost under his breath. "Is it time to shoot him yet?"

"I haven't decided."

"Can I shoot him when you do decide?"

"No. Vienne can."

"Aw," Jenkins says. "I never get to have any fun."

CHAPTER 17

Hell's Cross, Outpost Fisher Four
ANNOS MARTIS 238. 4. 0. 00:00

We find Ockham leaning against the bishop's statue. He has peeled off his armor, his wad of clumpy hair tied at the neck, and he stands observing Jean-Paul Bramimonde. The boy crouches low, unmoving, naked except for a linen loincloth, while a group of six miners form a loose ring around him. There are cuts on his back and shoulders, his body caked with guanite dust.

He's attached by the ankle to a cable. The cable is spiked to the ground. It's one of the barbaric methods the old Regulators once used to train their acolytes.

The miners are laughing, each of them wielding a makeshift weapon—crowbars, heavy wrenches, and a welding torch—and egging the boy on. Jean-Paul's eyes widen. Flecks of foam fly from his mouth as he lunges at Jurm. But the cable tied to his ankle snaps taut, and he belly flops onto the ground. He comes up spitting dust and frothing.

"Tch, boy," Jurm teases him. "Is that all you've got?"

"Use your ears, lad." Ockham spits on the steps. Wipes brown juice from his mouth. "Not your eyes."

Tobacco, I think as Vienne and I close in on the circle. Where did he get the coin for tobacco? "Ockham," I say sharply, "explain yourself!" Although I already know the answer.

"Training," he says, not looking at me.

"Training?" Vienne says, taking her place beside me. "That boy is about to get his brains mashed out."

"Care to wager on that?" Ockham says. Then bellows at Jean-Paul, "I said, stay low. That's it. Low! Balance and leverage. Put your weight on the back foot. Back foot!"

"Do something," Áine calls to me, entering the Cross from a corridor.

Vienne snarls, "It's not for a miner to tell a chief how to handle his Regulators."

"This is my home," Áine snarls back at her. "So I'll say what I like. Want to make something of it?"

I can tell Vienne wants very much to make something of it, but she can't hurt someone she's sworn to protect. It's in the Tenets. Otherwise, I'm sure Áine would be finding herself in horrible pain and a part of her body in a cast.

But the fact remains that Áine challenged my authority in front of my davos. So, now, even though I was about to call a halt to the exercise, I have to stand and wait. Just to prove to her and the rest of the miners that they can't give us orders. It's a piddling contest, and I despise piddling in public.

Áine is huffing in frustration when, without a word, I turn my back on her. Vienne looks pleased. Wish I were.

"Piddling contests are in the job description," Mimi says. "It's part of being chief."

I ignore her, too. Focus on the fight. The real problem at hand.

Jean-Paul drops back into a crouch. He makes a chuffing sound to focus his chi. It's classic Regulator hand-to-hand combat training—a fighting style called tai bo that fuses Earther martial arts with physics. In battle school I was trained in the same style. But we faced other acolytes of the same age and size. Not grown men who outweighed us three-to-one and carried heavy, metal tools.

"Mimi," I say.

"Yes?"

"Nothing," I say. "Just a random reflex." But in my mind's eye, I'm picturing myself standing at attention in front of my first davos while Mimi, my new chief, sized me up.

"You look like a movie cowboy in that new symbiarmor," she said. "Did your daddy buy you that?"

"Yes, chief," I said. "When I graduated from battle school."

"Battle school?" The rest of the davos laughed.

The one named Vienne spoke up. "Another schoolboy, chief?"

"I don't understand what's wrong with battle school," I said.

"That's because you went to battle school." Mimi put an arm around my shoulder and led me away from the group.

Though I was tall for an age-six, she still towered over me, a tall, muscled age-nine with cropped black hair and a jagged scar across her forehead. "Look, kid, you can't learn to be a Regulator in school. You have to train with a master. You have to learn to follow the Tenets. Or you'll never be a true Regulator, just a movie cowboy."

"I can follow the Tenets," I said. "Where can I get a copy?"

Mimi laughed. "The Tenets aren't for reading." She tapped her head then her heart. "They're here and here."

"I—"

"Rule number one: Stop starting your sentences with *I*. It's *we* now."

"I—"

She smacked the back of my head. "Rule number two: The base of the skull is your symbiarmor's weak point. An object is only as strong as its weakest point. The same is true of a davos. Are you going to be my weak point, cowboy?"

With Mimi's words echoing in my head, I shake the memory away. Ever since Mimi's brain waves were implanted to control the nanobots in my body, memories have become more vivid. More real.

"That actually was *my* memory," Mimi says.

"It's getting harder to tell," I say.

"For me, too, cowboy."

A cold shiver runs down my spine. What does that mean, *for her, too?*

Another lunge by Jean-Paul catches my attention. There's blood on his ankle where the cable cut him, and the miners are getting nastier. Moving closer and closer to bait him.

Time to end this. I signal Vienne to move behind Ockham. Just in case things don't go well. "Jean-Paul is paying your fee, Ockham," I say.

Ockham grunts. "So?"

"So maybe you don't want him dead. At least until he pays you."

"I'm not worried. This kid's got giant yarbles."

"Giant yarbles make bigger targets," I say. "Maybe he ought to wear more than a loincloth."

Ockham laughs. Slaps me on the back. "Didn't know you had a sense of humor, chief."

"He does," Vienne says. "I don't." She bumps Ockham with her shoulder, a reminder that she's there.

"Order your miners to stand down," I tell Áine and Maeve.

Áine curls her lip, and I can see that she's not happy. "What miners do is their business," she pouts. "They don't need a chief to tell them how to act."

Ouch.

"Especially when we're getting paid coin," Jurm pipes in.

"Paid?" I get in Ockham's face. "You paid them to beat a boy?"

"Not me." Ockham starts laughing, but stops when no one else joins in. "My acolyte paid them himself."

"He did wh—" I say.

A scream interrupts me. As I turn toward the source, Jean-Paul, the miner wielding the arc torch charges. He swings the long, angled rod of the torch high over his head. Bears down on Jean-Paul. Who stays low, his weight distributed evenly on the balls of his feet. Hands in blocking position.

"Wait," I yell—it's too late to stop it. Roll into the rooter, I think, urging Jean-Paul to use the miner's weight and momentum against him.

But the boy doesn't move. Instead, he stands his ground. Takes the charge. At the last heartbeat, he pitches forward to duck the welding rod. His hands useless against the miner's pumping legs. A knee catches his chin. He flies backward.

The miner stumbles, his legs tangled up in the boy's, and they fall together in a mass of flailing limbs. Proof that neither one of them is a trained fighter. The miner is first to his feet. He brings the welding rod up again. Ready to rain blows on Jean-Paul's back as the boy rises on hands and knees, trying desperately to catch his breath.

"Halt!" I shout as I jump down the steps. "Stand down! Now!"

The miner looks befuddled as I step into the circle. He turns to Áine, then to Ockham for direction. I take the chance to snatch the rod out of his hands.

The boy's mouth is bloodied. Droplets roll down his belly, staining the dirtied, white loincloth.

I give Jean-Paul a good shake. "What were you thinking? That man could've killed you."

"I want," Bramimonde says stubbornly as he yanks his arm away, "to be trained the way a Regulator acolyte is supposed to be trained."

"That? That is not how acolytes are supposed to be trained. Acolytes don't train against grown men," I say. "Especially ones carrying hand tools for weapons."

"Aw, we wasn't going to hurt him bad," Jurm says. "He paid us to fight, so we figured it ort to be a good one."

"Save it for the Dræu," I say. "Ockham, untie the kid." I drop the welding rod to the ground. It clatters on the stone, the sound echoing off the walls, and I'm a little surprised by the noise it makes.

Jurm picks it up and backs into the circle. But the boy isn't taking no for an answer. He drops into a fighting crouch. "Come back, coward!"

"I said," I scold Jean-Paul, "stand down. Get yourself cleaned up."

The boy wipes his mouth on the back of a forearm. "I'm fine. All systems copacetic."

"Where did you hear that phrase?"

"From you," the boy says, "when you saved my life."

"I—" Then I notice that Ockham, followed by Áine and

Vienne, is joining us. "This is stupid, Ockham. Find another method for training the boy."

"Durango," Ockham says, whistling. "This method's been good oil for generations of acolytes."

I point to the stains on the boy's loincloth. "You call that good oil? I call it stupid."

"A speck of blood? Think what the Dræu would do to him if they laid hands on an untrained fighter."

The tendons in my jaw start working. "We are not the Dræu."

"He's got to be trained to fight them." Still whistling.

"Not this way," I say, stepping into his face, staring down at him. "It's barbaric."

"Barbaric? Who was your master, then?"

"I didn't have one." I can hear Mimi's voice from my memory: *you'll never be a true Regulator, just a movie cowboy.* "I trained Offworld." And because I'm full of pride, I add, "At battle school."

"Battle school? That means you're a rich brat officer?" Ockham says, stepping closer. "But you're *dalit*."

A hush falls over the miners. I try to ignore them, especially Áine, who crosses her arms and scowls at me.

"What of it?" I say.

"Rich brat officers don't turn into *dalit*. Here I was thinking you were some cast-off pretty boy, but turns out, you're worse. Officer *dalit*. Hah. 'Oh how the best-laid schemes o' mice an' men, go awry.'"

"Don't quote poetry at me, Ockham. I hate poetry."

"He stole my line," Mimi says. "Misquoted it, too."

Ockham huffs tobacco in my face. His nostrils flare. I can smell the harsh stink of his breath. Here it comes, I think. But hold my ground. "Got something stuck in your craw, oldie?"

"Maybe I do. Maybe I'm thinking," he says, and spits a string of tobacco juice on my boots, "a man ought to have to prove himself before he's fit to lead."

With a flick of my boot, I sling the spit back at him. "That sounds like a challenge to me."

"That's because, pretty boy,"—he thumps my chest with the heel of his hand—"it is."

CHAPTER 18

Hell's Cross, Outpost Fisher Four
ANNOS MARTIS 238. 4. 0. 00:00

Ockham's punch glances off my symbiarmor. But I feel the force of it disperse through my body, and I almost take a step backward. Almost. The old man still has power, and he knows how to use it. But I'm younger, faster, and my armor's a few pay grades above his. If Ockham thinks he's facing a soft Offworlder, he's in for a surprise.

To answer the challenge, I pound his chest with both fists. He comes back at me, grinning through tobacco-stained teeth. He needs dental work. Lots of dental work.

And a sprig of mint.

"Strike fast and hard," Mimi tells me. "You should end this as quickly as possible."

"Yes, Mother," I say.

"I formally challenge you for command of the davos," Ockham says. Then he bows, palms pressed together.

"Challenge accepted," I reply.

But the words no more than pass my lips then Vienne

interrupts. "Chief," she says. "This fight is mine."

"Vienne, no." This has to be my battle, because I'm fighting the miners as much as I'm fighting Ockham. "Not this time."

"I'm your second," she says stubbornly. "It is my right to take on all comers."

I start to argue when Mimi chimes in, "To refuse her is to dishonor her."

"I know that!"

"If you dishonor her, she will never forgive you."

"I know that, too!"

"But if you let her fight in your place, the miners will never respect you."

"Yes! Yes! I've got it. This is one of those *gǒu pì bù tōng* messes that go with being chief. I know I'm damned if I do, damned if I don't. Okay?"

"Just making sure," Mimi says.

If she weren't flash-cloned to my brain, I would knock her silly.

Taking a deep breath, realizing that all eyes are on me and Vienne, who is standing beside me frozen in the Regulator salute, I make the decision to hurt her.

"Vienne, you are excused. I will fight Ockham."

She blanches. Then regains her composure and bows. Only I know the truth: My words burn like battery acid. Only seconds pass, but I can feel a chasm opening between us.

"Yes, chief." She stands aside. "As you wish."

I can't look at her. Turning away, I strip my armor down to the skivvies. Then stand calmly before Ockham. My body is lean and hard, the muscles rippling in my stomach as I flex, calling forth my chi.

Ockham tosses his head back. Laughs. "Nice belly, pretty boy. But you best not expect me to go easy on yo—ack!"

A chop to the windpipe silences him mid-sentence. Ockham grabs his throat and staggers back, trying to catch his breath. Pressing the advantage, I launch a scissors kick to the side of his head. Then drop into a crouch as I leg whip his knees.

The old warrior lands hard on his butt. Groans. As I move in to deliver a stomp to the ribs, a blow I've seen Vienne maim men with, Ockham rolls away. My foot stomps bare ground, and the old man kips up to his feet.

"Too slow," he says, laughing at his escape.

His breath comes in wheezing gasps, but he's able to drop into a defensive stance. I recover quickly. Throw a round kick at the side of his head. It's a killing blow, but Ockham catches my foot easily in his thick-calloused hands. Draws my foot into his belly, then shoves hard and sends me spinning away.

"Too slow again. You ought to let the suzy fight your battles."

For an instant it looks as if I'll crash headlong into the stone floor. But I twist like a goring drill and land on my toes. The soles of my feet smack the stone. The sound echoes in my ears.

Damn it, this needs to end now.

Before the sound fades, I attack again. This time, with a series of rapid-fire kicks to Ockham's chest. He blocks the first three with his forearms. But I drive a rock-hard heel into his solar plexus. Softly I land in the dust as he gags and heaves. His body bends at the waist like a steel bar melted in the center. The muscles in his face slacken, the skin on his cheeks turns red like he's been burned. His eyes droop and close halfway, the pupils dilated.

I slide behind Ockham. As he falls to one knee, struggling for breath, I step in to deliver the coup de grace—an overhand punch that Vienne taught me, aimed at the base of the neck. Where his brain stem is unprotected. The correct term for it is a rabbit punch, but Vienne is no rabbit. She's a cobra, and her strikes are lethal.

What am I doing? "No!" I yell the instant before the blow lands.

The sound of my voice causes Ockham to twitch his head to the side. My calloused knuckles land anyway. But the turn of Ockham's head has changed the target. Instead of the soft tissue of the neck, I hit boney skull.

Crack!

A bone breaks.

I think it's mine.

"It's yours," Mimi says. "You delivered the punch at precisely the wrong angle."

"Thanks for that crumb of recon," I say. "Which one?"

"Fifth metacarpal. Hairline fracture. Treatment protocol requires ice and elevation above heart level to reduce swelling—"

"Remind me later," I say.

Ockham slumps forward, eyes rolling into his head, and topples almost gently onto his side. I stand above him, take three calming breaths, and flex my hand. It burns like hot mercury. I bend down to check the old man's pulse. He's alive. Thank God.

"You hurt yourself," Vienne says.

"Just a metacarpal," I reply.

"You should have killed him," she says. "It's your right."

"We need him to fight the Dræu. Besides, now that I've kicked his ass, he has to fall in line. It's in the Tenets, right."

She nods, satisfied. "Right."

We step away. Allow the miners to minister to him. Spiner and Jurm check Ockham for injuries.

"Is he still alive?" I ask.

"He's breathing," Jurm says.

"I reckon that counts as living," I say, and then wait until Mimi tells me that his injuries are minor. "Don't move him until we check him out. Call your medic down here."

The miners shrug, and no one moves. A few of them murmur about taking orders from a *dalit* and helping a damned Regulator.

"Do it," Áine says, striding toward us. "There's no arguing when a man's hurt. Jurm, I'll get Maeve. You and two others, fetch a gurney from the infirmary. *Now.* If you don't mind." She pauses and then adds, "Please."

She catches my eye. Shakes her head. Walks up the stairs. There is frustration there. And fear. How can I blame her? Dissension in the ranks. Two Regulators injured, one possibly crippled, with a cannibalistic enemy in the wings, waiting to attack fortifications that aren't finished. I feel like a mountain climber whose only toehold is a thin lip of crumbling rock.

"Will Ockham die?" Jean-Paul asks Vienne, his body colored rust from the fight, the blood from his mouth drying black on his belly.

His voice gives me a start. I almost forgot he was there.

"No," I hear Vienne answer. "He's too mean to die."

Jean-Paul flashes that same determined look I saw back in the New Eden bazaar. "What about my training? How will I become a Regulator now?"

"Here's some advice," she says, leading him away, "and it won't cost you a penny. If you want to become a Regulator, try to learn from the man who won the fight, not the one who lost it."

CHAPTER 19

In the dream, I'm lying on a stainless-steel table in a white room. A blue light is burning above the gurney. My hand reaches up, trying to block it and succeeding only in barking skin from my knuckles. There is a coarse mesh basket protecting the light. This is a field hospital, and I've been fighting death with my fists. A respirator tube is stuffed down my throat, and two surgeons in scrubs stand over me.

"Theoretically," the man says, "it will work."

"Theory is fine and good," the woman says. "But what if his mind can't accept the symbiont? It could lead to psychic breakdown, schizophrenia—"

What could? I try to say, but something stops me.

"Let me remind you who his father is," the man says, and places a mask over my face. "If CEO Stringfellow wants this to work, it's going to work."

"In theory."

"Now you're catching on."

Catching on to what, I think, but then the dream ends. It always ends right there.

I awake in a sweat. Is that the way the flash-cloning process really happened, or is it the version my mind has concocted for me? Even Mimi doesn't know. It happened before she joined me.

My heart thumping, I roll to my back to find my center. Breathe in. Breathe out. When I'm calm, I open my eyes. The quarters are dark.

Although the mines where shut down years ago, I can imagine hearing the ceaseless whir and clang of the ore being run up to the tipple and then dropped into the conveyor belts that separated it for shipping. I can almost smell the acrid scent of the ore, the stink of the enzymes the Big Daddies secreted during their tunneling. I stretch, exhale noisily, and roll from the cot.

"That was not eight hours of sleep, cowboy," Mimi scolds me.

"Close enough." Though from the way my body's buzzing, I know that it wasn't even half that.

I've lived on two, maybe three hours of sleep for weeks on end now. I'm tired. It's not that I don't want to sleep, to dream my own dreams for once, instead of revisiting past nightmares. But I can't. My brain won't let me. And there's the matter of this job I accepted. It's my duty to protect the miners, and I can't do it from slumber land.

After pulling on my symbiarmor, I pick up my boots and tiptoe across the floor. On my way out, I check the other cots. Ockham is in the infirmary, sleeping off the fight, and Jean-Paul's at his side. Jenkins lies snoring loud enough to cause a cave-in. Fuse's cot is empty.

So is Vienne's. A pang of jealousy stings me. It isn't a good idea for them to wander off in the night. The miners on guard duty might think they're Dræu and accidentally club them with one of those heavy wrenches.

"Mimi, locate Vienne and Fuse."

"*'But, Och! I backward cast my e'e. On prospects drear!'*"

"I'm too sleepy for obscure literary references. Just locate them, please."

She gives me the bearings, and I set off to find my crew. Without a clear idea of where to go or where I'm going, I follow Mimi's directions to the letter. I'm beginning to see how living in the mines disrupts your biorhythms. There's no natural day and night here, so the signals that your body needs to regulate itself aren't there. The miners try to simulate the natural passing of a day by raising and dimming the lights.

But it doesn't work that well. Because people had been living underground as long as there were people on Mars, the effects of life underground are well-known, including chronic insomnia, acute claustrophobia, and vitamin D deficiency due to the lack of exposure to sunlight. Gene therapy helps alleviate some of the problems. The simple truth, though, is that the human body needs sunlight to live. Here, there is none. Maybe that explains why miners are so ornery.

"Mimi, switch my bionic eye to night vision lens."

"Cowboy," she laughs. "Your ocular implant does not have a night vision function, and you know it."

"Switch to laser vision, then," I tease her. Sometimes, though, it would be nice to have special powers.

"The phrase *if looks could kill* is still just a saying."

"What good is a nanoprocessor visual prosthesis if I can't see in the dark or shoot things with my eye?" I miss seeing a low-hanging cable and smack my forehead into it. "Ow!"

"So that you can see objects with low clearance." Mimi laughs. "And then duck."

Mimi isn't the only one laughing. Áine, who is having a good giggle at my expense, appears in the corridor ahead. "That's why you ort not walk around in the mine."

Oh no. Not her. I swear I hear Mimi laugh. Raising a glow light on a lanyard, Áine holds the light up to her face. Then shines it on mine.

"You laughed at my pain," I say. "That's not very nice."

"I laughed because you were clumsy, and clumsy's fair game." Áine slips her arm in mine. "What brings you out at this hour? It'd officially be nighttime, and that means sleep time. Or is two days of constant work not enough for you?"

I rub my forehead. Just a small goose egg. "I don't sleep much."

"Because you miss the sun?" she asks, resting her hip against mine. The shape of her face is outlined in yellow light, giving her skin a soft glow. "Or is it because you're lonely?"

My mind flashes to Vienne and the hurt, angry look she gave me after I wouldn't let her fight. "Lonely? No. In general, I don't have much time to sleep. It's difficult—"

"To always be in charge? To never have time to rest your head?"

To have another person's nightmares in your head, I say to myself. "Right, to be in charge. Something like that. What about you? Why're you out and about, since it's sleep time?"

"Sentry duty, silly. We all got to do it." She pulls me by the good hand and doesn't let go when I try subtly to shake loose. "Follow me. I'll show you something that will help you relax."

Locking my heels, I say, "I should stay here. Keep an eye on things. Like you said, I'm the chief, and it's been a hard day."

She gives me a tug. "Though they might be lousy soldiers, miners know how to keep watch on the tunnels. Your mean old Regulators are safe. Come along now."

Towing me along like a space barge, she heads down the corridor for several meters, then makes an abrupt right turn. It's darker here. I have no choice but to follow the glow of her lanyard.

How did I get myself into this? Wandering dark hallways

with a suzy. If Jenkins and Fuse find out, they'll never let me live it down. And Vienne. Though physical contact with females isn't technically against the Tenets, being alone with one is. Vienne thinks Regulators should be above reproach. Especially the chief.

"That armor," Áine says. "It feels scaly. Don't you ever take it off? Other than fighting, I mean."

"Mimi, get me out of this."

"Come again, cowboy," she says. "Your signal is full of static."

"I, um, need to check the, ah, work on the corridor back there. Make sure we told the miners which of the secondary tunnels to use explosives on."

"The charge's already been set. We miners know how to knock down tunnels quick as spit."

"Well, then there's the barricade building out by the Zhao Zhou Bridge."

"Quit worrying about that, too." She makes a turn, and the tunnel slopes downward. "I'm here to help you relax, no? So, tell me, how'd you got to learn how to fight like that? The miners all thought your face was too pretty. That you'd got that suzy to do your fighting for you."

I laugh. "That suzy taught me how to fight."

"Oh?" She tilts her chin up toward me. "She's not the only suzy who knows how to teach a boy a few things."

"Mimi! How do I get out of this mess without offending her?"

"Got yourself in, cowboy. Get yourself out."

"Look, Áine, you seem like a nice girl—"

"I *am* a nice girl," she says, and pulls a lever hidden by the darkness. "You ought to see how nice I can be."

There's a rumbling sound, and an air lock in front of her begins to open. She turns to face me, her body now a silhouette, and I realize that she's wearing a dress with leggings, not coveralls. "Welcome to the sun."

Bluish light pours into the tunnel. A rush of frigid air makes the downy hair on my temples rise. She pulls me through the lock and rolls it shut.

"Hurry," she says, her face bathed in blue light so strong, it overwhelms the glowing yellow of her lantern. "Before the cold leeches inside."

"Amazing," I say. "Mimi, map this locat—"

"Mapped, slowpoke."

I step over a high threshold and onto a sheet of ice. Before us, the tunnel opens into corkscrew-shaped ice cavern. Its ceiling towers a hundred meters above us, and its walls, made of ice like stained glass, stretch up like spires of a cathedral. Light from an unseen opening above whispers to me, beckoning me.

"What is this place?" I ask, my head raised in awe.

"It's an ice cave. There's a glacier above Hell's Cross. When the terraforming melted the permafrost, the runoff created these."

The possibility that the harsh tundra could hide beauty

like this lifts my spirits. "You mean there are more?"

She shakes her head. "Not that we know about. When the old miners found the first few, they made the mistake of trying to walk on them. One miner hit the ice with a pick, and the crack ran the length of the walls, all the way to the surface. The cavern gave out, and two of them died."

I test my footing on the sheet of ice. "So I shouldn't try sledding."

"Not if you want to live." She tilts her head. Smiles. Touches her stomach.

Lifting my head, I let the light and the chill wind sweep over my face. "Do all the miners know about this?"

She squeezes my hand. "We don't keep secrets from ourselves."

No, I think, just from outsiders. "It goes all the way to the surface?"

"That's where the light comes from, silly."

"Right," I say, and then realize that I am silly. No, an idiot. Being in an ice cave with a girl who's changed into a dress and—

She pulls closer to me. "Want a lick?"

"No thanks," I say. Time to put the Áine express in reverse. "I really have to get back."

Áine reaches up. Breaks off an icicle. "Try one. This is where we get most of our fresh water." She runs the tip of the icicle over her bottom lip. Then leans her head back and drops of frigid water fall onto her outstretched tongue.

"Cowboy," Mimi interrupts, "I am reading signs of distress, but my external sensors indicate no proximal threat to you."

"Oh, there's a threat," I say aloud by mistake. A clear and present one.

Áine cocks her head. "Threat?"

"Sorry. I was, ah, talking to myself."

"You were telling yourself that there's a threat here?"

"More or less."

"Tch." She puts the icicle into my free hand. "You think I'm threatening? I'm flattered."

"That's not what I meant." I bite the tip of the icicle like it's a carrot. Pulverize it with my molars. Hand it back to her half-eaten. "I notice you're really good at twisting everything I say."

"You do that a lot." She throws her arms around my neck. "Try to draw attention away from yourself. I'd noticed it when we met in New Eden. Why so humble, soldier boy?"

I unclasp her arms. "Not humble. Just have a job to do. And I don't want to insult you, but I do need to go." Now. Before I get myself in deep trouble with my crew.

"Okay, I'll let you go." Áine runs the tips of her fingers down the inside of my arm. "If you tell me how the symbiarmor works? Can you feel this?"

"It tickles," I say. "The fabric has a million microsensors woven into the fibers. It transmits electrical signals to my skin, and my brain sorts them out."

"Your brain?"

"Nanobots in my nervous system sort the impulses and then send feedback to the bioadaptive cloth in the armor."

She puts her hands on my belly. "Mmm, warm. You're better than a pair of mittens. We could use a big, strong, handsome young man like you around here. I've got ways to make it worth your while."

I push her hands back and step away. "That's about enough."

Then she surprises me by pointing at the line that runs from the corner of my eye to the edge of my ear. "How'd you get that scar?"

"I lost a fight with a Big Daddy."

I expect her to coo over the scar, but seeing it changes the look in her eye. She hikes the sleeve of her blouse to reveal a thick scar running up her forearm. "I got that from a live wire. The shock knocked me ten meters."

"Oh yeah?" I say, because two can play this game. I lift the back of my shirt, showing her a splatter pattern of thick, purple scars. "Before it split my skull open, the Big Daddy sprayed me with its acid."

"Tch," she says. "That's not so bad." She pulls back her hair. Exposes a jagged line of scar tissue. "I jumped off a crane and landed on the treads. Almost scalped myself. And I didn't have no high-priced sawbones to stitch me back up, either. Maeve had to do it."

Squinting hard, I reach up to my eye. Give it a hard twist.

There's a clicking sound, and I pluck the eyeball from its socket. "Synthetic eyeball. Beat that." I smile triumphantly and reinsert the prosthetic.

"Nothing but a flesh wound." She rolls up a legging to show the wound that had made her limp. The skin is raised like the caldera of a volcano, with the inside a glossy mass of red and puce colored tissue. It's still fresh, barely begun to heal. "The Dræu shot me right there. They killed the two girls I was with. Then left me on the ice to die."

A faraway look comes to her eyes, and she angrily rolls down the legging. Competition over.

"I'm sorry," I say because I can't think of anything else.

"Tch. Just look at me." She moves into the mouth of the ice cavern. Her heavy breath freezes in the air. "Making a damned fool of myself. Over a boy. A Regulator, too."

"No," I say.

"Yes! A fool!" She breaks off an icicle and flings it at me. It shatters against my chest. "Better than a pair of mittens, I say. Look at my eyeball, he says." She breaks off a handful of icicles and starts firing them, one after another. "Warm that up, Regulator. And that! And that!"

I let the ice explode against my chest. What happened? One second, she's trying to seduce me, and the next, she's chucking icicles at my head.

I move toward her. "Is this about the other girls who died?"

"Don't talk to me," she barks. "Go!"

For a moment I watch her breath freeze in the blue light. See her wipe her nose with her sleeve. Count the number of times her chest heaves. I'm torn between trying to comfort her and getting away as fast as my feet will carry me.

"Take option b," Mimi says.

But I don't listen. "Áine, I'm sorry for what I said. I—"

"Get away from me!" she screams, her eyes blotchy and red. "Get out! Just leave!"

Gladly, I think, ducking back through the air lock into the dark tunnel. Life would be so much simpler if all problems could be solved with an armalite.

CHAPTER 20

Hell's Cross, Outpost Fisher Four

Once when I was still a kid, before battle school, I went with Father to a corporate function. The staff told me I was going to a party and they dressed me in a formal suit that matched his, down to the ties and patterned hose. For three hours I stood by his side greeting other executives, unable to have a drink, food, or even go to the latrine, wondering when the party was going to start and being befuddled that we left before it ever started. That's how I feel about Áine's tour of the ice cave. I expected to see a strategic area, and it turned out to be a setting for a romantic interlude.

For hours afterward I walk the subterranean roads, learning the lay of the land and getting a good feel for our territory, while running the argument with Áine through my mind. Did I lead her on? I'm still asking myself hours after I return to quarters, when Maeve knocks on the door and calls out.

"Breakfast!"

"Breakfast!" It takes Jenkins less than three seconds to jump out of his cot, pull on his suit and boots, and make a mad, stumbling dash for the door. It takes him an additional six seconds and a flattened nose to realize that said door is closed and that the lock mechanism requires him to lift the handle, not pull on it. I know because he's disturbing my morning prayer, and because I'm timing him.

"Oy, Jenks!" groans Fuse, who rolls off his cot and hits the floor with a boney thump. "Give a jack a tinker's minute to shimmy on his skivvies, no? What's the rush?"

"My belly's empty, and this carking door's fig-jammed."

"Lift," Vienne says. She's sitting in the lotus position next to me in the corner of the room, our backs to the room. An altar is open before us, and our quarters are full of the sharp odor of burning incense. Twice each day she has prayer and meditation. In the morning I join her for the meditation. It calms me. Clears my mind. Helps me focus.

"Huh?" Jenkins says. I can hear him scratching his head.

"Lift the handle," Vienne says. Her voice is like still water.

"Got it! Last one to the table's a rotter!"

"You lot coming along for breakfast?" Fuse says after he's dressed.

"Soon," I answer.

"Right, then."

He leaves. Air blows into the room, sending the incense

swirling toward the ceiling. My eyes stay with it, watching as it dissipates. A sure sign that I have lost concentration.

"You're uneasy," Vienne says, eyes closed, hands resting on her crossed legs, fingers forming an O.

"Tired."

"But there's something else?"

How can I tell her, I woke up last night and you weren't here, so I went to look for you and was shanghaied by a suzy who first tried to jump me, then wanted to slug me. And that now, as I feel you next to me, your head held just so, your eyes closed, your lips slightly parted, I have trouble holding my breath, much less holding my chi.

"Just tired," I say.

"Ah." She says, and lets my lie hang in the air, like burned incense.

But the moment is interrupted by the feral sound coming from the mouth of Spiner, his eyes wide in stark terror as he bangs on our open door. "Chief! Come quick!"

"What is it?" I call to him.

He falls to his knees, gasping, his breath spent from running. "Dræu! In the tunnels. Scouting party. Headed for. Crazy Town."

Damn it! Too soon. The demolition crews haven't closed those tunnels yet. "Mimi, do a scan. Fast." I haul Spiner to his feet. "How many are there?"

"Too many," he says, gasping. "Chasing a tram."

"A tram? Who took out a tram?"

Spiner shakes his head. "Don't know."

"Lock down the Cross," I tell him. "Keep everybody inside."

"But—" he says.

"Don't argue! Keep everybody inside and arm them with anything you've got. This might be just a scouting party, but we can't take chances."

There's a shout, and when I look over my shoulder, Áine is running toward me with a spanner wrench in hand.

"What do you think you're doing?" I say.

"Going with you," she says, running past me. "I've got a score to settle, and now's as good a time as any to do it."

CHAPTER 21

Hell's Cross, Outpost Fisher Four
ANNOS MARTIS 238. 4. 0. 00:00

The corridor from Bedlam is the longest of the four from Hell's Cross. It leads to a rise, the same one we came down when we entered the Cross the first time. The miners have blocked the main route, strategically closing the tunnels and shafts using C-42. We pass through an open iron gate made of vertical shafts topped with sharp barbs. They look like spears. On the deck the wind picks up, blowing my hair in my face. I pull my cowling up and stuff my hair underneath.

"Watch for rust!' I call ahead because here, halfway across Bedlam, the steel beam supports and bare rebar of a crumbling viaduct are the only things to walk on. Who knows if the metal still has enough integrity to hold our weight? Vienne has point, but she's not the one I'm worried about. It's Jenkins, with his heavy boots and clumsy feet. "And watch your footing!"

My voice is lost in the wind, which both whistles and rumbles, an effect of the squat concrete buildings and the cavern roof above us. To my left, the quick-pour construction is already failing. The buildings that once held, according to the dilapidated signs, the Orthocrats' Ministry of Weights and Balances is a crumbling pile of concrete and rebar, all sliding onto the rail bed.

Ahead, Vienne raises a hand, the signal for us to stop. I see why. The middle of viaduct has collapsed, and only a few planks tossed haphazardly across the span connect the two parts. We cross quickly, except for Jenkins, who seems to have other phobias beside darkness.

"I'm afraid of heights," he says, his knees shaking as he takes baby steps up to the planking.

"Come on, you great git," Fuse says, and tries to drag him across.

"No!" he says. "I'm not doing it."

"Okay," I say, and start walking away. "Stay here."

After a few seconds he calls, "Wait!" Then charges past me, cheeks puffy with held breath, eyes locked on the far side.

"Piece of work, that one is," Fuse says ruefully, and jogs ahead.

At the end of the viaduct, we enter a building made of marble, not concrete. High, buttressed ceilings, Doric columns, and a roof with a massive hole in the middle of it. Whoever built this mini palace wanted it to be special. We pass through a vestibule to a ballroom that is at least fifty meters across, but it's littered with fallen columns, huge chunks of marble, and a thick layer of dust. In the middle is a dried-up fountain with a dais for a shattered statue. Only the ankles remain. Dirt-colored molds grow in every crack, corner, and crevice. Just being in here makes me feel like a relic.

Inside, the air is so still, I can hear everyone breathing, the sound of our footsteps echoes all around, and Mimi's voice when she says, "Alert! I'm picking up biosignatures approaching from twelve o'clock."

Which means the far side of the room. There must be another entrance.

"Here they come! Spread out!" I whisper. "Take cover! Vienne, take the point. Check the far entrance."

"Affirmative." Crouching, she runs to the far side. Slips out of view. But I know she's safe because Mimi is tracking her.

With trained precision, the other Regulators move into position behind the columns. I move into position myself, near the fountain in the middle of the room, where a high circular basin gives good cover. Áine follows on my heels. I signal her to back out of the room. "Get back to the viaduct!" I whisper.

"No," she protests. "I want to shoot the damned cannibal rooters myself!"

"You've got no weapon and no armor," I say. "Just one stray bullet can take you out."

She eyes the armalite on my back. "Lend me yours."

"Not unless you'd like your arms blown off."

Before Áine can argue, Vienne pings me to open a vid link. "I mark seven targets, chief. On foot. Carrying plasma weapons, metal plate armor. In pursuit of three targets. They're Dræu, confirmed."

"The three targets they're pursuing?" I ask.

"A thin man, an older woman with a blue face, and a girl. The man and woman are running—strike that, crawling—for their lives. The girl is jogging backward. Laying down suppressing fire with an armalite. They're heading this way."

Armalite? "Ebi Bramimonde?" I ask Mimi.

"And her mother," Mimi adds.

"What're *they* doing here?

"Fleeing from the Dræu," Mimi says.

"You think?"

"The evidence is as plain as the pimple on your cute little—"

Smart aleck. I grab Áine by the wrist. "Out! Now! This zone is about to get hot!"

"But—"

"No buts! Move!"

For a second, she considers arguing, but the look on my face must be carking fierce because she starts bubbling up and takes off for the exit.

"Hope I wasn't too harsh."

"Bullet wounds are harsh, cowboy."

True, but bullets don't have to answer for their actions.

"Vienne, fall back. Take a firing position so you can cover the friendlies. We'll take out the Dræu."

The Bramimondes crash into the ballroom, the Dame's screams filling the space. She's pulling the man along but stumbling over him, out of her mind with fear, her chalk-painted face freakishly luminescent in the half darkness. Ebi follows them, expertly laying down suppressing fire in a figure-eight pattern. She steps behind the entryway, tosses a stun grenade at her pursuers, and calmly reloads a new clip of ammo.

"Hurry, Mother," she says. "I cannot hold them much longer."

"I *am* hurrying," the Dame shrieks, now dragging the man by the arm. "Do I not look like I am hurrying? Is this the face of a woman talking a leisurely stroll on the Meridian Sea?"

"More like the face of an asphyxiated harpy," Mimi says.

"Now be nice," I say. "To the harpies."

Once the stunner effect wears off, the Dræu mass like a pack of scavengers at the doorway shouting and screeching, their snoutlike faces streaked with blood and dirt, their body armor rattling. Our sights are trained on them, ready to make gut hash, when the Dræu taking point suddenly stops. He takes a sniff of air and shouts a word I can't understand.

Good time to act. "Vienne! Lay down smoke! Give the friendlies some cover."

"Affirmative." She chambers a smoke grenade and steps

out into the clear for launch. The grenade sails over Ebi's head and lands a few meters ahead of the pursuit. The ball-room fills with acid blue smoke, and we hear a scream as one of the Dræu takes a round from Ebi's armalite.

"Make that six pursuers now." I press the aural link, wince from the prickling sensation behind my eye, and bark orders to Fuse. "Three friendlies passing by me, closing on your position. Meet and greet only. Do not fire."

"Yes, chief. Meet and greet," Fuse says.

"Jenkins," I say. "Move up past me. Concentrate your fire on the entryways. Take out the Dræu."

He passes us. Kneels behind a fallen column. "What entryway? I don't see nothing but smoke."

"Shoot the smoke then." If he gets lucky, he might hit something.

Fuse interrupts, "And Jenks? Don't shoot at the friendlies this time."

"That wasn't my fault!" Jenkins protests. "I said I was sorry!"

I break the connection an instant before bullets shower the entryway. Jenkins lays down his own textbook figure-eight pattern. So much for his whining about low visibility.

The bullets find their targets, too. The screams of the Dræu ring out over the clatter of spent shells falling to the marble floor. The sound quickens my pulse and chills my blood.

"Get ready to move," I tell Vienne.

"On your mark, chief."

The fire from Jenkins's gun stops, which means that he's reloading. Hope he doesn't waste bullets, I think, and make a mental to note to have Fuse hide the rest of the ammo for when we really need it. The smoke clears. The noise dies. Crouched behind the empty fountain, I wait for the Dræu to show their hand. *Ponder and deliberate before you make a move.*

For a few moments it seems like the firefight is over. I instruct Fuse to help the Bramimondes to get their wounded man to safety, send Vienne and Jenkins back out to the viaduct, and then I move back to cover our exit. If we get lucky, we'll get through this extraction with no casualties while doing a little damage to the enemy.

Then the sound of a child's voice drifts up to me.

"Jenkins?" A sandy-haired girl appears in the vestibule. Dressed in a pair of floppy overalls with the cuffs rolled up. Calling for Jenkins to come out. "Are you playing hide-and-seek? I want to play, too."

How did she get here? I turn and try to wave her away, but she takes that to mean come forward. She starts winding her way through the debris, coming toward me, calling out, even as I wave like a madman, not speaking for fear of drawing fire.

From the clearing smoke, I see the line of a laser site searching for a target. Be quiet, I think, trying to will the girl to be silent. Don't give away your position. For a few seconds she is silent. Then the dot of a laser sight dances across her face.

"Ow," she says, and covers her eyes. "That hurt me."

Oh damn. Move! In the time it takes for the little girl to utter a sob, I'm jumping over a shattered column, only a few meters away from her, holding my breath and trying to get to her before the shooter pulls the trigger. I don't look. Don't look at the Dræu. Don't look at the kid.

My heart stops as I grab her and roll to protect her, my back hitting the floor and then sliding three meters, stopping only when my skull cracks into the wall. A cloud of dust rises around me.

I start to stand. See the laser sight on my chest. Then wrap the girl in my arms and turn away from the Dræu as he opens fire.

Brppt! The three-burst rounds sting my back. Reflexively, my spine arches, and I let out a howling scream, even as Mimi solidifies the fabric, sending the bullet ricocheting in all directions. Shielded by my body, the little girl doesn't realize that I'm protecting her. My scream is terrible, and she scrambles back away from me.

No, you don't, kid.

With bullets still striking me, I scoop her up, pull her tight against my chest, arms pinned within mine. Carry her to the safety of the vestibule.

The bullets stop. The Dræu shooter is reloading. I have three point six seconds—the length of time it takes to drop a spent clip, pull a full one from an ammo belt, and jam it into the magazine well. I scoop up the little girl and run through the vestibule. Outside, Jenkins and Vienne are taking position past the viaduct, and I know that there's no way I can make the length of bridge before the Dræu spot me.

Stairs.

To the right.

My boots clanking on the metal steps, I carry her down to the rail bed, where I spot a rusty door leading to the basement. I kick it open and slide the girl inside.

"Stay here," I fuss at her. "And don't come out again. For anything."

She's already on the brink of tears, and the gruffness in my voice sets her over the edge. "I-It's too dark. I'm ascared."

"No, no, no," I say. "Don't you start crying. Just hide. You can do that, no? All miners are good at hiding."

She nods her pixie head, pretending to be brave, and I realize that it takes more bravery, more sheer guts, for that little girl to slide into a dark, scary space than it does for me to face the Dræu. I've a weapon and body armor. She's only got herself.

"Good girl," I say, feeling as awkward as Jenkins trying to dance a waltz. "Don't worry. I'll be back soon."

After closing the door, I take cover behind the debris on the rail bed. From here I can cover the basement door and keep the Dræu in my sights. Above me on the viaduct, my crew is holding their positions.

I reach Vienne on the aural vid. "Stay put. Cover the friendlies till they're safe."

"Affirmative," she replies.

I see that Ebi has stopped shooting. She and Fuse have hoisted the wounded man by the armpits and are half dragging him to cover near the tunnel.

Another burst of gunfire. The thin man squawks. Grabs his thigh. Blood pours down the leg of his trousers, and he stumbles forward, taking Ebi down with him.

"Jenkins!" I bark into the aural link. "Damn it! Don't shoot the friendlies!"

"It wasn't me!" he shouts back. "I ain't even reloaded yet. The gun's jammed."

"The Dræu!" Vienne points at a figure emerging from the smoke.

He stands a head taller than the others, it seems, and he wears two bandoliers crisscrossed on his chest, his uniform a mix of CorpCom black ops and regular military issue, probably stolen from a dead man. His weapon is an armalite fitted with a laser scope. The same scope he's now using to sight Dame Bramimonde.

The Dame works to untangle herself from her bleeding companion, while Fuse and her daughter drag her by the arm, trying to get to shelter behind an abandoned rail truck. Only a few meters away. They'll never make it.

"I have the shot," Vienne says.

But I've already raised my armalite, and I have the better

angle. I lay the crosshairs of my sights on the Dræu.

"May I help you aim?" Mimi asks.

"No thanks," I say.

In the heartbeat of time before I squeeze off the round, I feel the caress of the stock against my cheek. I feel the recoil, a slight kick that my body absorbs reflexively. I open my sighting eye as the bullet enters the target's skull, three centimeters above the left temple. Then exits the opposite side of the brow.

The Dræu drops his battle rifle. A rivulet of blood trickles into his beard. He steps back, blinks, and jiggles his head, as if trying to shake something out of his ear.

"It's not a kill," Vienne says. I can hear the disappointment in her voice.

Shake it off, Durango. "Stand ready."

I train my sights on the Dræu. Waiting for his next move. The bullet, I guess, has only damaged the frontal lobe of the brain. Except for two holes in the sides of his head, he probably will live. We'll let him live, too, as long as he doesn't go for his weapon again.

"Mimi," I say, intending to ask her to scan the wounded man's vitals.

"Scan?" she replies.

"Negative." If he's dying, I really don't want to know after all.

The smoke from the ballroom begins to waft out over the wounded Dræu. He's standing in the same spot on the viaduct, turning in circles, listening to a sound he can't quite hear. I could eliminate the target now. Easy shot. But I can't take it.

"What're you waiting for?" Áine says as she steps out from behind a rail car. So that's where she went. I thought she'd obeyed orders too easily. "Kill him while you have the chance."

"No," I tell her. "Regulators don't shoot wounded targets."

"You're having a go at me, right?" she says. "You just shot him. Do it again!"

The smoke has almost cocooned the Dræu, who seems to have no interest in picking up his battle rifle. "The Tenets forbid it."

"That's stupid!" she protests. "Save yourself the trouble of having to kill him later. Finish him off before he can get away!"

Shaking my head, I ease off the sights. The Dræu isn't going anywhere, and we may be able to capture him, interrogate him. He'll be more valuable alive than dead. "The Tenets aren't about doing what's easy. It's about doing what's right."

"Bugger your damned Tenets! That's an animal, a bloodthirsty jackal! They're not even human anymore."

"And if I shot an unarmed, helpless enemy," I say as I start moving closer to the basement door where the kid is hiding. "What would that make me?"

"A man!"

"Yeah, well," I say, thinking of Father's last words to me. "That's not the kind of man I want to be."

She crosses her arms and stamps her foot. "Damn you!"

"Say whatever you want," I say as I push her behind a huge chunk of decking fallen from the viaduct above. "Just keep your noggin under cover. Mimi, scan and store the wounded Dræu's biorhythmic signature."

"I can't," she says. "That Dræu is no longer within range."

"What?"

"He's gone."

She's right. When the smoke clears, the viaduct is empty. The Dræu have disappeared.

CHAPTER 22

Hell's Cross, Outpost Fisher Four
ANNOS MARTIS 238. 4. 0. 00:00

"Jenkins," I say through the link. "Keep eyes on that viaduct. Shoot any hostiles stupid enough to come back."

"Heewack!" he booms, and the feedback zaps my eardrum.

"I'll take that as an affirmative," I say, wincing. I start to jog over to the basement to get the kid, but Fuse pings me.

"We need you here, chief," he says, breathing hard. The rescue effort has taken his wind away. "Stat."

I glance at the basement door. The girl will be okay for a minute. On the way, I grab Áine and take her with me. She doesn't need a gun to help now.

When I reach the rail truck where the Bramimondes have taken cover, I find a dying man. Ebi leans over him. The Dame stands a meter away, a gauzy kerchief pressed to her lips. Although she isn't crying, her eyes are wide with shock. She watches Fuse as he kneels down and tries to resuscitate the man. Ebi is pressing a makeshift bandage over the wound, but each time Fuse pushes on the man's chest, blood seeps out below the bandage.

Femoral artery, I say to myself. Plenty of soldiers have survived battlefield wounds to the thigh, but not when the main artery is hit.

"His vitals are fading," Mimi warns me.

I stand back to let Fuse do his job. A moment later he glances up. Shakes his head slightly, confirming what I already knew. It's useless to continue trying to save a life that's beyond saving.

"Fuse," I say. "Stand down."

Ebi hears me but doesn't argue. She steels herself, her spine erect. Battle school training.

"We're done here," Fuse tells Ebi, who stops applying pressure to the wound.

They both stand, then Fuse tells her to go wash up using the anti-pathogen wash in his med kit.

"What?" Dame Bramimonde says. "Keep trying! You cannot stop now!"

"Mother," Ebi says flatly as she cleans blood from beneath her nails, "he is dead."

Dame Bramimonde's knees bend, and I instinctively reach out to steady her. But she slaps my hand away.

"Do not touch me! Do not lay a single filthy finger on me, you traitorous wretch. It's your fault he's dead—all of you!"

"Our fault?" Fuse says as he drapes a work tarp over the

body. "The only reason you're still alive is because of us."

I shake my head no at Fuse. "Dame Bramimonde, why did you come here? Who is this man?" The words are no sooner out of my mouth than I recognize him—a silver-haired man in a brown, plain tunic. It's the servant who took me to see Ebi.

"The man's name, Chief Durango," she says, almost spitting, "is not important now. What took you so long to come to our defense? Why did you not respond to our distress calls?"

I look to Vienne. The look on her face is clear. There were no distress calls. "Mimi?"

"No distress calls, cowboy."

Why would Ebi lie?

"Mother," Ebi says, sticking out her chin, "I am a Regulator. Regulators do not ask for help. I did not send the distress call."

Regulators don't ask for help? Since when? Nothing could be further from the truth.

"Someone needs to study the Tenets again," Mimi says.

"You defied me?" the Dame says, turning a scowling face to her daughter. "When I tell give an order, Lisette, I expect it to be followed to the letter. I did not rise to the position of CEO by tolerating insubordination."

"You are a *retired* CEO," Ebi says. "And I no longer take orders from anyone except a Regulator chief."

"You impudent little hussy!"

"Words are not bullets, Mother. My name is Ebi, and I do not fear your name-calling anymore."

I clear my throat. "A man is dead. Stop bickering long enough for us to give last rites and put his body into cryo. Then you can tell me who he is and what the blazes you're doing here."

"The answers are simple, Durango. First, we are here to retrieve my misguided son." Then the Dame sneers, "And second, that man was my husband."

If that's how the Dame treats her husband, I think as I head back to the kid's hiding space, I would hate to be someone she dislikes. Of course, I am somebody she dislikes. Dislikes intensely.

"Quit whining," Mimi says. "Weren't we trying to find a little girl?"

"*I* was," I say. "I think *you* were just trying to drive me crazy."

"I don't have to try to do that," she says. "You do a fine job yourself."

"Hello?" I say, pulling the panel and peering into the dark basement, half afraid of what I'll find. All it would take is a stray bullet to find the crack—

"Don't think about that," Mimi fusses at me "The worst-case scenario doesn't always have to play out."

"If it does, then I'll be prepared for it."

"That's a lie, and you know it," she says. "There's no being prepared. Only less surprised."

"Hello?" I repeat. "It's me, Durango. It's safe to come out now."

Seconds pass. No response. And then a small, sweet voice. "I want Jenkins."

"Thank you," I whisper, and peer into the darkness. "Hey, kid. Jenkins is sort of busy right now. We need to go to some-place safe, but when he's not busy, I'll tell him—no, *order* him to come play with you."

"Pinkie promise?"

"Pinkie." Please, please don't let anyone else hear me saying this. "Promise." To show that I'm true to my word, I extend a hooked pinkie finger—the one I have left.

"Okay," she says, and I feel the tug of her finger pulling mine. "I'll come out."

As she does, I take her hand. Then sweep her up in my arms. I carry her up the steps leading to the viaduct.

"I can walk," she says. "I'm age-three now."

"I'm sure you can," I say, and swing around with her. "But I don't mind giving you a piggyback ride. I always wanted a little sis—Vienne?"

There she stands, hands on hips, an impish smile on her face, like she's just heard a juicy bit of gossip. "Picking up young girls again, chief?"

"I—ah—I."

"We played a hiding game," the little girl says. "Then the chief made me a pinkie promise."

"Is that so?" Vienne extends a hand. "Well, that's good.

But you need to run as fast as you can back to the Cross. I'm sure Maeve is looking for you."

"Can I stay? Please?" She clings to my arm when I set her down. "He's very nice."

"I know he is," Vienne says firmly. "Except we're in a hurry right now. Come on, be a jewel."

The little girl kicks the dirt. "Aw. Okay."

"That's my big girl."

The kid runs along the viaduct and easily crosses the broken span, headed for the Cross.

"You handled the kid like a professional," I tell Vienne. "I'm impressed."

She jams a fist into my ribs. "And you are getting soft."

"Ow!" The punch takes me off guard. My armor easily absorbs the blow, but it's enough to throw me off balance. "I didn't see that coming."

Vienne tucks a strand of hair behind her ear and smiles, causing my knees to bend involuntarily. Didn't see that one coming, either.

Phweee! "Plasma blasters!" Nor that one. "Duck!" I shout, and pull Vienne down to the deck with me. My head jerks toward the source of the blast—the vestibule. Damn it, the Dræu are back for more.

"How many hostiles?" I ask Mimi as we take cover behind a skinny concrete railing post.

"Indeterminate. They are all clumped together."

"Distance?"

"Ninety meters and closing fast. Your current position will be compromised. Move to safety, cowboy."

"You read my mind."

"I always do."

For cover fire, I ease off a few rounds. Then sprint for the far end of the viaduct. We clear the break with a long, adrenaline-fueled jump. Plasma bolts fly past us and ping off the deck ahead. They ooze to the ground below, hopping and hissing like water in hot grease. The air fills with the stink of thermite, and the metal begins to melt.

"They've got a pulse cannon," I say out loud. "Damn. Double damn." I open an aural link as we're running. "Jenkins, get your carcass out here. The Dræu are back, and were taking fire—"

"Come again, chief," Jenkins yells as he steps from behind the rail truck, laying down cover fire. "Can't hear you over all this shooting. Take that, you farging rooters! Ha! Ha-ha!"

"It appears," Mimi says, "that Jenkins is already in position."

"Astute observation, Mr. Watson." He probably was there the whole time, I think, having a good time watching us ducking those plasma rounds.

With a lunge, I launch myself across the hood of the truck. Another round of plasma shots slam the metal skin, and its passenger door sags on its melted hinges. A second later, Vienne pulls the same stunt and lands behinds me.

Our heads turn. Eyes meet. And we both start laughing.

"Regulator!" we yell, and touch fists.

A volley of plasma gels come flying over the truck. "Time to bug out," I say.

"Affirmative," Vienne agrees.

With the Dræu still filling the causeway with fire, we run for the tunnel. We follow the trail of blood underground, expecting to find the Bramimondes, but seeing nothing but a puddle of blood, three sets of footprints, and one of the plumbing bombs Fuse has been teaching the miners to build.

"Find them," I tell Vienne and Jenkins as I close an iron gate behind us. "Follow the footprints to wherever they got to. When you find them, follow these directives."

"Yes, chief."

"First, cover them against advancing hostiles. Second, when you see Fuse, give him a good hard slap for leaving his station."

"A slap on armor or bare skin?"

"Use your discretion." I smirk. "I trust your judgment."

She salutes. "Yes, chief."

"Jenkins, you go with her."

He slings the armalite to his shoulder. "Aw, I wanted to shoot more Dræu."

"Plenty of time to do that later."

Like that, they're gone, and the tunnel is quiet. A few seconds later I hear a noise, a high-pitched battle cry that raises the hairs on my neck. The Dræu are caterwauling. And they're coming for me. "Mimi, how many hostiles now? And don't tell me indeterminate!"

"A bunch."

"Thanks," I say. "A bunch is much, much more specific. Distance?"

"Fifty meters and closing. Their weapons are fully charged."

Slipping into an alcove in the tunnel wall, I snap a new clip into my armalite and pull my side arm. With two weapons, I can hold them off, unless they rush me. Then any of them could fire a plasma, and I'd be a dead man.

On second thought. Setting the weapons down, I unhooked one of Fuse's special C-42 bombs from my belt. "This'll do," I say, satisfied with the weapon's capacity to commit mayhem.

Seconds later the Dræu slam into the iron gate. They don't bother to try opening it, but climb with freakish ease to the top, fighting one another to get a shot off, their lips dripping wet with foam.

"Don't move now," I say, and toss the bomb at their feet. Then pull the trigger.

A half second later the blasting cap triggers the explosion.

Fuse does good work.

The Dræu scream. The sound sends shivers up my spine, and my instinct is to run. But I walk toward the gate, my finger hard on the trigger until the canister is empty and only spitting flames come from the end of the pipe. I see little, but I can smell everything.

When the smoke clears, and I step into the tunnel inspect the damage, I find nothing but a damaged gate and scorch marks on the wall and an empty spot where the Dræu had been.

"Mimi," I say, "where are they?"

"Gone," she replies.

"Gone where?"

She pauses. "Across the viaduct, according to my sensors."

"So I didn't kill them?"

"No."

"And that's possible how?"

"I—" She pauses, sounding almost embarrassed. "I have no data to explain this occurrence."

"Me, neither." So Dræu could step into a raging fire and not be burned to cinders? Bad news. Really bad news. Are they flame retardant or just so tough that they can ignore third-degree burns? How do you defend against an enemy like that?

"Is that a rhetorical question?" Mimi asks.

"No," I say, "I want answers. Real answers that will help us fight these monsters." As I start walking back toward the Cross, I call Vienne. "How's the situation with Fuse?"

"He's red-faced about his error, if you know what I mean."

There's a note of mirth in her voice. Maybe it's the thrill

of a good battle. Or maybe slapping Fuse has something to do with it.

"Rendezvous in the courtyard," I say. "We've got a little bit of a tactical problem on our hands."

"What's that, chief?"

"It's the Dræu. They can't be killed."

CHAPTER 23

Hell's Cross, Outpost Fisher Four

Dealing with the fallout from the Bramimondes' sudden entrance takes hours away from the job I want to do—getting ready for the real Dræu attack. Instead, we take care of her late husband/servant. We lay him in a makeshift grave and cover his body with a heavy tarp.

Ebi and Jean-Paul join us Regulators and a few miners to pay respects, but the Dame is too traumatized by the ordeal and demands a hot bath and a lie down. The lie down she gets. The bath—hot or otherwise—is a luxury nobody's going to worry about getting her.

And then the hard part. Finding out what the deuce the Dame is doing here, a thousand kilometers from home. So I call a meeting of all parties concerned. We gather in a room next to the infirmary on the arcade.

"We seem to have a new batch of visitors," I say as we gathered around the table. "Mind telling us why you're here? Since they'll be staying with us for a while."

"Staying here? I certainly shall not," the Dame sniffs.

"It's not like you'd got much choice now," Áine says. "Like it or not, you're stuck here."

"Do not insult my intelligence," the Dame says. "Do you really expect me to take the word of a group of emaciated dirt worms? Now, where is my son? I've come to—"

"Dirt worms?" Áine launches halfway across the table. "You bring the Dræu to our doorstep, and you insult us? I ort to spit in your face."

"*Ort?*" the Dame says, mimicking her. "Is that a word? I don't recall it being part of the bishop's Academy of Language. Although, I must say, your kind never had the benefit of hearing very much civilized speech."

Áine curses under her breath. The Dame smiles, then looks to Maeve with a mocking eyebrow raised. The old lady only smiles in return.

It's not, I think, the reaction the Dame is wanting. But I'm getting tired of the game. We have to finish the redoubt before the Dræu attack again, our defensive tactics need tweaking, and I need to debrief my crew—the Dræu are much more than your common cannibalistic marauders.

"How is it," I ask, keeping my voice calm and commanding, "that you came to be here, Dame Bramimonde?"

"Do you not listen? I told you that I have come to retrieve my son. Where is he? And that old man who led him here?"

"That's not what I asked you."

"How dare you ask anything of me, *dalit*. I can barely tolerate sharing the same air with you."

I ignore the insult. "You, your daughter, and your husband came to Fisher Four alone? For a son you don't care about. I find that hard to believe." She cuts me a look, so I force the issue. "Wealthy folk like you not hiring bodyguards? That's unusual."

"We did hire protection," the Dame says. "The cowards fled as soon as the Dræu appeared."

"Where are they now?" I ask.

"The Dræu pursued them."

A pall falls over the room. We know what happens to people that the Dræu chase. "Where exactly did the Dræu appear?"

The Dame waves away my question. "As if I know anything about this wretched place."

"Outside the station," Ebi interjects. "It was an ambush. We were expected."

"We, as in any humans?" I ask Ebi. "Or we, as in the Bramimondes?"

"We as in Bramimondes, I believe."

"What difference does it make?" the Dame sneers. "Those animals only wanted to kill us. It is nothing short of a miracle that we found our way to safety."

I doubt it's a miracle. More likely dumb luck. "It makes a very big difference, Dame. Was this a random attack, or did they target you specifically?"

The Dame flicks imaginary dust from her cuticles. "How would I know?"

"They knew it was us." Ebi says, coming to the table, where she plants her hands firmly on the rough hewn stone. She stares fiercely at me. "The leader called us by name. He even introduced himself. I killed three of them in the firefight before our bodyguards deserted us."

"The leader?" Fuse says. "The one that the chief shot?"

Ebi nods. "Yes, that was the leader. His name is Kuhru."

"And he was specifically targeting you?" I say, the hackles on my neck rising. I don't like the idea that the Dræu were waiting for them. "Why?"

"He said that their queen wanted us," Ebi says.

"Mimi, is she telling the truth?"

"Affirmative," Mimi says. "Her heart rate and respiration indicate that she is telling the truth, as she knows it."

"Thanks for the disclaimer."

"Lie detecting is not an exact science, cowboy," she says. "The standard disclaimer always applies."

"So," I ask Ebi, "why would the Dræu queen want you?"

"Easy," Jenkins butts in before Ebi can answer, "she's hungry. Can we go now?"

I order him to pipe down, then ask Ebi, "Why does the queen want you and how did she know you were coming to Fisher Four?"

"Kuhru didn't say, but before the shooting started, he told the other Dræu to search us for the treasure."

"Treasure?" Jenkins's ears perk up.

"Which was ridiculous," the Dame says. "We carried nothing of value with us. Our departure was rushed, so we took only the bare essentials."

"Along with a group of bodyguards," Fuse adds.

I feel the situation slipping out of my hands—too many people are interrupting me—so I clear my throat. "Back to my original question: How did the queen know you were coming to Fisher Four?"

"I don't know," Ebi says.

The Dame rolls her surgically sculpted eyes and taps a fingernail on the table. "As my daughter says, we do not know. We are not zoologists, after all, and I am weary from travel and from this inquisition. Lisette, accompany me to my quarters."

"What quarters?" Spiner scoffs. "You've not been invited to stay amongst us. You'll be damned lucky the miners don't drop you down a chigoe hole."

The Dame stands. "I will not be addressed in that manner."

"You high-faluting hag!" Spiner launches off his stool. "Up in New Eden, they might put up with your crap. While you're on miner ground, you'll act like you've got some manners."

The Dame huffs and scoots for the door. Spiner, furious at the slight, starts to follow her.

I let loose with an earsplitting whistle. "Nobody's going

anywhere until I get some answers. What's this treasure the
Dræu are after?"

"Durango," the Dame says, stretching out my name like
a threat, "I have no idea. But I am exhausted, and I must
see my son. Lisette, follow me." She leaves the room. Ebi,
though, doesn't follow her right away.

"Chief," Ebi asks me, "may I be dismissed?"

"Dismissed," I say, and she follows her mother. I've had
enough arguing. I need to talk to the one person who can
answer my questions directly. "The rest of you go, too. All of
you. Except Maeve."

Áine objects, "I'll not be taking orders from the likes of—"

"Áine, please," Maeve says. "Go take care of the children."

Reluctantly, she follows the others out of the room. But
not before flashing an obscene hand gesture in my direction. She slams the door behind her.

"You've hurt the girl's feelings," Maeve says. "What happened between you?"

"Nothing," I say, and even I don't believe myself.

"*Nothing* can be *something*," she says.

"Exactly my point," I say, trying to change the subject.
"You keep telling me the Dræu don't want anything, but
they clearly want something: treasure. I agreed to take this
job, but I need honest answers, and I need them now."

Maeve stands up. "If it's answers you want, then
follow me."

That was easy, I think.

"Yes, it was," Mimi adds. "Too easy."

"Is she lying?" I ask.

"The standard disclaimer always applies."

I have no choice but to follow Maeve. With the hem of her robe leaving a thin trail in the dust, she leads me up to the arcade. At the corner she presses on a panel, which slides open, revealing a hallway I hadn't discovered yet. The hall leads to a room, and inside is a single table made of wood, two matching chairs, and a glass lamp. The walls are covered with shelves and the shelves are filled with books. Books made of paper and bound together.

"A library," I remark. "I've only seen one at battle school."

Maeve takes a seat and motions for me to do the same. "It belonged to my family. Books were more precious to us than food. Each of us brought them with us when we immigrated."

"Immigrated?"

"I was born on Earth," she says. "My family left Boston after the plague caused the fall of the United Corporations of America. My father said that it was our chance at a new life, but I knew it was a life sentence. Argued with him the whole time he sold off most of our belongings and left us with nothing but the clothes on our backs. He kept saying that the Orthocracy would take care of us. But even at seventeen, I knew that wasn't true." She pauses. "Seventeen. That's the age you and Áine are now, if you count in Earth years. Tch. Children grow up so much faster on Mars.

Live less long, too. Not such a bad thing, I think."

"You were going to give me answers."

She spreads her arms wide and sweeps past the shelves. "Treasure you sought. Treasure you've found."

"A library?" Somehow I doubt that the Dræu are interested in books. They don't eat paper. "It's precious to you, maybe, but it's not treasure."

"Define treasure."

"Coin. Precious metals. Things so rare or in demand they have value."

"Guanite."

My brow wrinkles. Why is she cursing me? "I'm not following you."

"Once upon a time," Maeve says, "guanite was the most useful resource on Mars. Not valuable, but useful. The Phase Two engineers decided that polluting the planet was the fastest way to build up an atmosphere, so they built mining outposts all over the southern lands. The Fishers were the biggest, and Fisher Four was the grandest of all. An underground wonder, it was. You've seen the ruins. The Cross is all that's left, now, but before, ah, I've seen the digigraphs. This was before the Orthocracy tried to lay Fisher Four to waste because the miners wouldn't leave when the Manchesters and the ovens shut down. Now all we've got left is a few crumbling buildings and a million kilometers of empty tunnels to call home. We're like the guanite. Once treasure, now useless."

I rub my head. "So what you're trying to tell me is that you have no treasure."

"No," she says, rising to her feet. "What I mean is that if the Dræu think we have treasure, it doesn't matter whether we do or not. All that matters is that they are willing to do anything to get it, and that makes your job that much harder."

"A more cynical man would say impossible."

"Then it's a good thing you are not a cynic." She gestures toward the door. "May I show you out?"

As we're leaving, Maeve locking the door behind us, Mimi chimes in, "Did you believe her story?"

"Not a word of it," I say.

"That's good, cowboy. Because according to her heart rate and breathing patterns, she—"

"Was lying?"

"Through her rust-stained teeth."

CHAPTER 24

Hell's Cross, Outpost Fisher Four
ANNOS MARTIS 238. 4. 0. 00:00

The queen sits on her throne looking down on Kuhru. The miserable worm, he has failed again. Such a disappointment. When she took the Dræu in hand, she thought he would be the valiant, true warrior she could hold up as an example. His battle school record was stellar—freakish physical skills with an aptitude for sharpshooting and a thirsty ambition.

That's probably where I failed, she thinks. I mistook ambition for intelligence and intelligence for the ability to follow simple, straightforward orders.

"What possessed you," she says, pulling the dagger from her sleeve, "to attack Bramimonde? Your order was plain. Threaten her. Remind her that we were watching her every move. Remind her of the fate that awaits her if she dares to betray us. At what point did I tell you to chase her across the tundra like a pack of wild jackals?"

"The old woman slapped me, my queen," he says,

bowing, but looking at her through fierce eyes. "It's was an insult. I had to save face before the Dræu."

"Your little feelings got hurt, so you almost killed my spy?"

"That was not my intention."

"And that bullet hole in your temple?" she says, tittering. "Did you mean to get shot or was that not something you intended, either?"

Absentmindedly, he touches his forehead. "No, my queen. I meant to kill the Regulators."

"The Regulators are nothing!" She takes the dagger, slides it into his cheek, and pulls. The razor edge of the blade slits the skin, and his mouth flaps open, blood pouring onto the floor as he groans and cups his hands beneath his chin. "Bring me Postule. And clean up that mess."

CHAPTER 25

Hell's Cross, Outpost Fisher Four
ANNOS MARTIS 238. 4. 0. 00:00

An alarm sounds. A moment later Áine appears at the door. She beckons for the old woman to follow her in. "It's the Dræu," she says. "They want to confab."

"With me?" I ask.

"With Maeve," Áine says. "Nobody else."

We all jog to the Cross, where Vienne is directing the miners to take their positions on the redoubt. As my Regulators wait for orders, Maeve looks to me. I can read the question in her eyes: What should we do?

No choice here. I tell her to meet with the Dræu. "You do the talking. We'll provide a show of force."

"Should you be letting the animals know you're here?"

"Too late for that," I say. "They already know you've got Regulators on board. They just don't know how many. Let's not let them find out."

"What about me and my children? I have no desire to meet with that filth," Dame Bramimonde calls out to me.

She is standing with Ebi near the exit that leads to the Zhao Zhou Bridge. So much for needing a rest, no?

I look to Maeve. "Can you hide them?"

"Mother can hide," Ebi says, and pulls her armalite. "I will go with you."

"Guess that settles the question," I say. "You can join us, but you have to follow my orders."

"Yes, chief."

"The most important of which is to stick with Vienne and do only what she tells you to. Got that?"

"Yes, chief."

"You say that, but it's only fair to warn you that Vienne breaks bones when folk don't do what she says." I give the order to go and we all began to file out, except for Jenkins, who remains on near the exit, unmoving.

I elbow Jenkins as I pass. "Snap to it, Regulator."

"But—but where is everybody going?" He reluctantly pulls his armalite. "I heard the word *treasure*. I thought there'd be treasure."

"Sorry, Jenkins," I say. "No treasure this time. Just one old lady fussbucket."

"How about we just feed the fussbucket to the Dræu?" Fuse says as we move down the stairs to the path that leads to the Zhao Zhou Bridge

"Right. It would solve two problems. Get rid of her and poison the Dræu that ate her." Fuse laughs.

But I don't feel like joining in on the joke. There's

something wrong here. Back in New Eden, Dame Bramimonde didn't give a rip about her son's life. She wanted to leave him with the kidnappers, so why would she travel to the end of the world to rescue him?

I don't believe her story about Ebi wanting to rescue her brother, either. The girl may love her brother as dearly as she says, but I doubt seriously that she holds that much sway over her mother. There has to be another reason.

"Chief?" Vienne points to a phalanx of Dræu crossing the Zhao Zhou Bridge. They carry a white banner tied to the barrel tip of a rifle.

In formation, we move forward to meet them. Maeve walks a meter ahead of us. Áine is directly behind her, and I'm after her. A few meters ahead, a man steps out from the phalanx and walks toward us. He wears long, flowing robes. His head is shaven, and his Buddaesque belly precedes him. He could pass for a monk if not for the sidearm holstered to his waist on a black leather belt that creaks when he walks. When he's close enough, I can smell perfume oils, sweat, and underneath it, the uniquely spicy odor of Rapture. It's in his pores, on his breath, and in his ruddy face like a perpetual blush.

"You!" Ebi shouts at the man.

"Him?" Vienne asks me. "Chief, what is going on here?"

"I have the same question," I say.

Fuse turns back to me. "Who is that man?"

"His name is Postule. He specializes in kidnapping

children and squealing like a stuck pig. Used to work for
Dame Bramimonde—"

A high-pitched scream fills the hall. Jean-Paul rushes out
from nowhere, wielding a miner's wrench like a club. "I'll
kill you, Postule!"

"—then he kidnapped her children and tried to ransom
them."

Before we can make a grab for him, the boy races past us.
Jumps onto the wall. Moving faster than a neutron particle.
Ebi starts to follow, but Vienne snags her by the wrist and
pulls her back into ranks.

"Wait for orders. Chief?" she says, asking if we should do
anything about the boy.

"Let him go," I say. There's nothing we can do about him,
anyway, unless we want to start a firefight.

Jean-Paul covers the distance quickly. Then takes one
final leap and raises the wrench high. Postule lifts his arms
to cover his face, and the boy takes the chance to land a
thumping blow to the fat man's belly.

The wallop knocks Postule backward, but as the boy is
raising the wrench to attack again, one of the Dræu grabs
the weapon and lifts Jean-Paul into the air. He continues
to fight and scratch, using his heels to draw blood on the
Dræu's shins.

"What happened to the children that Postule kidnapped?" Fuse says.

"We rescued them."

Fuse smirks. "But the kidnapper got away, no?"

"Affirmative. He beat me in a footrace."

"Tch! Thought you were lighter on your feet than that, chief. The fossicker's just a couple biscuits short of a half kilo."

"Fuse?"

"Yeah?"

"I was having a laugh."

"Oy!" he says. "Give a jack a hint or summit, if you're going to give his nose a yank, no? Thought you were serious, what with them Dræu but a few meters off."

"And now," I continue, "Postule is apparently working for the Dræu."

"I'm surprised they didn't eat him," Fuse says. "He's fat enough to feed their lot for a fortnight."

"I'm sure he's useful in some ways," I say. "Or they realized he'd taste like guanite."

Fuse laughs. "See, chief. That time, I knew what you was up to, and it tickled the funny. See what happens when you soften up the audience."

"Call off your dog," Postule yells. "This is a diplomatic visit."

"Acolyte," I call to the boy. "Stand down."

Instantly Jean-Paul stops fighting. His body goes rigid, and the Dræu has trouble holding his dead weight off the ground.

"Oh, for pity's sake," Postule barks at his escorts. "Let him go."

A line of drool run from the Dræu's mouth and down his neck, but he reluctantly obeys. Jean-Paul sprints back to us. "Master, my first skirmish!"

Maeve steps forward to meet Postule. "We see your flag, so you've got protection as long as you raise no weapon. What is it you want?"

Postule offers a practiced bow. "The queen of the Dræu wishes to negotiate terms."

"What terms would that be?" Maeve says warily.

"Terms of your surrender."

The miners laugh, and Maeve cocks her head. "I'll humor you. What are the terms?"

"Simple. Turn over the treasure, and she'll only kill the Regulators. You may keep your children."

The old lady laughs again. "Treasure? We've not got enough food to eat, and you've come here asking for treasure. You're mad."

Postule blanches. Behind him, the Dræu are growing restless. Standing at attention obviously isn't their nature, and I can tell that their hinky mood worries the fat man. How did they travel here, I wonder. Postule is too fat to walk far. That means that their camp has to be close by.

"Don't play games with me, ruster," Postule says.

"Speaking of games," I say, "how'd you come to work for the Dræu, Postule? Last time we looked, you were spread-eagled begging for your life."

"The last time you saw me," he sneers, "I was escaping

from a piddle-poor excuse for a Regulator. I wondered when you would open your mouth, *dalit*."

Vienne cocks her armalite.

"Is that a threat?" Postule says. "Just for that, I'm going to ask the queen to kill you myself."

"Ask away," Vienne says.

"You didn't answer the question," I say. "How'd a high-class kidnapper like you end up with the Dræu? Or is it all thieving to you?"

The fat man puffs up. "I have always worked for the Dræu. Did you think they're just a bunch of wild animals living the end of the wilderness? There is more to the Dræu than you ever thought of, *dalit*. But let's consider your situation: a thousand kilometers from civilization. No food, no water, no communication. Only a few Regulators and a handful of malnourished miners against a ravenous horde. Who would be stupid enough to accept a job like that?"

"Here." Ebi tosses a ring to Postule, who cups it in his puffy hands. "You want treasure to leave these people alone, take this and go."

Postule sizes up the ring. It's yellow gold with a four blue diamond setting. Since there's no gold mined on Mars and the metal is embargoed, the ring is obviously imported from Earth. It is, I think to myself, worth a fortune.

"That ring will bring enough on the black market for a long retirement," Ebi says.

Or several years' worth of easy prison time for my

imprisoned father. What would it be like to have so much that I could toss a fortune into the air like it's nothing? Even when Father was a CEO, we never had that much coin. Ebi is a very different kind of Regulator from me.

"You're very different kind of Regulator, too," Mimi says.

"Not so different. Maybe from Fuse and Jenkins, but not from Vienne."

"Oh?"

"Yeah. Of course," I think, watching Postule.

He examines the stone in the light. "Very pretty, missy." He pockets it. "But it's not the treasure. Is it, miners? You know what my queen is looking for."

"Give me back the ring if you are not going to leave!" Ebi shouts.

Postule laughs and pushes her away. "You can ask the queen for it."

"Thief!"

"Stupid, spoiled brat."

Furious, Ebi lifts her armalite. Only a quick swat from Vienne keeps her from putting a slug into Postule's gut.

This is getting us nowhere. I walk straight up to Postule. "You've wasted your breath and our time. There's no treasure here, just megatons of guanite and a whole lot of Regulator bullets. Which is what you're going to find between those beady black eyes of yours next time you show your face in Hell's Cross."

Behind Postule, the Dræu start laughing.

"Shut up!" Postule screams at the Dræu, then turns back to Maeve. "Ruster, you had your opportunity. The queen offered you good terms, and you spit in her face. Personally, I knew you were too stupid to do anything but lie. There is treasure here, and the Dræu will find it. Makes no difference to her how long it takes or how much flesh she's got to flail to get it."

"You've got five seconds to get off our land." Maeve spits in his face.

"Witch!" Postule backhands her. As she falls, he draws back his hand to deliver another blow. Vienne snaps her armalite out and blows a hole through his meaty palm.

"My hand! She shot me!"

"Nice aim," I tell Vienne. Then I point to the opposite side of the bridge. "Go! Before my Regulators fill you full of chigoe holes."

On cue, the Regulators bring their weapons to bear. The Dræu, realizing that it isn't an idle threat, grab Postule by the shoulders and steer him away. He stumbles, holding the bloodied hand against his chest.

"My hand, my hand, my hand."

They kick his rear end to keep him moving. One Dræu covers their retreat, lobbing a smoke grenade for cover. When they reach the safety of the other side of the bridge, he roars out of frustration and fires off a few rounds of plasma into the billowing smoke. The shots carry a hundred meters, then drop impotently into the chasm below.

"So much for negotiations," I say a minute later, when the Dræu have gone. "Let's get back to the Cross, we've got—"

"Chief," Ebi calls. "Jean-Paul. I cannot find him anywhere."

"He was just here," I say as we all start to look around for him. "Mimi, locate Jean-Paul's biorhythm signature."

"Negative," she responds. "No biorhythms can be located within a half-kilometer radius."

"Which means?"

"He is not here, cowboy. He's gone."

CHAPTER 26

"Chief," Ebi says as I'm giving Fuse and Jenkins instructions on protecting the Cross in my absence. "I request permission to join the rescue party."

"Denied," I say.

The rescue party, as she calls it, is me, Vienne, and Ockham, who's looking better after his time in the infirmary. We're gathering at the Zhou Zhoa Bridge. Once we're gone, I've instructed them to collapse every tunnel except the one leading here. The miners aren't happy about the idea of dropping three tunnels near the Cross, but I'm not crazy about another sneak attack from Bedlam.

Because we could never catch up to the Dræu on foot, the miners have found us an ancient snowmobile, and Fuse has got it running. It's our only chance of rescuing the little fool Jean-Paul. Ockham is his mentor. That's why he's going along. But before we head to the snowmobile, I pull him aside.

"You're fit for this duty, right?" I ask him, knowing he'll catch the drift of my words.

He nods and winks his vacant eye. "You're the chief, chief. One eye. One hand."

"One heart," I say, finishing the oath. Then we move on.

"Wait! Chief," Ebi says, trailing after me, "Jean-Paul is my brother, and I am responsible for rescuing him from his kidnappers."

"Like I told you, Ebi," I say. "I don't think Jean-Paul's been kidnapped. The little idiot probably chased the Dræu out of here."

Our plan is follow their trail. With any luck, it will lead us to the Dræu camp. With even more luck, Jean-Paul hasn't gotten himself captured. Or worse.

"Request for reconsideration," Ebi says after a few seconds.

"Okay." I pause long enough to count to three. "I've reconsidered."

"Thank you, I—"

"And you're still not going. Three is enough for a rescue party, and I need you here to keep your mother under wraps. This job was hard enough, then she showed up. Where's she now, by the way?"

"Resting in quarters. She took her medication and needed to lie down." Ebi's lips tighten. "But you need me on this mission."

"Why is that?"

"Because I know where Postule is."

I stop walking. Look hard into Ebi's lineless face. The proportions perfectly symmetrical. Her brows plucked and shaped. Teeth whiter than any I've ever seen. The skin is flawless, like porcelain. She should be beautiful, but every detail is so perfect, her visage looks like a mask and not a face.

"How'd you know that?" I ask her.

"The ring he stole from me. It has a global positioning microdot under the stone. With a receiver, I can track him down anywhere. If we find Postule, we find my brother."

"A microdot?" She's pretty savvy for a newly minted Regulator. "You tricked Postule into taking the ring?"

The corners of her mouth turn down, her version of a smile. "So you see, you have to let me go."

"Just hand over the satellite tracker. We can find him just as easily as you can."

I hold out an open palm, and she looks like it's diseased. After a few seconds she slaps the transmitter in my palm. "I am twice the warrior Vienne is. If something happens to my brother, my mother will have you to blame."

"You're dismissed," I say, the tendons working in my jaw.

"Yes, sir." She salutes and heads for the exit, shoulders straight, head erect. The walk of defiance.

Ockham shakes his mane of gray hair in dismay. "These new Regulators."

"More disrespectful every year," Vienne agrees, shaking her head in unison.

"Enough reminiscing about the before days, oldsters." After looking over the tracker, I hand it to Vienne. "Here, Vienne, you be my compass. Ockham, get the vehicle ready. Fuse," I say, pulling him aside for a private word. "While we're gone, I've got a project for you to work on."

"What's that, chief?"

"Your barricade wall isn't going to work against the Dræu. They're too aggressive, and they've seen it, so we've lost the element of surprise." I roll out a sheet of electrostat. "Here's the basic idea of what we need."

Fuse whistles and rubs his head. "You drew this, chief?"

"Affirmative." With help from Mimi.

"Help?" Mimi says. "I created ninety-nine percent of the design."

"Eighty percent."

"Ninety."

"Eighty-five is my final calculation," I say. "Take it or leave it."

"With your math skills, I'll leave it," she says.

"Let me get this straight," Fuse says, studying the drawing. "You want me to tear down the redoubt that we've not yet completed and build a whole other structure?"

"And I want it finished by the time I get back."

Fuse laughs, "Good one, chief."

"I'm serious, Fuse." I smile ruefully. "Our defensive strategy has been completely revised."

"Oy! By—by myself?" He puts both hands on his cheeks,

like a kid who's been asked to clean his quarters. "It can't be done."

"It can," I say, "and you will do it. I've got faith in you."

"I'd feel better," Fuse says, "if you had less faith and more manpower."

Me, too, I think.

"One more thing, chief," Fuse says. "What happens if the mission goes figjam and you cark it?"

"We won't."

Our journey takes us across the bridge and several kilometers up into the cavernous access tubes that once allowed Manchesters to harvest tons of guanite every hour. The way is laid with tracks, the rails as high as my hip and as wide as my shoulder. In days past the sound in the tunnels would've been worse than deafening. Now there's only the whine of the mobile's engine.

Outside, the terrain is a mix of high, jagged hills covered with snow and low-lying stretches of land dappled with threadbare, frozen soil. I feel exposed, especially as we approach a line of hills to the north. We're wearing heavy coats the miners provided. They're filled with synthetic down, and the shells are waterproof.

"Mimi, see what you can do about getting us some camo. Eventually we'll have to dump the coats, and this regulation black color makes us stand out like a—"

"Sore thumb?" she interrupts.

"Yes, sore thumb. Just run the program and transmit codes to the others' suits, no? And Mimi?"

"Yes, cowboy?"

"I hate when you finish my sentences for me."

"Someone has to."

A jolt of static electric sweeps over my body. My armor changes from black to digitized white and various shades of grey. I touch Vienne, then Ockham, and their armor morphs to mimic mine.

"That's some trick," Ockham shouts over the engine, clearly impressed.

The morning sun is a heatless yellow globe that casts cold light on the streaks of ice that make our road, and I can smell our exhaust in the air. The mobile's four cylinders roar as I gun it. The speedometer climbs. Sixty. Seventy. Eighty. Eighty-five.

Behind me, Vienne wraps her arms around my waist and squeezes my hips with her knees. This, I could get used to.

After bouncing over the tundra for almost an hour, we come to a place where the path splits. One way is west to a line of high mountains. The other is north, where there's a valley surrounded by foothills.

"Which way?" I ask as we stop to stretch our legs. I'm talking to Mimi, but Ockham answers first.

"Tracks head to the north." He bends down to the glass-hard ground. "The tracks ain't from no snowmobile. They're driving something with bigger footprints and a bigger engine."

"How far ahead of us?" I ask.

"About twenty clicks." Vienne holds up the tracking device. "And they're still moving."

"Show-off," Ockham mumbles. "Damned newfangled toys. Like to see what happens when the power pack gives out."

"Good work. Both of you." I fire up the engine. "Let's go."

After a while we reach the foothills, where the GPS signal shows that our target has become stationary. Below us, the Dræu camp spreads out like a stain. Dozens of metal habipods form an uneven circle around a central structure, a clear dome that contains several more habipods, and in the exact center is a polydome at least two hundred meters in circumference. I recognize the design—CorpCom army issue. The Dræu don't lack for resources.

The dome bustles with activity, and it is surrounded by roving packs of Dræu. Their backs are turned to the rest of camp, their faces toward the dome, as if they're posted to keep individuals from getting out instead of getting in.

"He's there," Vienne says, checking the tracking monitor. "Postule is inside the dome."

"What about Jean-Paul?"

"Negative," she says. "I don't see him."

"Mimi, do you have a fix?" I ask.

"He's here," she says. "Give me time to sort his biosignature from theirs."

Ockham hands me a pair of omnoculars. "Take a look at

this. Looks like Postule is in a bad spot. Right in the center, on the throne."

I dial in to the location. The throne is surrounded by Dræu carrying battle rifles, which are aimed at Postule. The fat man is on his knees, genuflecting, his gaze fixed on the woman sitting on the throne. She is thin with long black hair that falls in heavy ringlets down to her waist, and she's dressed in brightly colored, gauzy fabric, her legs tucked beneath her bottom. Both hands are adorned with rings, and her face is hidden behind a porcelain harlequin mask.

"The queen?" I say. How could something so beautiful lead a band of vicious cannibals?

"He's a dead man," Ockham says after he pulls out another pair of omnoculars. "Just a matter of what the carking beasties do to him before they gut him."

My stomach tightens. Even though I know it's true and that Postule made his own bed, it still sickens me. The queen takes Postule's shaking hand in hers, smiles, then slides a meat cleaver from beneath her cushion.

With one deft swing, she lops the hand from the wrist. Holds it up by the ring finger. It's adorned with the ring that Postule stole. The fat man's body shakes like he's got the tremors. Behind him, the Dræu gather tightly. A pack of hungry animals. The sight of blood is too much for them, and only the queen keeps them swarming Postule.

"My God," I whisper, and then hear Ockham curse softly.

The lens of the omnoculars fog, and I have to wipe it

clean. When I adjust the lenses, the queen has removed the ring. She holds it up to the light, like a curious kid who's just found a sparkly toy. Especially when she opens her mouth and pops the ring inside.

"Chief," Vienne says, and holds up the tracking device. "Signal's dead."

"She ate it."

"The signal?"

"The ring. The queen swallowed it like a tasty morsel."

But the queen isn't finished. Hooking Postule in the corner of the mouth with a finger, she lifts him from his knees. Gently she pushes his head forward, and his chin touches his flabby chest. She raises the other hand high. I see the flash of light on metal as she swings the cleaver again. Blood sprays the queen, dappling her gauzy dress, and leaves red dots splattered across her face.

The kill is too much for the Dræu. They swarm the fat man's body as the queen slips gracefully to the seat of her throne. She hits a button, and the dais rises a dozen meters above the feasting cannibals. From there, twirling one of the hundreds of ringlets of black hair, she watches the horde devour Postule.

"She's not a forgiving one, that's for sure," Ockham says.

"What happened?" Vienne asks as she gives up on her tracking device and stores it in with her other gear.

"The queen killed him," I say. I tap my vid screen open. "Mimi, anything on Jean-Paul's biorhythms?"

"Affirmative. I have triangulated a weak signal one thousand meters to the west. I'm displaying it on aural vid . . . now."

I move my head so that the blip is in the middle of the screen. "There." I point toward the parked power sleds. "That's where our boy is. Ockham, move ahead to see if you can get a visual."

"Aye-aye," he says, and begins picking his way across the terrain, the camo pattern on his symbiarmor making him almost invisible to the naked eye. Within three minutes, he's back. "Got him. The little rooter's hiding in one of the power sleds. Looks like he hitched a ride and got himself in a big pickle."

I sigh. "Let's go get him."

"Right," Ockham says. "We need to disable those power sleds while we're at it. If the Dræu figure a way to get them into the mines, those turrets will cut us to ribbons."

"Negative." I count six sentries posted. "Even if we take them out, we're bound to raise a ruckus, and the Dræu will come running. The risk's not worth the reward."

"C'mon, chief, live a little." Ockham grins. "What's the worst that could happen? We cull a few Dræu from the herd, make a little mayhem, and it all goes fig-jam, we jump a power sled and race the beasties back to the Cross. What'd you think, Vienne?"

"That's my kind of mission," she says.

"This is not a democracy," I say, though I hate to

disappoint her. "Maybe it would be smart to even the odds, but we're not going to take the power sleds."

"No?" Ockham says.

I pull a box of C-42 from his gear bag. "No, we're going to blow them up. Courtesy of Fuse and his bag of tricks."

"Now that," Ockham says, "is my kind of leadership."

CHAPTER 27

South Pole
ANNOS MARTIS 238. 4. 0. 00:00

Staying low and running in a crouch, we take a wide loop around the perimeter of the camp and count on the symbi-armor's camouflage to hide us in the blindingly white ice sheet. It's only a half a kilometer, but my thighs are burning and my lungs tighten. I want to cough badly, but I hold off until we're in position behind a knoll above the habipod that protects the vehicles.

Six Dræu sentries guard them. They carry plasma pistols, except for one, who holds a battle rifle. I mark him as the leader and signal to Vienne that he's the primary target.

She confirms the order with a nod. Then quickly digs a trench on the knoll. Fits her armalite with a scope and a sniper barrel equipped with a silencer. Silently she inserts a clip of armor-piercing ammo.

"Mimi," I say, "watch my back."

"Backside being watched, chief."

"I said *back*."

"Same general area, correct?"

While Vienne locks in on her target, Ockham and I move closer. Once Vienne takes out the leader, we'll rush the other five and make quick work of them. Hopefully before they can sound the alert.

I pull a combat knife from my boot. Ockham does the same. Then moves ahead to the next cover.

"Let's do this the old-fashioned way, no?" he whispers.

"Vienne," I say through the aural link, "eyes on our target?"

"Target acquired, chief. I see the boy. He's under a tarp on the third sled. Give the word."

"Thirty seconds. We're almost in po—"

Ahead, Ockham slips on a patch of ice and slides to one knee and flattens himself on the ground. The noise catches the attention of the Dræu leader, who turns toward it. He grunts at one of the sentries, the smallest of the crew, who reluctantly follows the order. The leader trudges up the hill away from the habipod, mumbling what have to be curses and wiping drool from the side of his mouth.

From my vantage point, I can easily take the sentry down, he's so tantalizingly close. But because it would wreck the mission, I do nothing. Nothing but wait and hope. And pray that Ockham's camouflage is good enough to hide him.

The sentry takes two steps forward. His heavy boot lands atop one of Ockham's hands. He turns in a semicircle, using its foot as a pivot point. Then he aims the pistol toward the hill where Vienne's attention is focused on the leader. She's not aware of the reflection from the weapon aimed at her chest.

I hear a click and smell the discharge of magnesium fuse. In three seconds the plasma will heat to critical mass, and the Dræu will have a kill shot.

"Now!" I shout to Vienne over the link and leap from cover and strike the Dræu at the base of the neck with my knife. The sentry collapses.

Vienne fires the shot. I hear the leader's body collapse onto a power sled. The Dræu call out in surprise when I grab the charged plasma pistol. I toss it to Ockham, who is already on his feet. The old man fires three quick shots, taking out a Dræu with each blast.

A plasma glob zips over my head as I charge the remaining sentries. I take out the first one with a front kick to the solar plexus. Then spin to the next one, who has picked up the battle rifle. I reach for my armalite and realize it isn't in the holster.

"Oops," I say. "You wouldn't shoot an unarmed man, right?"

A nasty grin splits the Dræu's face, and he begins to squeeze the trigger as an armor-piercing bullet enters and exits his chest cavity. He's still grinning when he pitches forward and lands atop the body of his leader.

With the crew taken out, I signal Ockham and Vienne forward. Then I check the perimeter, making sure that we've not been spotted yet. When Vienne reaches the third sled, she tosses the tarp aside and pulls Jean-Paul by the ear out of the cargo bay.

"Oy!" he manages to say before she claps a hand over his mouth.

The boy bites down just as hard, clamping his teeth on the exposed webbing between her thumb and forefinger. Vienne, after letting out a quiet huff of pain, punches him at the base of the skull. His knees wobble, and he collapses in a pile of shivering, unconscious flesh.

"Blighter," she says, sticking her bleeding hand into a pile of snow.

I look to Ockham, who shakes his head sympathetically. "Feisty little beast, no?"

"Put him in a sled," I tell Ockham. "And cover him up with the tarp. Him carking of hypothermia's no better than getting fragged by the Dræu."

"Yes, chief," Ockham says. He cocoons Jean-Paul in the tarp, then lays him behind the jump seat of the sled.

"Vienne," I say, opening my gear pack, "keep watch. Ockham, help me place this C-forty-two."

I hand three charges to Ockham. "There are two more sleds than we've got charges for, so we'll need to do double duty on two of the sleds. Those two in the back parked closest together. We'll leave that one in front for ourselves." After checking to make sure the fuel tank is full, I move as many boxes of chain gun ammo that will fit into the cargo hold.

"My apologies, chief," Ockham says as we work. "I almost fig-jammed the mission. Damn these old legs. There was a day when I could walk a tight wire forty meters off the ground. Now I'm lucky just to tie my own boots."

"No harm," I say. "Let's finish the job first. We can whine about the old days when we're back at the Cross."

I'm joking, but Ockham doesn't want to laugh. "It's not the way of the Tenets, chief. A Regulator buries his face while a beastie's centimeters from slaughtering him like a feed animal." The joy he showed just a few minutes ago has evaporated. "Better to go out in a glory blaze. Die a beautiful death."

"Enough philosophy, no?" I say. "Let's finish the job before the Dræu finish their supper."

I set the last timer. Then look up to check Ockham's progress. My eye catches a flicker of motion from the front of the habipod. The Dræu I kicked in the face—he's awake. And reaching for an alarm on the open door of the shed.

Twip! Vienne's shot hits the Dræu in the chest. He pitches forward. Blood pours out of the wound. But it isn't a kill shot, and the Dræu raises his hand as another round catches him. His hand falls onto the alarm. A siren sounds.

"Ockham!" I shout. "Fire up this power sled. Vienne! Cover us! We're moving out!"

Jumping into the seat of the sled, I punch the starter button. The turbine squeals as the fuel hits, and I let her roll out of the habipod. Then from the knoll above us, Vienne empties a clip of ammo, the spent cartridges ejecting in a steady stream around her. Although I can't see anything yet, I know it can mean only one thing.

The Dræu are coming.

Coming for us.

CHAPTER 28

South Pole
ANNOS MARTIS 238. 4. 0. 00:00

"Man the chain gun!" I yell to Ockham over the noise of the engine. I twist the throttle, and the sled leaps forward.

But the old man is already bringing the massive barrel to bear. A line of Dræu charge up the hill, carrying plasma pistols. Ockham releases a burst of fire. They fall like their legs have imploded.

"Get in!" I call to Vienne. She jumps down from the knoll into the deck, careful to avoid Jean-Paul's tarp cocoon, and slides into place while swapping the sniper barrel out of her armalite.

Jet flames erupt from the sled's turbine. We shoot forward, the force of the sudden acceleration snapping our heads back. The front skies bounce over the knoll, and the weight of the extra ammo causes the rear to lift. For a long second we hang there, teetering between escape and collapse, until Vienne throws herself forward onto the cowling.

I steer hard left, following the path we took into the camp.

The Dræu crest the hill again, and their pistols are primed to fire. With an earsplitting *phweee*, a wave of plasma globs sail over the sled and sinks into the ice two meters ahead, leaving dozens of holes in the permafrost ahead of us.

"Steer for me!" I yell to Vienne.

While she reaches over to take the handle bars, I pull the detonator from my pack and hit the button. For a second, nothing. Then *popoppopopop*! The habipod explodes. Fiery debris flies a dozen meters into the air, and the concussive blast knocks the Dræu's skirmish line flat. There's nothing left of the 'pod except a few tattered sheets of corrugated metal and twisted sled parts.

"Heewack!" Ockham lets out a victory whoop. "That'll show them beasties what the Regulators are made of. Breathe easy, Regulators."

After taking control of the sled again, I steer over the last of the foothills. The tundra spreads out now, putting distance between us and the horde.

"Mimi," I ask. "How's the pursuit?"

"There are no signatures on my scans," she says. "Yet."

"Meaning I shouldn't be breathing easily."

"Meaning you may not want to breathe at all."

"What's that noise?" I ask aloud, then realize that the sled's engine is straining. I check the tachometer. We're only reaching fifty percent of potential speed, and the sled sounds like it's chewing up its drive train.

Only a minute passes before Mimi pipes up. "You didn't

hold your breath enough, cowboy. Sensors are picking up a mass of biosignatures closing fast."

On cue, Vienne shouts over the silence. "Chief! We have trouble. Bogies at six, eight, and five o'clock. It's the Dræu. Riding snowmobiles."

"More fun for me!" Ockham shouts. Begins loading another ammo belt into the chain gun. "I see 'em!" he shouts. "Ten bogies bearing down hard at seven o'clock. Let the murderous rooters come on! I'll give 'em a taste of Regulator breakfast!"

"Cowboy," Mimi chimes in. "At their current rate of speed, they will overtake this sled in approximately three minutes."

"Damn," I say, and twist the throttle harder. It's no use, of course. The sled is already maxed out. It's the weight, I realize. I packed the cargo bay with too much ammo, and it's slowing us down.

"Ockham!" I shout. "Dump the ammo belts!"

But Ockham doesn't seem to hear me. "Eyes on the target! Opening fire!" and he releases a long burst of fire that rains shells into the air. The spent cartridges hit the floor of the cargo bay like falling sleet. I snap my head around in time to see two snowmobiles explode.

There are two Dræu on each mobile. One driving. One shooting. The last of the mobiles is larger than the others, with armor plating on the cowling. The leader, Kuhru, is driving, but the passenger is the remarkable one—the queen of the Dræu stands on the backseat, the porcelain mask hiding her face, a mortar launcher resting on her shoulder.

A mortar launcher! If she hits the sled with that, we're dunny pie. "Ockham! Dump the ammo! Now!"

"He can't hear you," Vienne yells into my ear. "Too much noise."

I look back at the queen. She is sighting us through the launcher's viewfinder.

"Duck!" I yank the handlebars hard to the right. The sled fishtails, and Ockham stumbles from the turret. He lands on a box of ammo and rolls almost into Vienne's lap.

"Pardon my buttocks, young miss," he says.

"Get back on the gun!" she screams. "And dump the ammo!"

A mortar shell flies past our sled and skitters across the ice a few meters in front of us. Then explodes and blows ice chunks across the cowling of the sled.

"They're closing in!" Vienne yells.

"Hold on!" I bellow as the front skis hit the edge of the mortar crater.

The front of the sled pops up and we jump the hole, the treads throwing up a curtain of debris. The wash hits the driver of the lead snowmobile, who steers into the hole. The ski digs into the crater, and the mobile pole-vaults, slamming the Dræu face-first into the ground.

"Got one!" Ockham whoops. He tries to scramble to the back of the sled.

Vienne catches him and yells into his ear. "Chief says to dump weight! We're too heavy!"

Ockham makes the okay sign. "Got it, chief!"

When I accelerate again, Ockham bounds to the back of the cargo bay. He hoists a box of ammunition waist-high, then tosses it overboard. I feel the rear end lift and look back. Ockham is perched on the edge of the sled, his armalite in one hand and a sidearm in the other.

"No Regulator worth his salt," Ockham yells to me, "wants anything but a blaze of glory, chief! I'll stop these beasties. You get the girl and this buggy home." Somehow, he bows and then executes a backflip. He lands on his feet and sprints for the box.

"Man down! Man down!" Vienne shouts. She vaults the jump seat and takes the grips of the chain gun in hand. "Bring her around, chief!"

I pull hard on the handlebars, and the rear end fishtails wildly. Their weight and momentum carries us two hundred and twenty degrees, the sudden swing disrupting the fuel lines to the turbine. The engine stalls. "Damn it! *Esena mori poutana!* Piece of crap!"

As the Dræu close in on Ockham, I hit the starter button again. And again. Vienne aims the gun at the approaching snowmobiles. A very quick burst scatters them as they veer hard in both directions to avoid fire.

"Can't get a clear shot, chief!" she yells back. "Ockham is in my line of fire!"

The Dræu peel back, out of range of Vienne's gun. They circle Ockham, gunning their engines, dodging in and out to draw his fire. One snowmobile makes a run at Ockham. The old man dodges easily, the plasma blast bouncing off his symbiarmor and falling, sizzling, to the ice.

Ockham takes aim with his armalite. Fires a single round. *Foof!* A green mass shoots out of the lower barrel. It strikes the gunner between the shoulder blades. Screaming, the Dræu reaches behind, twisting, trying to yank the plasma off. A second later the plasma explodes, taking the mobile and the driver along with it.

"There's plenty more where that came from!" Ockham pumps out two grenades. They find their targets, and two more mobiles explode. Then he turns toward my stalled power sled. "Damn you, chief! Don't you dare try a rescue. Finish the mission! Finish—"

Crack-a-boosh! A mortar shell from the queen's launcher knocks Ockham off his feet. Seeing their chance, the Dræu gun their engines. Roar toward him.

"Chief!" Vienne yells. "Go! Go now!"

Saying a prayer, I hit the starter button again. Nothing. "Come on, you old whore," I say softly.

Then hit the button again. Ignition! The ski lurches forward, taking Vienne and her gun farther from the Dræu. She fires out a burst in frustration anyway. The stray bullets send the Dræu scattering again, which gives Ockham enough time to climb to his feet. He kicks open the box of ammo as a barrage of plasma fire turns his sidearm into a puddle of metal.

Ockham tosses the gun away and brings the armalite to bear. He squeezes off a half dozen rounds of explosives that strike Kuhru's snowmobile, sending the vehicle tumbling end on end. But the queen is too quick. Before the rounds hit, she leaps from the backseat and comes up firing her mortar launcher. The shell rockets for Ockham, a trailing vapor line in its wake.

"Ockham!" I yell.

At the same instant a second snowmobile rushes him. It crosses into the path of the mortar, and the explosion takes out the driver and the gunner. The rest of the Dræu swarm in for the kill. But the old man still has one trick up his sleeve. He pumps a light-mass grenade inside the box. Then slams the lid and jumps atop it.

"Reg-u-lator!" he bellows. Chills run down my spine.

Without the weight of its cargo, my sled accelerates to ninety-five percent of capacity. Wind laced with snow rips past my face. Ahead, the tundra opens up like a table, and I don't look back at Ockham, even when a series of explosions rocks the landscape and sends up a black plume that blots out the sun. My shoulders sag. A beautiful death is what Ockham wanted, and he got it. But that doesn't soften the blow. Another man down. Another life sacrificed. Another Regulator lost.

A quiet moment passes with nothing but the drone of

the turbine and the sluicing of the skies over the packed ice. Then Vienne breaks the silence. "It's Ockham! He's still alive!"

Impossible. "Mimi?"

"His signal is still registering, cowboy."

"Why didn't you tell me?"

"You didn't ask."

I turn the sled in a wide arc. It's true. On the rise, one of his arms hanging like a thread from his shoulder, his armor in shreds, Ockham stumbles along. His helmet is shattered. His face burned and bleeding.

"Go back!" Vienne yells.

But I can't. He's done for. And the Dræu are coming. I hear them before I see them, their howls echoing across the tundra. Ockham looks back over his shoulder. Wild fear forces his legs to move, and for a few seconds he's running. Then they're on him—a pack of Dræu. Furious. Ravenous. They ride the old warrior to the ground. Lift him prone over their heads. Mouths open to catch the blood hemorrhaging from his wounds.

Twip! Twip! Vienne snipes two of them.

"Shoot Ockham!" I shout to Vienne.

"I cannot! He must have his beautiful death!" she yells.

"It's not beautiful," I yell back at her, "to be eaten alive!" Though my sniping skills aren't in the same class as Vienne's, the target is close enough.

"Chief, please," Vienne says. "Don't take this from him."

"I'm sorry." I take aim. Pull the trigger. Watch the old man's head snap back. Watch him die at my hand, the hand of a brother.

Vienne looks up at me, her hazel eyes rimmed with red, full of accusation, hurt, and disbelief. "How could you do that to him? He will never reach Valhalla now. You . . . you took that away from him. How could you?"

I bow my head, ashamed of the way that I have diminished myself. "How could I not?"

CHAPTER 29

South Pole
ANNOS MARTIS 238. 4. 0. 00:00

The sled slams into a snowbank ramp. Sails over the barricade. Threads churning frantically. Turbine pouring vapor jets.

We're going to die, I think, and cling to the handlebars.

Vienne pumps a thousand rounds into the Dræu, whose snowmobiles weave like choreographed dancers in a mechanized tango. Three mobiles charge into range of the gun, and Vienne feeds them a strafe of bullets as we land.

Hard.

The nose of the sled hammers the ice, and the handlebars almost rip loose from my hands. Behind us, two Dræu snowmobiles hit the snow ramp. They soar high into the air—engines and drivers screaming—then crash, scattering the savages like grotesque rag dolls across the permafrost.

They're all dead, I think.

Until one of them stands up. Raises a battle rifle to his shoulder as my sled bears down him—Kuhru!

"Vienne! Get down!"

Kuhru fires a three-shot burst. *Brrrp! Brrrp! Brrrp!* The barrel burns orange, and the bullets whistle past my head.

"Wà kào!" I curse. "That was close!"

Then Vienne stops firing. "I'm hit!" she yells and leans against a box, a hand covering her heel, one of three weak spots in symbiarmor. Blood seeps between her fingers. Then I see a laser sight dance across her face.

"Down!" I bellow, and veer right.

Kuhru's second burst whistles past. But now his mouth drops open, the sudden realization that the sled's not stopping. He fires wildly, panicked, and breaks into a run.

"Qù sui!" I bellow. "Nobody shoots my crew!" Then slam the brakes.

The sled whips around, and the treads slam into Kuhru, knocking him out of his boots. His body floats off the ground, then falls, as if a giant hand has lifted it gently and placed it on a row of rusted-out generators that are half buried in snowdrifts.

It's a beautiful death. Too beautiful for a killer, I think as I veer toward the mine entrance, where Fisher Four opens like a black mouth.

As we reach safety, I sneak a glance backward. The queen stands atop her machine, marshaling her forces, shouting for them to form up. Clearly she's not ready to give up and go home.

Then I turn my attention to the pitch-black tunnel ahead, steering between fallen boulders and wreckage.

"Status report," I ask Vienne. "How's the foot?"

"It has shrapnel in it."

Ask an obvious question, get an obvious answer. "How bad are you bleeding?"

"I'm bleeding pretty well." She's leaning against an ammo box. Her knee's propped up, and she's applying pressure to the wound.

"Mimi," I ask, navigating around several hunks of scrap metal. "How is she?"

"My scans suggest that the injury is minor."

"Signs of shock?"

"Affirmative. She should administer a dose of epinephrine."

"I'll be sure to tell her you said that."

A junked mine car appears ahead of the sled, and I cut hard to avoid it. The passageway is getting too bumpy, so I cut power. Letting the Dræu catch up.

"Stupid miners!" I shout. "Don't they ever throw their crap away!"

Then the lights come on. The tunnel is swamped by floodlights placed high in ceiling. I can make out the shape of the rocks as we pass, the colors of the stone walls, and the shapes of the shrapnel still stuck into my armor—it's going to take hours to pull all of it out.

"Greeting party ahead," Mimi says.

"Please tell me they're ours?" I say, taking a worried glance at Vienne, who's beginning to shake.

"Affirmative. It's the good guys."

Beyond another broken-down harvester, Jenkins, Fuse, and Ebi are positioned in a skirmish line. They kneel behind a concrete partition, ready to fire.

Mimi opens an aural link with them. "Regulators," I bark. "The Dræu are crawling up our backs! Hold position. Do not advance!"

Fuse confirms the order. "Hustle your buttocks, chief. The miners say there's fifty Dræu heading this way. At least fifty. Might be more. You know the miners and their lack of counting skills."

Fifty? Impossible. There were only about a hundred in the base. How many did we take down? Twenty? Thirty? Makes no sense.

"Mimi," I ask. "Am I counting wrong?"

"Negative, cowboy. I estimate thirty-nine Dræu fatalities and twenty-one wounded."

"Then the miners really can't count."

"Negative," she says. "Sensors now indicate several dozen Dræu biorhymic signatures."

Damn. A moment later we pull up to the concrete barrier. "New plan," I tell them. "We're bugging out. Now!"

Fuse takes one look at Vienne and runs to the back of the sled. "What's happened to you, love? You look pale as a dungy worm."

"Don't . . . call . . ." Vienne's head wobbles to the side. "Shoot . . . you . . ."

"She took shrapnel," I say, and give up my seat. "Fuse, you drive. Jenkins, Ebi, get on this bucket!"

Fuse slides into the driver's seat. "In the heel. That's where they always get you, innit? You'd think the minds sharp enough to dream up bioadaptive cloth could figure out how to make a decent boot."

"Shut up and drive!" I bellow.

Ebi helps Vienne into the jump seat, then joins me at the back of the sled. "Did you find Jean-Paul?"

"He's wrapped in that tarp." I have to fight the urge to give it a kick. "Check his pulse or something. Make sure his worthless hide is still intact."

"Yes, chief."

Jenkins vaults into the cargo bay, his arms thrown wide. "Oh, baby, it's been too long. Come to papa." He hugs the chain gun. "You're so beautiful. And look at all this ammo. It's like Christmas, and Jenkins's been such a good boy. Yes, he has."

"*Re malaka*," I mumble, then shout, "Fuse, get us out of here!"

"What about Ockham?" Fuse asks, revving the engine.

"We lost him on the tundra," I say. "He's dead."

Because Fuse is a better driver than either Vienne or me, we quickly reach the Zhao Zhou Bridge and the wide gorge it spans. A contingent of miners, led by Maeve, Spiner, and Áine, is waiting when we cross the long bridge.

Fuse kills the engine. Ebi hops down from the seat and draws her armalite. She takes position beside the sled while Jenkins aims the chain gun at the black hole of the tunnel.

Behind us, the sounds of the snowmobiles grow louder, then fade.

"C'mon, c'mon, you fine cannibals," Jenkins mutters. "Baby's itching to dance. C'mon, ain't you wanting to dance?"

"What happened?" Áine says when she sees the blood on my hands. "You've got yourself hurt. I knew it! I knew you couldn't ride off without coming back in pieces."

"It's not me. It's Vienne," I say, then brace for impact as Áine throws her arms wide.

And slams into Fuse. Lays a great sloppy kiss on him. "You're safe! I'd got afraid that it was you'd been shot."

Fuse, embarrassed, unclasps her arms from his neck. "Not now, lovey," he says. "We're on the job."

"Step to, people! The Dræu are crawling up our ass!" I sweep Vienne up in my arms. Her head lolls to my shoulder, the touch of her forehead on my cheek colder than it should be, and her teeth are chattering. "She's going into shock." I say, turning to Maeve. "We need to keep her warm and get the bull—"

Maeve bunches up her face. "I've been pulling metal of one kind or another out of miners for twenty plus annos. I know shock when I see it. Spiner!"

Spiner opens his arms, motioning for me to hand her off. "We'll take care of her, chief," he says.

But I can't let go. She's so light in my arms, so fragile, even as her whole body shakes against me, and I find myself wishing that I could draw her inside my suit, let my armor wrap around her, to protect her the way that Mimi protects me. The Dræu are coming. My davos needs me. But how can I just give her away?

"Chief," Mimi says. "Her vitals are distress—"

Yes, I know, *a broch*! I know. "Be careful," I tell Spiner as I slide her into his arms.

"We'll get her right," Maeve says. She pats my arm and smiles sympathetically as they hurry Vienne away.

Brrppt! A burst from Jenkins's chain gun gets my attention. "Heewack!" Whooping joyously, he sends bullets flying into the tunnel, where a Dræu advance party has emerged into the light.

I grab the omnoculars. Like before, the Dræu are screaming and leaping around, jumping on one another's backs, growling and raging like they're in the last stages of rabies. I can almost smell their feral stink from here.

"And some things never change," I say. "Jenkins, hold your fire. You're wasting ammo."

Fuse leans over to me. "So Ockham's carked it?"

Vienne's accusation rings in my ears. *How could you do that to him?* "That's what I said."

"Heads up, chief!" Jenkins barks. "Looks like the beasties brought the heavy stuff."

Jenkins points to the tunnel on the other side of the

bridge. In the cover of darkness, the Dræu have gathered silently, showing restraint that's definitely not barbaric. They march out in three lines. The first line drops to the ground. The second line kneels behind them. The third line stands, and they all aim their weapons at us.

"Ha!" Jenkins snorts. "Like them plasma dots can make it halfway across the bridge."

"Is that her?" Fuse asks as he points toward the slim, dark-haired figure striding from the tunnel, a mortar launcher on her hip.

"One and the same," I say.

Then I watch frozen in awe as she hops onto the back of kneeling Dræu. Then vaults to the shoulders of the tallest Dræu.

Raises the launcher.

Fires.

"Move!" I yell.

We sprint away from the sled. Jenkins, reluctant to leave his chain gun, is the last to go. His boots hit dirt as the shell strikes the bow.

The explosion flips the sled. It catapults. Slams against the stone walls. Slides down with an earsplitting squeal, coming to a rest on its side. Fuel begins to leak out, and the stink of it fills the air.

"My gun!" Jenkins starts toward the wreckage.

"Wait!"

But Jenkins doesn't listen. He runs to the sled, and with

fuel pooling under his boots, begins throwing boxes of ammo aside, trying to reach the latches holding the gun to the sled.

"She's about to fire another mortar, Jenks!" Fuse shouts.

"Take cover!" I gesture for them to get behind a rock formation. "Jenkins! Hit the deck!"

Foosh!

The mortar leaves a stream of bluish exhaust at it roars toward the sled and Jenkins, who is working on the fourth and final latch.

"It's all bent up, I—" he says.

"Incoming!"

"Outgoing!" Jenkins yells.

He forgets the latch. But not the gun.

With the shell bearing down on him, he rips the chain gun from its last latch, then dives across the slick stone floor. His momentum and a burst of accidental fire push him ten meters from the sled as the shell lands.

A spark lights the fuel, and as it burns, the air swells in an ever-expanding series of pockets that move so quickly and violently that it breaks the sound barrier. The explosion throws the sled twenty meters into the air, a twirling, whirling twisted metal mass that seems to hang like a kite for a few seconds, and then falls with a woofing sound into the Zhao Zhou gorge.

"Gah!" Jenkins cries out, and I think it's just a reflex reaction to being so close to death.

Then I do a double take. The explosion has also ignited the trail that Jenkins left in his wake. Fire rips toward him at lightning speed. Flames hit his boots. Ignite the soles.

"Gah!"

He stomps his feet. Tiny fireballs fly out around him like he's dancing on fireworks. The flames race around to the back of his symbiarmor and flare out on his buttocks, whereupon he starts jumping around and smacking himself on the rear end, alternating hands when they get too hot.

Mimi starts laughing.

"Is he in danger?" I ask.

"Only to himself." She cackles. "The suit is fireproof, you know."

"Stop dancing!" Fuse says. "It'll burn out, you great barking fop."

"It's hot!"

"Jenks always says he has a hot butt," Fuse says, laughing. "Now he has proof."

"This is not the time for humor!" Ebi fumes as she fires a few rounds toward the queen, who ignores the gunfire as if it can't hurt her. "We are being attacked!"

"*Au contraire, mon ami,*" Fuse says. "Things are always funnier when you're under fire."

I'm about to tell Jenkins to roll around to put out the flames, but they die out before I can. Jenkins is smoldering, inside and out, his gloves blackened with soot and his face red with rage.

"Fragging rooter cannibals!" He hoists the chain gun, aims in the general direction of the Dræu, and opens fire. The bullets bounce impotently along the Zhao Zhou Bridge. A useless waste of ammunition. But a good show for the Dræu. Let them see that we're not going to lie down for them.

When the belt is empty and Jenkins's rage is out of ammo, the queen comes forward out of the darkness, striding ahead of the Draeu. She's confident, I'll give her that much.

Then she rips the mask from her face and tosses it aside, and the porcelain shatters on the stone. She lifts her chin proudly. Her face is as beautiful as the mask.

I feel myself gasp. That face. *Vittujen kevät ja kyrpien takatalvi!* I know it.

"Jacob Durango," the queen calls out. "The queen of the Dræu would parlay with you."

"She knows your name?" Ebi raises an eyebrow.

Fuse looks shocked. "Oy, chief. Your first name is Jacob?"

"What did you think it was?" I ask.

"Durango."

"And my last name?"

Fuse scratches his head. "Er, Durango?"

"Durango Durango." I tap my head like I'm thinking. "Interesting name."

"Eh," Jenkins shrugs. "I once knew a Regulator named Peter Peter."

"What happened to him?"

"Chigoes digested him."

"Thanks for that pleasant image." Standing, I remove the armalite from my back. "Ebi, she'll be in range of your sniper rifle once we meet. Keep an eye on her. If anything goes wrong, drop her where she stands."

"With pleasure, chief." Ebi checks the safety on her weapon.

"Jenkins," I say as Jenkins joins us, wisps of smoke still rising off his buttocks, "not a single shot from that chain gun. I don't want to be sawn in half because of your itchy trigger finger."

"It's not itchy. Just toasty."

"Jenkins," I scold him.

"Yes, chief. I promise not to accidentally kill you just so I can cark out the farging rooters who lit my ass on fire."

"Good man." I hand my weapons to Fuse. "Watch these for me, no?"

Fuse accepts them, but says, "You're going out there unarmed? Either you're the bravest son of a dunny rat I've ever laid orbs on, or the stupidest."

"She asked for parlay. You go unarmed. It's our way."

Fuse blocks my path. "The way of Regulators, sure, but the way of the Dræu is to eat first and grunt questions later."

"She's not a Dræu," I say as I step around him and start for the bridge. "It's worse than that."

"Maybe she's just a pretty Dræu or something?" Fuse calls after me. "The *only* pretty Dræu. How do you know that she won't kill you?"

"Because," I say without looking back. "I went to battle school with her. She's a Regulator, too."

CHAPTER 30

Hell's Cross, Outpost Fisher Four
ANNOS MARTIS 238. 4. 0. 00:00

The face of the queen has hardened since we graduated battle school. Her hair is longer, too. Of course. Cadets keep their hair shorn close to the scalp, male and female alike, and the first thing graduates do is stop cutting it. Cadets. That's how I remember her.

Younger. Gentler.

Human.

"Cowboy," Mimi starts to say.

"Let me handle this, Mimi. Off-line mode, please."

"But—"

"Off-line mode."

There's no noise when Mimi goes off-line, but I know when it happens. Like I know when someone's watching me and then isn't.

The queen carries herself like royalty. Shoulders square and level. Chin held just so. A quick flick that sends her curly tresses behind her shoulders. When we're a meter apart, I call her by the name I knew: "Eceni."

"No one has call me that since—"

"Since you decided you liked the taste of human flesh? Or since you joined a band of murderers?"

She laughs. It sounds different, too. Deeper. Meaner. "I meant to say, since the end of battle school. Of course, you went by a different name then, too. Didn't you, Jacob?"

"That's irrelevant."

"Do the rusters think so? I suspect they would find your real name to be very relevant."

"I am not my father."

"Obviously not. Else you'd have committed ritual suicide in the New Eden square alongside his other Regulators. Instead, you let them chop off half your little pinkie finger. Ouch. I bet that smarts. Sort of like pulling off a hangnail."

Unlike the Dræu, who stink of body odor and rotted cheese, Eceni smells like fruit. Strawberries. My god, that means she bathes. Washes her long black hair. Tries to keep her humanity while living among a pack of savages. But how can you stay human when you live among predators?

"Is that why you wanted a parlay?" I catch myself hiding the mutilated hand behind my back. Forget that, I think and make a fist with it. "To rehash old news?"

"I don't, you know? Like the taste of flesh. I'm no cannibal."

"You just enjoy the company of killers."

She taps her teeth with a painted fingernail. "You have

the same taste. How many medals of valor did your sweet Vienne own? One for every soldier she's killed, no? What does a girl do with over a thousand medals? Keep them in her dowry chest for her future husband?"

Future husband stings in a way that I hadn't expected. "Regulators kill for a reason," I say, almost snarling, "and only because we have no other choice."

"Of course, you do. That's what the Tenets say, and we must only do what the Tenets tell us. The Dræu have rules, too, Jacob. They're just more simple and easier to remember."

"What rules would that be?"

"Eat, drink, and take whatever you want." She chews the tip of her fingernail, the same way she did when we were in battle school. "And what I want is treasure."

"Then you came a long way for nothing. These folk don't have enough water to drink, much less some treasure."

"Reckon I'll have to kill them all to find out." She runs a hand down my arm. "Your symbiarmor's looking a little worse for wear. Too bad. You always looked so sharp in a uniform. And not so bad out of it, either."

She winks. It makes me want to chunder. But she moves closer. Lays a delicate hand on my shoulder. "Know why I stopped wearing symbiarmor, Jake? It makes you lazy. You start thinking that nobody can hurt you, and you stop paying attention to the details."

"Like what?"

"Like the fact that I just stuck a shiv into your gut."

I look down. A blade sticks out of my armor.

"Didn't even feel it, did you, *mon cher*? You won't feel it the next time, either, except it will be in the base of your skull, where your symbiarmor can't protect you."

I pull out the shiv. Toss it over the side of the bridge into the gorge. "You sicken me."

"What is it, Jake?" she whispers into my ear. Her breath is warm and moist against my face. "Can't believe I'm the girl you loved? Is it so hard to believe that people change? Look at you. Once upon a time you were the privileged son of a CorpCom CEO with the makings of a great general. Now you're leading a *dalit* davos protecting a group of rusters who would strip your body for coin if they had half the chance."

I shrug. "It's true."

"Glad to see that you've come around. Now about that treasure—"

"It's true," I say. Take her by the shoulders. Push her away. "That you're not the girl I knew. She was a damned good soldier and a human being."

"I'm still a damned good soldier, Jacob." She smiles. Skips around me. "I married after you dumped me, you know. A CorpCom golden boy with a pretty face and a thick bank account. Guess where he is now."

I stare straight ahead. "No thanks."

"I fed him to the Dræu. It was easier than divorce." She presses her back against mine and giggles. "You know, I have friends. Powerful friends who can do almost anything. Anything like free a sick old man from the gulag."

"Impossible."

"Everything is possible, Jake. You of all people should know that. After all, you're above average intelligence." She twirls around me, the hem of her dress rising about her knees. She moves like water, her dress like growing rings. "Far above, from what I read."

"What have you read?" I steel myself against her. She's sparring with me, just the same as if we were fighting with knives.

"Just a little information in some old files I found. Isn't it kind of creepy having another person in your brain? Sure there's room in that big head of yours?" She leans into my chest and brushes my lips with hers. "Get me the treasure, Jacob Stringfellow, or I'll feed you to the Dræu after I bring this mine down around the rusters' heads."

I flex my jaw. Turn my lips into a thin, hard line. Push her gently to my side. "I think that's an empty threat."

"Try explaining that to the rusters, Jake." She taps me on the nose, then turns heel. "They know all about the Dræu and empty threats." As she walks away, her skirt sways with the rhythm of her hips. I watch until she's halfway across the bridge.

"Awake up, Mimi," I say. "Record her biorhythm signature."

Precisely thirteen point six seconds later, I feel Mimi's presence. "Done, cowboy."

I stand on the bridge, arms folded, acting like Janus guarding a toll bridge.

When Eceni reaches the safety of her soldiers, she turns and shrieks, "Cowards! Fools! Know this! You have one day to surrender the treasure to the Dræu. Or we shall kill you all, starting with your anointed savior, Jacob Stringfellow."

Laughing, she grabs the launcher and fires a mortar into the ceiling. Behind me, the miners scurry for shelter. Rock rains down on me, bouncing off my suit. It feels like an avalanche.

CHAPTER 31

Hell's Cross, Outpost Fisher Four
ANNOS MARTIS 238. 4. 0. 00:00

The infirmary is small, clean, and comfortable, and it stinks of alcohol and bleach.

I knock twice and wait to enter.

Maeve and Áine are attending to Vienne, who is lying in the bed farthest from the door.

Maeve waves me in.

As I pass the first bed, I see Dame Bramimonde lying there asleep, her face washed clean of the blue makeup, her cerulean dyed hair unbraided and combed out. So that's where she spends her time. I'd assumed the Dame was holed up in quarters making the miners wait on her hand and foot. "Didn't know she was sick," I say in a hushed tone.

"Lots of things you don't know, Regulator." Áine draws a curtain around the Dame's bed, and I feel ashamed of myself.

Maeve leads me to Vienne's bed, then draws the curtain to give us privacy. My uber warrior's face is gaunt, pale. Gray lines under her eyes. She looks frail and wan, almost weak, and I feel something inside me torque. Her hair is freshly washed and combed out, smelling of soap. The wounded heal is bandaged well and elevated. Her toes, poking out of the bandages, are swollen black and purple.

"Nice piggies," I say, trying to be light and perky, but I feel like the air is catching in my lungs.

Vienne turns her face to the wall.

"The wound," Maeve says, clearing her voice, "was as clean as you could hope for. The shrapnel went straight through. You got her here fast, so I don't expect much in the way of infection. If something does come up, we've got a good store of antibiotics and debridement larvae on hand. Yes, well, have a good visit. Call for me if you have the need."

Maeve draws the curtain behind her as she goes. I stand beside the bed. If I had a hat, it would be in hand, and I'd be working it between nervous fingers. When we started this mission, I told Fuse that we wouldn't get hurt. Shows that fortune telling is not one of my talents. Maybe being a chief isn't, either.

"How's the foot?" I ask quietly.

The wall remains the only object of her interest.

"Mimi, how is she?"

"Vitals are normal," she snaps. "That's all I can tell you."

Her snappishness annoys me. *Can* or *will?*"

"Is there a difference?"

"Feel free," I say with a flash of anger at being treated

poorly by my own AI, "to go into silent mode."

After another long minute, I put my fingertips on Vienne's arm. It the first time I recall touching her bare skin, and it makes the tips of my fingers tingle. I wonder what it would feel like to touch her face, to feel the soft glow of her cheek on the back of my hand, the velvet touch of her lips on—I clear my throat to clear my head. "Vienne, how are you?"

"I'm alive," she says, unmoving, "thanks to you."

I force a fake chuckle. "You mean, *no* thanks to me."

"Twice you've saved me." She pulls her arm away from my touch. Speaks in a hoarse whisper. "That means I owe you two life debts. No Regulator has two lives to give."

"Oh that. Then let's say this one's on the house." Trying to be chipper again. It fails miserably.

She rolls her shoulder away from me. "There is nothing you have to say that I want to hear."

"You're still angry," I say.

Silence.

"This is about Ockham."

Silence.

"You think I ruined his beautiful death." And because I would rather provoke a response than be ignored again, I add. "But you're wrong."

"The Tenets are never wrong," she snaps, then rolls back over.

I sigh heavily. "The Tenets tell us that dying in the service of your comrades is a beautiful death, and Ockham would have died either way, serving all of us by allowing us to escape. The fact that I didn't allow the Dræu to eat him alive will not keep him from reaching Valhalla in the afterlife."

"Your bullet ended his life, not the enemy."

"So?"

"So he did not die by the enemy's hand."

"You're splitting hairs, Vienne." My father's voice rings in my head: *It is the thinnest lines that define us.* "The Tenets say nothing about whose bullet should end a life. If death can be beautiful, then his sacrifice was beautiful. I acted out of mercy. Why can't you see that?"

"It is not your job to show mercy," she hisses. "It is to be chief."

I cross my arms. "A chief can't show mercy?"

"Not when it is weakness."

I feel myself draw back, like I've been slapped. "So I'm weak now?"

She takes a few seconds to respond. Time to chew over her words first. "When it is my time, will you deny my beautiful death?"

So that's what's on her mind. "If there's one thing I know, Vienne, you will outlive me."

"You have saved my life twice," she says. "Answer me, please. When it is my time, will you deny me a beautiful death?"

"No," I say.

"Thank you."

"But I will do everything in power to keep you alive. I don't care how many life debts you end up owing me."

"Why?" she says. "Why would you do that?"

"Because I couldn't bear it." I lean in, touch the nape of her neck with my fingertips. "Because I—"

"Don't say that!" She slaps my hand away. Claps both hands over her ears. Squeezes her eyes shut. Doubles over like she's in great pain. "The Tenets forbid it. One eye. One hand. One heart. You can't serve the Tenets with a full heart, if . . . if . . ."

"The deuce with the Tenets," I whisper, "I'd rather talk about ifs." She pretends not to hear me, curled up in her ball, trying to shut me out, her wounded foot purple and swollen in its bandages, reminding me of the pain she's in. "Talk to me." Silence. Taking the leg of the wheeled bed in hand, I swing it out so that she is no longer facing the wall. Now she's facing me. "Talk to me, Vienne. We've fought too many battles together to let—"

Her eyes open. They're full of tears. She takes her hands down from her ears. Her voice is hoarse from the pain. "This is all I have to say: You are less the man I thought you were. I am less the Regulator for serving under you. I swore lifetime service, and I'll keep my vow. But now, I've said all I'm willing to say and wish . . ." She buries her face in the pillow. "Wish you would just leave."

I return the bed to its proper spot. Take a deep breath.

Nod. Tell Mimi to wake up, since the conversation's over. If only I'd never come into this room. Never let those words *almost* slip from my lips. If I had it to do over again, I would change that. But I wouldn't take back the shot I fired, even if it changes how Vienne sees me forever.

I draw the curtain and walk past the Dame's bed, breathing deep to clear the image of Vienne's face away. Instead, I can smell the soap from her hair, hear her voice clear in my ears, as if she's standing right next to me, whispering my name. My breath catches in my lungs so hard, it feels like I've swallowed something that's stuck. It aches, and I feel myself wince, then try to breathe again. Then I tell myself to let it go, that nothing will ever happen between the two of us. Yet there's that quiet voice, hoping, hoping, hoping.

"Poor little brain," Mimi says.

"Stow it," I tell her. "I'm not in the mood."

"Which mood is that?" she says, mocking me. "Because my sensors say otherwise."

I huff. "Can't you just leave me to wallow in my own self-pity?"

"Sure," she says. "Just don't expect me to watch while you do."

"Okay, Miss Smarty-pants. Mark and track the biorhythms of every Regulator and miner. Let me know if anybody goes anywhere out of range."

"Affirmative, cowboy," Mimi says. "Anything else?"

"Negative," I say. "It's been a long day, so while you're

keeping watch, the rest of us are going to get some sleep."

"Including you?"

"Including me. I just hope there's something left to defend when I wake up."

But when I leave the infirmary, Maeve is waiting for me on the arcade, leaning on the rail and watching the children playing hopscotch with Jenkins.

"Seventeen," she says to me.

"Seventeen what?" I can't handle this right now.

"That's how many children the Dræu have stolen from us. One of them was Áine's little sister."

"I'm sorry. I didn't know it was that many."

"There are many things you don't know about us, Durango." She turns away, and her smock slides down her shoulder, pulling loose a bandage and revealing a thick, purple mass.

"That's a keloid," I say. I've seen marks like that before. On the battlefield. On my face. On Vienne's back. "That wound is fresh. It wasn't there before. I was on the battlefield the day the Orthocrats turned their mining chigoes loose on us. They killed most everybody and everything in their path, and those they didn't kill ended up with keloids that looked just like that. So I've got a question for you, Maeve. *Where is it?*"

To her credit, she doesn't bother to lie to me. But she doesn't respond, either. Just chewing her chapped bottom lip. Thinking.

"You have a chigoe," I say. "Show it to me. We've got less than a day before the Dræu come back, and I need to make a measure of the situation."

Maeve looks into my eyes so intently, it's like she can see Mimi. "Tell me, Regulator. How do you measure infinity?"

Infinity, apparently, is measured by taking a secret passage from the Cross, down a flight of stairs through an old air lock, and into an ancient sewer access tunnel. I seem to be spending a lot of my time in sewers lately. Ducking low, we follow the tunnel for a few hundred meters. The path slopes sharply downward, then takes a sharp left turn, and I can see light ahead. Maeve stops at the end of the tunnel. Beyond her, I can see the sheer rock of the gorge, and above that, the bottom of the Zhao Zhou Bridge. I look down and see nothing but infinite darkness. The gorge goes on forever.

"It's a long way down," I say, staying at least two meters away from the edge. My mouth goes dry. Pulse is increasing. Breath becoming more shallow.

"Breathe!" Mimi says, and zaps my butt with a sly jolt of static.

"Yow!" I yelp in response.

"Quite the view," Maeve replies, thinking I was referring to the scenery. "Ready?"

"Ready for what?"

"For the next tunnel. It's about fifty meters below this one." She lifts a climbing rope from the floor of the tunnel.

"Know how to rappel?" she asks as she takes rappelling position on the edge, her voice sounding very far away.

My voice squeaks, "Affirmative." Rappelling was part of basic training in battle school. They made us slide down more ropes than I can count. "But don't you need a harness?"

"Harnesses are for rooters," she calls, then drops out of view.

"Maeve!" I drop to my knees and crawl forward. At the lip, I press flat against the ground and pull myself along. From forearm to palm, I'm doused with sweat, and the metallic stink of fear wafts from my armpits. I look down. The horizon pitches to the left. Below, the rope is empty.

"Mimi," I dare ask. "Did she make it?"

"My sensors are still registering her vital signs."

"Seriously, does she expect me to follow her? So I'm going to have to rappel, too?"

"The evidence would suggest it, yes."

"Bugger."

"Cowboy, may I offer a suggestion?"

"I'm open to anything."

"Grow a pair."

"Already got 'em. You of all people should know that."

"Durango!" Maeve's voice drifted up from below. "Are you coming? You've not turned rooter, have you?"

"I've not turned rooter," I mutter. "I've always *been* rooter."

"Keeping going," Mimi says, encouraging me.

Several deep breaths saturate my lungs—if I stop

breathing halfway down, I won't pass out. Then, grabbing the rope and wrapping my left leg around it, I back over the edge and slide into space. The first step is bad. The second is worse. By the time my body slithers into open air, my mind has gone into free fall.

Vertigo sends wave after wave of nausea through me, and my hands start to lose the stranglehold on the rope. I am going to fall.

"I have you," Mimi says. "Close your eyes."

The symbiarmor goes rigid. She has taken control. What happens next is a mystery, because I feel nothing until she gives me another dose of static. When I open my eyes, I'm standing in the mouth of another tunnel. The rope is still grasped in my hand, and I fling it away as I take three hurried steps away from the gorge. My heart is hammering, and I see floaters drifting across my vision. But I'm on solid ground.

"Thanks," I tell Mimi.

"My pleasure," she replies. "It is my job to keep you alive, after all."

Maeve's back is to me. She squatting in front of a very small, very tight tunnel, like she means to go inside it.

"It's a bit tight at first," she says, and shimmies into the black emptiness.

"You don't say," I grunt as I try to copy her motions. Impossible. My shoulders are too broad, and I never once in my eight and a half years even tried to shimmy.

"Hurry," she calls from the darkness.

"Wait." I climb out of the hole and shuck my symbiar-mor and holster. Check to see that the armalite is on safe. Then slide into the tunnel feetfirst and pull the armor in after myself.

The going is actually easy. After the tunnel runs straight for a few meters, it turns sharply to the right and then right again.

"Where are you?" Maeve calls from somewhere down the tunnel.

"Behind you!"

"How far?"

"Can't tell. It's dark."

"Doesn't matter, either way. You're almost to the end. Watch out, though, there's a bit of a decline coming up soon."

I push again and then start to slide. "Mimi!"

"Bottoms up, cowboy!"

I try to wedge my elbows and hands against the side of the stone. But the sides are too slick. "Damn it!" I yell as I slide faster. "Whoa!"

"Relax!" Maeve calls up the tunnel.

I can see the dot of her head now, getting larger as I accelerate, a broad grin on her face. What's she smiling about? I'm about to be dashed on the rock, and she's smiling? Cruel, heartless—

The bottom drops out. I fall almost straight down, toward

a brown mass of stone. No, it isn't stone—it's something else. I hit the brown mass feet first, and I stick like a knife in a target.

It's sand. Nice, soft sand—I'm not dashed on the rocks. The armor flies out of the tunnel after me and lands with a smack at the back of my head. "Ow!"

"Duck," Mimi says.

Ha-ha. "Can I get a hand?" I ask Maeve. "This stuff kind of chafes."

"Sorry, Durango." She braces herself on the edge of the sand pit. Then offers a hand. "I didn't mean for that to happen." Then she nods at a steel door a couple of meters away. "That's where we keep our treasure."

"That's not what I call them."

"That's not how we think of them, either. But the Dræu do."

She rolls the door open and steps inside. Warm air meets my face, and I find the source of the fecund odor I smelled on the way down the tunnel chute. Lights flicker near the ceiling, illuminating the pathway, which is barely wide enough for me to navigate.

She pushes a photocell, and a huge multivid lights up. "What do you think?"

The screen shows a cloud-filled blue sky and the side of a green mountain with tall trees growing on it, rolling foothills, and a line of forest to the right. In the foreground a batch of tall grass sways in the breeze, and a crop of red flowers grows among it.

"It's beautiful." I touch a palm to the screen. "Where is this? Earth?"

"This is the Eden of Mars," she says, sounding like a virtual reality tour guide. "Outpost Fisher Four as the founders designed it, a new world of a perfectly harmonious, balanced biosphere. In Phase Blue the permafrost will melt away and leave land ripe for forestation and settlement."

"What happened?"

She switches to her normal voice. "The planet warmed up, all right, enough for the Orthocracy to close us down. The equator was livable, so they thought, why keep feeding the skies with smoke when the job was finished for them? Who cared if a few thousand indentured miners got what'd been promised to them?"

I stare at the screen. It's beauty that I've never seen on Mars. "I didn't know." I look from the screen to her. "It's not the story that the Orthocracy told. There were lots of stories they told wrong."

Her eyes are bright, her expression a half frown. "What about the CorpComs? What stories have they told while you were off fighting wars with one another?"

"The CorpComs are better than the Orthocracy."

"Maybe to you," she says, and switches off the multivid. "But to us, there's no difference twixt one and the other."

I'm sad to see the picture fade. "Why turn it off?"

"Because they're not fond of the light," she says, and hands me a pair of phosogoggles.

First I pull on my symbiarmor and buckle my holster into place. Then I put on the goggles. *"They?* I thought we were talking about an *it."*

"Depends on your definition of *it.* If you're thinking in terms of a hive mind, then it will do you." She opens the door. "But if you think there's only one of the beasties inside, you're in for a bit of a shock."

Along the walls of the cave are many long tanks filled with an amber liquid. Moving slowly in the liquid are hundreds, maybe thousands of creatures the size of my palm, with eight legs, a thick carapace, and a long proboscis. Floating along with them is a viscous liquid that I fear as much as any high-caliber sniper's shell or any blast from a plasma weapon. The common term for it is snot, but in reality, it's a highly corrosive secretion that can dissolve rock.

"Chigoes!" I shout. *"Ja vitut!"*

"CorpCom exterminated the Big Daddies, that's true. But they didn't know about these."

I bend down for a closer look. Watch them swim in the nutrient broth. Absentmindedly finger the scar on my temple. "You've got to destroy them. Think of what damage they could do when they're full-sized."

"Nonsense," she says. "They are full-sized, and they don't do anything except suck down nutrient soup and take care of their queen."

"Queen? All the chigoes were males."

She dips a hand in the tank, careful to avoid the snot, and uses the back of her fingers to stroke the shell of one of the chigoes. "Do you believe everything you're told? Or just the more blatant propaganda?"

For a second I can't believe my eyes. Then I spring forward. Yank her hand out of the tank. "Don't! You'll get— wait. How?"

I flip her hand over, expecting the same wound I saw on her neck. "No burns? How's that possible? I can see snot floating in the liquid."

"Thanks for coming to my rescue," Maeve says, and smiles. "Even if it wasn't needed. The chigoes can't hurt you if they're in the tanks. The nutrient bath neutralizes the acidity of their secretions. As long as they don't get loose, you have nothing to fear."

"What happened to your neck, then? That keloid came from somewhere."

"An accident. I was careless the first time we cleaned their tanks."

"I don't understand. How? Why?"

"How is easy." She gives the chigoe a playful push. Then washes her hands in a sink nearby. "They were born here, the only true Martians left living. The Earthers found some fossils and dug out the DNA, the way they learned to with dinosaurs and mastodons on their own planet. When they found out what the chigoes could do, they buggered up their DNA and turned them into slaves."

I shake my head no, "Only sentient species can be enslaved. Otherwise they're only draft animals."

"Define *sentient*."

"Capable of rational thought."

"That leaves off most of humankind."

"Good point," Mimi says. "I like this woman."

Pipe down, I tell Mimi. The last thing I want to hear is that the monstrosities that ruined my life—and took hers— are intelligent. "All humans have the capacity for rational thought, Maeve, even if they never use it."

"There's no difference between a man who can't think and one who chooses not to," she says, and I shake my head, thinking that what we really need to do is finish the job of eradicating these animals. "No, the chigoe aren't sentient, but they not dumb animals, either. They're like bees, with a queen and one single mind."

The mention of a queen reminds me of Eceni, which reminds me of what brought me here. Time is running out. We need to finish our business, so that I can finish it upside. "What's your purpose, then? What're you going to do when they're grown to size and start tunneling your whole outpost away?"

"Those would be the Big Daddies you're thinking of. These chigoes won't get any bigger than this."

"What's the point of keeping them? They're still dangerous without being able to mine guanite ore, which the CorpCom don't have use for anymore."

Maeve sticks a tongue in her cheek, then reaches into her pocket. "Do you think CorpCom would have a use"—she opens her hand, revealing a coarsely cut black stone—"for this?"

A diamond. For almost as long as Mars has been settled, the hunt for diamonds has been going on. Except for a few tiny slivers, no one had ever found any. "You're mining diamonds, and you paid my crew a hundred to save you?"

"Not diamonds. Diamond. We've only found one so far, and we can't sell it without losing our land to speculators or the CorpCom themselves."

I understand her point. Fisher Four is worthless now, but if word leaked out about diamonds—even one diamond—prospectors would rush to take over the mines. If the CorpComs don't beat them to it. Still, hiding chigoes doesn't sit well with me. "Where did you get it?"

"From one of the chigoes. It brought it out of a tunnel that goes a least a kilometer straight down. There's no miner alive, and no Manchester big enough, to dig that far down. We need the chigoes to do it for us."

"And the Dræu know about this?"

I watch the chigoes wriggling in the nutrient bath. They seem harmless, almost cute, as they bounce off one another and crowd near the surface in an attempt to get Maeve's attention. But then I feel a shudder of fear that's not my own. Mimi. She's afraid of them.

"Somehow they figured it out. How, I don't know. But

they want them bad. Imagine the coin they could extort by threatening to turn a few hundred omnivores loose."

"Mimi," I ask. "She's not lying this time, no?"

"All physiological indicators suggest she's telling the truth."

So the miners are at some point going to be very wealthy. The thought tickles me. I wonder what Dame Bramimonde would think if they became her neighbors. "Just one of them could destroy an entire greenhouse factory."

"Now," she says, "you're catching on. This is why we can't just give the Dræu what they want, no matter who they take away from us."

I have to remind myself that this is the same species that killed hundreds of soldiers. And Mimi. And almost killed Vienne. Then I feel a pang of guilt because of the fact that chigoes, even a small version of them, exist.

"You lied to us."

"Would it have made such a difference if you'd known the truth?"

"You know damned well it would," I say. "That's why you didn't say anything."

She lifts her palms like a cut-rate Buddha. "Wouldn't you lie, too, if it meant saving your people?"

"No!" I say. *Qí yán fèn tu yě*, she sounds just like Father. "Lying is never the right thing. My crew has to know the truth. They have to know what they're fighting for."

"They will quit us," Maeve says. "Leave us to the Dræu."

"Maybe," I say. "It'd be their right, seeing as how they'd been deceived."

"But what about you?" she says, "Would you stay?"

She takes my hands in hers. They're cracked like old leather, the rough, creviced hands of a miner. A lifetime of hard labor and pain is in them, and I know that her lies have nothing to do with the vow I made.

"I promised to fight the Dræu for you," I say. "I started this job, and I intend to finish it." Even if kills me.

"Which," Mimi says as I turn to go, "it probably will."

CHAPTER 32

Hell's Cross, Outpost Fisher Four
ANNOS MARTIS 238. 4. 0. 00:00

The funeral for a fallen Regulator begins with the build-ing of a small structure, the House of Mourning. It is con-structed of wood, if available. If not—and it almost never is, unless the Regulator is from wealth, because wood is one of the most precious commodities on Mars—then any flam-mable material will do.

A House of Mourning is one meter longer than the Regulator it will hold. Two meters wider. Three meters taller. The roof is angled at forty-five degrees. The peaks at either end are marked with a round seal. One seal represents the family of the mother. The second, the family of the father. These dimensions are in the Tenets, along with the rule that a fallen Regulator whose body is lost in battle must receive the same funeral as any other.

The seals on Ockham's house are a lion and a star, carved by Spiner from the same wood used to build the rest of house. The lion, from his mother, represents the fierce hunter. The star, from his father, represents the capacity of imagination. When I see the house, I know that Ockham was his mother's son.

Spiner, Jurm, and the other miners salvaged the wood from the old temple. They built it on the far side of the Zhao Zhou Bridge, across which we are carrying an effigy of Ockham on a simple bier. A linen shroud covers the bier. Maeve made the shroud herself, taken from a piece of table-cloth she smuggled on the journey from Old Boston. If we had it, his symbiarmor would be folded and placed under his head. His armalite would rest on his chest. Both of these are lost, like him.

Fuse, Jenkins, Jean-Paul, and I carry the bier. Vienne, on crutches, follows behind. Spiner walks beside her, and the miners trail after them. As we approach the house, Vienne swings open the doors of the building. We slide the bier onto a pyre made of fuel drums, then step outside. As chief, it is my duty to close the doors and seal them.

"Peace be with you, Regulator," I say, my palms pressed together as I bow low.

"Peace be with you at last," everyone responds. Like me, they press their palms together and bow.

"Peace be with you all," Vienne says, a mourning shawl draped over her head and shoulders. She bows, then, standing on one foot, spreads her arms wide, a gesture that symbolizes the rising of the soul.

"Fire," I say.

The miners move in. With hand torches, they set the House of Mourning ablaze. The flames catch quickly. The wood is old. Within a minute, the fuel barrels ignite, and a thick, hot fire consumes the house. I don't know how long it will burn, but when it finishes, Ockham as we knew him will be no more. His beautiful death will carry him to Valhalla where he will live forever among the heroes. That is my hope for him, to have the afterlife he imagined.

"Vienne," I say as we begin leaving.

She passes me without a word and without eye contact. I suppose I deserve it. Deserving it doesn't ease the sting. As we process across the bridge to the Cross, the House of Mourning turning to ash behind us, my legs feel like lead. Exhaustion has hit, and the only thing I want is a warm bed. The cot in the bunk room is all I'm going to get, and it will have to do.

In the dream, I am floating. I see myself sitting in front of the console that controls a beanstalk space elevator. I hear my thoughts: They say I drew this crap assignment because of my education. But I know the truth. Mimi thinks I'm a useless rich boy and stuck me here to make a point—she's the chief and I'm a boot straight out of battle school.

I yawn. It's the eighty-ninth yawn of my shift. I'm counting. There is nothing else to do but watch the loaded space elevator shoot into the atmosphere, then drift back down to the supply pad. Load. Unload. Repeat. Until a diode blinks on the multivid. Finally, some action. I tap the image with the fingertip of my nanoglove. A hologram of my chief pops up.

"Durango," Mimi says, "we've lost containment on a Big Daddy in Tunnel Two-E. The drone harness shorts out. It's tearing the place to pieces."

I hear screams over the audio feed. Mimi ducks, and the body of a technician flies over her head. "I've got nothing on my boards," I say.

"Tell that to the Big Daddy, cowboy."

"Uh, yes. I would but—"

"Shut your gob and convey these orders to the davos via the multivid. Clear the area. Establish a perimeter at ten clicks. Set up four EMPs in a square pattern. Order my Regulators not to engage the Big Daddy for any reason."

"Yes, chief! Will do!" I tap her image away. Hail the five other members of our davos—Squirt, Switch, Decker, Pike, and Vienne—and pass on Mimi's orders. "Chief says, do not engage the Big Daddy. For any reason."

"Roger that," Vienne, Mimi's second, responds.

Then I hit three buttons in rapid succession. Images of Tunnel Two pop up. One shows the high caverns that contain the holding pens for the Big Daddies. The second shows the catwalks above the tunnel, patrolled by handlers armed with electrostatic prods. The third is Tunnel Two-E. It's filled with wounded shock troops and the marauding Big Daddy.

That's where the action is. Where I want to be. Not stuck playing messenger boy. I keep my eyes trained on the Two-E feed. Watch Mimi take cover behind a shipping container. She shouts at the troopers, "Fall back! Fall back!"

But the Big Daddy blocks them with its massive carapace, a shell so thick mortar rounds won't pierce it. The troopers can't fall back, and their needle cannons are useless against the bioengineered chigoe. I lean close to the screen, my heart racing, as the Big Daddy snatches a trooper with its mandibles. With one easy snick, it splits the man in two. Then I see the Big Daddy starting to spin. "Chief!" I yell into the headset. "Behind you! Behind you!"

"Say again?" she yells back as the chigoe sprays thick liquid across the mass of the shock troopers. Including Mimi who is moving to the fatally injured man. The troopers fall screaming. Her symbiarmor seems to protect Mimi. But then she turns to face the multivid.

Half of her face is missing. "Chief!"

Mimi mouths a silent word. Reaches toward the camera. The feed from Tunnel Two-E pixilates. Then fails.

"Vienne!" I yell, watching our davos reach the tunnel. "Chief is down! Repeat, chief is down! I'm coming to you."

"No," Vienne says, "stay at your station. We can handle this, boot."

I tap on the headpiece, causing the signal to break up. "Can't hear you. I'm losing the feed." Then I throw off the headset. Grab my armalite. Sprint down the stairs to a power sled that takes me to the tunnel. When I arrive, I push through a legion of shock troopers taking position in the main entrance. Inside, the Big Daddy is still raging. I try to hail Vienne.

No answer.

They're all dead. I find their bodies strewn around. Mangled by the Big Daddy that attacked them.

But I keep moving. The Big Daddy drifts to the rear of the tunnel. I take cover behind another shipping container.

"What should I do?" I yell to no one. "Chief? Vienne? Anybody? What should I do?"

"Help me," the chief answers. Her voice, a hoarse whisper.

"Chief!" I find Mimi half buried in debris. What's left of her face is a twisted knot. My stomach almost chunders as I bend down to lift her. "I'll get you out of here, chief."

"No," she rasps, her misshapen mouth barely able to form the words. "Save others first."

"I can't. You're my chief."

"Do . . . it! I . . . order!"

"Yes, chief."

Turning my back on her, I pull Vienne out of the rubble. A streak of the chigoe's secretions runs from up her back, the armor melted away. The skin is bubbling there, and I am afraid the caustic chemical will burn to the bone. As quickly as I can manage, I carry her to the medics at the entrance of the tunnel.

"Take care of her," I say as I pass her off.

But duty returns me to Mimi. Again, I bend down. "Chief?"

"Others?" she says.

"Vienne made it," I say.

As the Big Daddy rampages, slamming its massive shell into the walls of the tunnels, which chokes the air with dust, I slide an arm under her knees. Cradle her to my chest. Though the pain should be excruciating, she makes no noise. My heart sinks. No pain means no nerve endings left. "Hang on, chief."

"Call me Mimi."

"Mimi, hang on."

She snatches at my chest with the claw of a hand. "Don't let . . . die, cowboy. This . . . not . . . beautiful death." With a shudder, she lets go of a last, rustling breath, and she dies in my arms. Then the tunnel goes suddenly silent, and I don't have the wherewithal to notice.

As I stand, I see an enormous shadow rise over me. There's a hissing sound. Something wet hits the cowl covering the back of my head. The air stinks of battery acid, and I heard a pop. My symbiarmor discharges a jolt of static electricity. My limbs go rigid.

The symbiarmor has shorted out. I am frozen. Unable to move. A mummy trapped in its sarcophagus. A dead man. As I struggle against my own armor, the searing pain of the chigoe's secretions burns through the disabled fabric. I scream as shock troopers pour into the tunnel. They aim their needle cannons and plasma blasters at the Big Daddy, driving it back long enough to set up a light-mass grenade launcher. Everything goes black.

Now a burst of static electricity jolts me awake. Mimi shouts in my head, "Wake up! The Dame went off the grid. I have lost her signature."

I drop to the floor, my symbiarmor absorbing some of the impact. I pull on my boots and buckle on my holster. "Why didn't you wake me up?" I slide open the door and jog down the hallway to the main door.

"I attempted to wake you for ten minutes. That was the third charge of static. Be thankful you were still in your armor."

"Open a vid link. Regulators! Form ranks at the cross in one minute. Jenkins! Jenkins! Stop snoring!" I close the link and run to the Cross. There, the remnants of the bonfire are emitting smoke and ash. A few miners lay sleeping around it. "Mimi, how long's the Dame been out of range?"

"Five minutes. Her last bearing was west-northwest from this point."

The direction gives us a place to start to looking, but in a mine, there's no way to tell where she is. She could be on the surface or in one of a thousand chigoe holes.

"Cowboy," Mimi says, "I have lost Jean-Paul's signature as well."

Damn it. "You were still tracking him, too?"

"You never told me to stop."

"Point taken," I say. "What was his last bearing?"

"West-northwest."

The same as his mother's. "He's going after her."

"So it appears."

"The first time I laid eyes on that kid, I knew he was trouble." I flex my hands—I'm going to throttle the boy.

A few seconds later my davos appears—Fuse coming from the tunnels, Ebi from quarters, and Jenkins from the miners' quarters, looking blurry-eyed and dragging the chain gun behind him.

Vienne is last to report, her foot in an air cast, using a pair of crutches. Even wounded, she carries herself effortlessly.

"You need to be resting," I tell her.

In response, she pulls off the cast and tosses the crutch aside. She pulls on her boot, which was tucked under an arm. "I'll rest when I'm dead."

I start to argue when Mimi interrupts. "Sensor readings suggest that she's using painkillers."

"Are they working?"

"I just provide information, cowboy. You get to make the decisions."

It would be easier to pin a diaper on Jenkins than tell Vienne she can't fight. And my plan depends on her.

"Regulators," I greet them when they're at attention. "We have a situation. Dame Bramimonde has left Fisher Four."

"Mother!" Ebi says, and Vienne cuts her a look.

"I'm tempted to let the Dræu have her, but it looks like Jean-Paul's followed her. As much as I'd like to throttle his skinny little neck, he's still an acolyte, which makes him one of us. Maybe."

"Mother, how could you!" Ebi says, bowing her head quickly, an odd ring to her voice. "Chief, I am humiliated by her actions. I swear to—"

"Later," I say, because I'm not buying it. "There's a job to be done. Here's the plan. Vienne and Ebi, follow the main tunnel out, then head northwest along this bearing for one half click. Scout for a trail, but don't go beyond a half click, got it?"

"Go." I turn to Fuse and Jenkins. "You two, same distance, but take a heading of fifteen degrees to the north. Stay on the main tunnels. No side trips, no chigoe holes. If you run into any trouble, signal me."

"This could be an ambush, chief," Fuse says.

"Keep your eyes and ears open, Fuse. That's exactly what it could be." Or it could be an evil old crone doing the worst possible thing at the worst possible moment.

"Yes, chief," Fuse says. "Come on, Jenkins. And stop dragging that chain gun. The squealing noise is killing me."

"Mimi," I say when they're across the Zhao Zhou Bridge. "Monitor all their signatures. I need to know the second anybody's out of range."

I open a private vid link to Vienne. "Let me know if anything odd happens."

"Yes, chief."

"I mean it, Vienne. Keep an eye on everybody. Trust no one. Not even me."

CHAPTER 33

Hell's Cross, Outpost Fisher Four
ANNOS MARTIS 238. 4. 0. 00:00

I hear the echo of the shots before anything else. They come from the main tunnel, I think. But with these acoustics, I can't be sure. For twenty minutes I waited alone on the Cross, perched on a skyhook container turned on end, the stillness of the air weighing on me, the stinking bones of the fire annoying me, waiting to hear from my troops.

At twenty-one minutes I receive a broken message from Vienne. "Chief, we're . . . fire . . ."

"Say again," I say. Then wait.

Nothing. Just a ringing sound in my ears and the fear that I made a huge tactical mistake, because the Dræu are about to rain down on us at any moment. "Mimi," I say. "Get a reading. Are they all still in range?"

"Yes, chief, all accounted for—wait. I am now reading signatures for Dame Bramimonde and Jean-Paul."

"Pinpoint their location."

"I cannot. There is too much chatter on the sweep. I . . . uh-oh."

"Uh-oh? What is *uh-oh?*"

"You are not going to like this."

"I already don't like it." I walk to the edge of the container for a wider view. "Spit it out!"

"I am picking up multiple unknown signatures along the perimeter of my field. Dozens. It is the Dræu. They didn't wait for the deadline."

"*Jumalauta.* I carking hate when guests come early for the party."

Using a metal pole, I swing to the ground and pull one of the alarms. The sound of whooping horns brings the miners out of their quarters, yanking on their boots and coveralls as they run. Among the first out are Spiner and Jurm.

"Tell me this is a drill," Spiner says.

"It's not a drill," I say. "The Dræu are attacking now."

Jurm shields his eyes. "Where? I didn't see none when I was busy putting on my drawers."

"The Regulators," Spiner says, ignoring Jurm. "They'd got in position already?"

"No," I say. "I sent them on a scouting mission. They're not back yet."

"Scouting for what?" Jurm asks.

"Dame Bramimonde," I say. "She's missing."

"You'd sent out soldiers for a useless crone?" Jurm whines, ignoring him. "What's the sense in that?"

Spiner pulls up his bootstraps. "There's no use crying about it, Jurm. Chief, what d'you want us to do?"

"Just like we planned," I say. "Get the operators on the cranes. Line up the rest in the chigoe holes. Wait for my signal."

"Gotcha." Spiner starts calling orders to the miners.

They snap to it and move quickly to their places. Not military precision, mind you, but good enough in a pinch. And better than I'd expected.

"Mimi," I say, "what's the story?"

"Two separate mass signatures. One approaching from twelve o'clock. The other from nine."

Since I'm facing dead north, she means the corridor leading to the Zhao Zhou Bridge. But to the west? There's no entrance from that direction. "We closed all of those tunnels down."

"Maybe the miners missed one," Mimi says.

"Where?" I say, noting the twin minarets and the zip line running between them, and two others running to the ground. Alongside them is the tall crane I noticed on the first day, also an important link in the chain. That's where Vienne and Ebi are supposed to be stationed. Without them, my defensive plan has a much lower chance of success.

"Indeterminate."

"Determine it, then, and alert me when you know." I turn to Spiner, who is still standing beside me. "Don't you have a post?"

"Yep. I'll take it when the Dræu is here."

Damn these obstinate, thickheaded, stubborn pains in the ass. "Trust me. They're here."

"I still dint see nothing," Spiner says. "Wait . . . uh-oh. Reckon I'll find my post now."

Uh-oh. I'm beginning to despise that phrase. Through the scope of my armalite, I see Jenkins and Fuse running for the Zhao Zhou Bridge. Each of them is carrying a body. Fuse, who has Jean-Paul, is in the lead. Jenkins, the Dame tossed over his shoulder like a sack of synthetic flour, brings up the rear.

When Jenkins reaches the edge of the bridge, he plops the Dame on the ground. Then opens fire on the pursuing line of Dræu with his chain gun. To support him, I fire several bursts into the lead fighters. The result is predictable. And messy.

Between the two of us, our bullets take down a half dozen Dræu. The rest of skirmish line retreats, pulling the casualties with them. But Jenkins isn't finished. With the barrel of the chain gun spinning empty, he charges toward the mouth of the tunnel.

"Jenkins!" I shout via the vid. "Retreat, you whacker! Get Dame Bramimonde to safety!"

"Aw," he says, and returns to the Dame, his shoulders slumped in disappointment. He slings her limp body over his shoulder again. Then trudges off toward safety.

"Is she dead?" I ask him on the link.

"I wish. She just had a fainting spell. The boy's hurt, though. Took a round in the gut. Or the butt. Whichever."

"Fuse," I say. No response, just static. "Mimi, check the link with Fuse."

"Link is down," she says after a few seconds. "And his symbiarmor is not responding to telemetry pings. That's odd."

That explains a lot. "Jenkins," I say, while keeping suppressing fire on the tunnel to cover their escape. "What happened to Fuse's symbiarmor?"

"It's fragged. He took a punch to the back of the head from that Kuhru." By then Jenkins reaches the end of the bridge. He spins Fuse around and points to me. Fuse nods, and they join me near the edge of the bridge.

"They ambushed us," Fuse explains after I demand an explanation as we retreat to the Cross. "It was her doing. The Dræu were waiting, and she was leading them right back to us."

"What about the boy?"

"You mean, did he betray us, too? Not if being bound and gagged and forced to walk barefoot over sharp rock is a sign that you switched sides." He touches the back of his head. "Sorry about the suit. I can reboot it when I get back to quarters. That Kuhru got me with the stock of a battle rifle before Jenkins could kill him."

We reach the courtyard, and I do a quick scan for hostiles. All clear. "So he's dead?"

Jenkins laughs. "I put a hundred rounds into his belly. If that don't kill you, won't nothing kill you."

About time. We owed that rooter some payback. "Get them both to the infirmary," I tell Fuse and Jenkins, "and report to your stations double time."

"Chief," Mimi says. "I have determined the exact location of the secondary entrance."

"Finally!" I say, stepping up on the statue dais. "Some good news."

"I am not sure this constitutes good news. Look up."

CHAPTER 34

Hell's Cross, Outpost Fisher Four
ANNOS MARTIS 238. 4. 0. 00:00

The first two bodies out of the hole are both human. Ebi falls first, followed by Vienne, who fires her armalite as she plunges from a height of over a hundred meters. She pulls the clip then drops the gun.

Halfway down, she and Ebi both tuck into a ball. Cover their heads with their arms. Rotate so that their backs will strike the ground first. I hold my breath. Ebi hits first. And hard. Her armor takes the impact from the courtyard tiles, but she comes out of the tuck too soon. Her arms flail. She rolls over to her stomach, groaning.

Sprinting, I reach her at the same time that Vienne lands. She shoulder rolls and lands on her good foot. Then grabs the nearby armalite and begins spraying the roof with fire.

"Get up!" I shout at Ebi, who's rising slowly. Too slowly. "Is she injured?" I ask Mimi.

"Her symbiarmor isn't signaling distress," Mimi says. "No broken bones. No internal injuries."

"Regulator!" I yell at Ebi. "You got the wind knocked out of you. Move! Before they kill us both."

Ebi shakes the cobwebs loose. "Yes, chief."

"Fall back!" I call to Vienne.

She nods. Backs up toward us. Firing until the clip is empty. That's my Vienne.

"Or mine," Mimi says.

The three of us retreat under the safety of the arcade, where I open a vid link. "Jenkins! Status report."

"They're back. And they got sleds."

I expected that. So we have a little surprise for them. "Tell Fuse to execute step one—but only after two of the sleds cross the bridge." I switch off the vid, knowing that I can count on Fuse, even as I hear the gunning roar of the sled's turbines. Above us, the Dræu start firing. Plasma rains down on us.

"We're pinned down!" Vienne shouts as she and Ebi take turns firing. "We have to stop their fire!"

"Fine with me!" I say. "I'm open to suggestions!" Neither of them has one, except to keep firing. In the distance I hear the sound of a power sled revving, which means the sled drivers are about to make their move. Where, I wonder, is the queen? I look up at the ceiling again, trying to do a head count. Five, maybe ten Dræu are looking down, aiming at us. It is hard to tell.

Out of the corner of my eye, I notice the tall crane sitting idly by. In the cockpit Spiner sits back with his feet on the panel, eyes closed, oblivious to the fact that he is only a few meters from a barrage of ammunition. "Give me some cover," I say, ready to make a run for the crane.

Vienne and Ebi stand, their rifles trained on the blackness. I take off. Race to another column. Then to the far corner. Behind me, I hear a crack. A Dræu falls to the ground. But I don't stop to celebrate as a round of plasma dots chase my trail. Out the back corridor. Across a tiled patio that leads to the closed tunnel.

Finally I reach the crane. Dive behind the treads just ahead of a large plasma blast, which explodes beside the cockpit and sends Spiner sprawling backward in surprise. "Out!" I yell as I swing open the door. Then pull Spiner from the cockpit. "And stay down!"

Grabbing the pilot's seat, I sweep the hook over the container. The hook drops down, and the magnet attaches. I lift the container. Swing it between the crane and the hole to block another barrage of pulses. "Stay under cover," I order Vienne and Ebi through a vid link. "This thing's going to start swinging."

The crane cable groans as the container swings back and forth, a three-ton stone. I yank back on the brakes, and the container sails high. It hits the cavern ceiling—huge chunks of rock cascade to the ground.

"*Kusottare!*" I yell. "Missed!"

With the container out of the way, the Dræu start firing on my crane. On the ground Vienne and Ebi return fire, giving me another chance to bring the container around. "Mimi," I say, "give me a hand, will you?"

"I believe that you are the one with the hands in this relationship."

"You know what I mean. Calibrate an angle that will ram this hunk of steel into that hole, then use the symbiarmor to guide my hand."

"It will be painful."

"Sorry it's going to hurt you."

"Not me, cowboy. You. Countdown. Three, two, one."

My back arches against the armor, which goes rigid to hold my body in place. It hurts, and I grunt. Only my arm and hand move, controlling the stick so that the container swings eight times like a pendulum, its massive weight causing the boom and the attached cable to groan.

On the last upswing, the magnet releases, and the sky-hook container shoots straight to the ceiling and slams into the hole. Taking several Dræu with it. "Who says you can't put a square peg in a round hole," I say, and try to shake off the effects of Mimi's control. "You do good work."

"Technically, it is a rectangular peg. But thank you. A girl always enjoys a compliment."

"Either way, it'll hold them for a while." I jump down and race back to the courtyard to join Ebi and Vienne. "You two, man your positions on the minarets."

Vienne directs Ebi to the sniper nest on the minaret, and

I run in the opposite direction, down the corridor toward the Zhao Zhou Bridge.

Boom-ba-doom!

An explosion rips through the cavern, and the shock knocks me to the ground, dust raining down on me.

"Was that Fuse's handiwork?" Vienne asks via vid link.

"Hope so," I say.

At the end of the tunnel, I find the source of the explosion. A fifteen-meter-long segment is now missing from the Zhao Zhou Bridge. It's been dropped into the gorge by two C-42 charges, courtesy of Fuse.

The Dræu's main force is stranded on the far side of the gorge, which is good. But they have two power sleds, which is bad, because each sled has a gunner, and they're spraying bullets at the miners.

"Jenkins," I say through the vid. "Status?"

"Fuse says to please shoot the fossickers shooting at us!"

"Will do." I call to Vienne and Ebi. "Snipers, take out the gunner."

Through my omnoculars I watch them raise their armalites in unison, sight a gunner, and squeeze their triggers. Each bullet finds its mark at the base of the Dræu's skull, and the targets collapse over the barrels of the chain guns. *Twip! Twip! Twip! Twip!* Four more Dræu on sleds go down before Vienne takes out the remaining two.

"She stole my kill," Ebi says.

"Get used to it," I say.

I bounce down from the container and run across the tops of the other containers until I reach the next crane. Áine is operating it. "Time for stage two. Drop the container."

She salutes. The boom swings around, and the container, which is missing both of its doors, drifts over the gorge. After two minor adjustments, Áine settles it above the gap that the C-42 has created.

"Jenkins," I say into the vid, "you and Fuse get those miners inside."

"Can I bring in the sleds?"

"That's the idea."

"Whoop!"

I signal the second operator to lift a container, which creates a gate, and the miners pour in, with Fuse and Jenkins behind them in the captured sleds. When they're safely inside, Áine drops her container into place.

"Think they'll take the bait?" Fuse asks me.

"They're not as stupid as we thought," I say, watching them as they begin to move en masse to the container. "But they are as bloodthirsty. I don't think they'll be able to help themselves."

"Won't their queen keep them back? She'll know it you've set up a trap."

"Haven't seen her at all." But I know she is out there. Somewhere. It isn't like Eceni to miss the action.

"Here they come!" Vienne announces from her high-vantage point. Then she abruptly fires several rounds into the area where the sled is parked. Ebi follows suit.

I tap open the vid. "Vienne! What the blazes?"

"They're back on their feet, chief. The Dræu we shot. Five of them are on their feet and moving into firing position."

"Did you miss?" I ask.

"No. Body shots to the heart and lungs. All on target."

Merda! "Keep shooting then." I tap out of the vid and have Áine swing the boom around. After I step onto the hook, she lowers me to the ground inside the maze. There, Fuse and Jenkins are waiting. They've stripped the chain guns from the sleds, which the miners are now hiding inside two of the containers.

"Look!" Jenkins says, hefting a chain gun in each arm. "Twins!"

"Glad you're having a double date. Fuse, stay close to me. With your aural link out, I can't open a vid, and this next part gets dicey."

Fuse agrees, and we take position for Stage Three. Jenkins remains on his mark, growling to psyche himself up.

"What's next?" I say.

"Tell the cranes to drop the second wall." Fuse mentally measures the spot where the containers would go. "And you might want to step back two point two meters."

"Let's make it three." I signal for the cranes to be dropped behind Jenkins. Creating a second wall. Leaving me as bait. Then I order Vienne and Ebi to stand down. We want the Dræu rushing the gate, not dodging sniper fire.

"Yes, chief," Vienne says, sounding disappointed.

From her crane, Áine shouts, "They're charging across the bridge!"

"Let a couple dozen cross unharassed!"

"They've already crossed!"

"Then lift the carking box off the bridge! Keep the rest of them on the opposite side."

The cables tighten on her boom, and I hear the sound of metal scraping as the container lifts.

"Done!" she shouts. "About twenty of the beasties crossed. The rest are caught in the box or—wait! One's hanging from the edge of container. You've got to get it off. It's throwing off the balance."

"Vienne," I say, "take out the dangler. But let the other targets inside the gate before."

"Yes, chief." *Twip!* "Dangler down."

We're interrupted by the sound of twin chain gun fire and Jenkins's gleeful roar.

"Heewack!" Jenkins roars.

"Get him out of here!" I order one of the crane operators.

A hook swings down, and Jenkins latches on, somehow wrapping his knees around it while holding onto both chain guns. As he clears the top of the containers, Jenkins steps off and swings the twin guns to his broad shoulders. The flashing blue lights from the cranes cast a purple shadow on his face, blanching the ruddy color away and highlighting the pockmarks on his cheeks. When he speaks, his voice full of the sound of gravels and dust, I don't know him. "I'm Leroy Jenkins, you cark-sacking cannibals! Bring it on!"

"Fuse," I say. "Step Four?"

"Right," Fuse says, intent on the Dræu who rushed in to kill Jenkins. "Close the front gate."

I make the call. Two containers drop. *Boom! Boom!* Trapping the Dræu inside. Howling in rage, they begin firing. But they have no targets.

"Chief," Fuse says. "We need the Dræu to spread out of the middle. Pronto. So we can drop the next containers."

"Jenkins," I say, "pin them against the walls."

Now safely unhooked and atop the wall of containers, Jenkins steps to the edge and opens fire. The Dræu dive for cover, spreading themselves like a layer of aminomite along one side of the maze.

"They're out of the middle," I tell Fuse.

"Let's drop walls one through three," Fuse says. Then shouts, "Miners! Keep 'em separated!"

I signal the cranes. "On my mark. One." *Boom!* "Two." *Boom!* "Three." *Boom!* The maze is now divided into four equal sections, Dræu trapped in each one. They scream in unison, a sound that makes the hair on my neck stand on end. On the other side of the gorge, the other Dræu howl in answer.

"On my order," I call into the vid as the last container falls into place. "Vienne, your target is area one. Ebi, area two. Jenkins, three. Fuse and I will cover four." Taking a deep breath, I pray that this is going to work. There has to be some way to kill these monsters—maybe filling them with lead was the way to do it. "Open fire!"

Two dozen Dræu. Their weapons useless against our cross fire. Penned in. Trapped. The maze turns into a slaughterhouse. Some try to scale the walls, their great leaps taking them halfway up the sides. But they're cut down before they can even get a handhold. Others close ranks and fire at us until their plasma weapons run out of charge. Then our bullets find them.

This is not who we are, and it shames me. The Tenets teach us to respect our enemy as we respect our friends, to honor ourselves, our ancestors, and our children with our actions. There is no honor here, just the killing, the need to destroy the enemy utterly in order to survive. Father would understand this action, would say that the Tenets were written for old-fashioned before days Mars, not the planet we've become. But it sickens me, and up on a minaret, I'm sure that Vienne is refusing to watch, her scope directed at the Dræu on the far side of the gorge. Her voice is in my ears: *You are less the man I thought you were. I am less the Regulator for serving under you.*

Finally, when the chain guns are empty and the screams have died out, I call for a cease fire to assess the damage.

"Mimi, scan the hostiles."

"Cowboy, you shouldn't feel—"

"Just the scan, please."

"No detectable signs of life."

"All targets are down," I say. "Let's clean it up."

The operators lift the containers, and the remaining miners, who're waiting safely in nearby containers, rappel to the ground. Their job is to remove the bodies before the next wave of Dræu is let across the bridge, and they take to it with gusto. On command, an operator drops a container in the middle of the maze. Quickly the miners load the Dræu carcasses to it.

"Cowboy! Alert! Alert! Multiple heartbeats registering! The Dræu!"

Down in the maze one of the miners yells and pulls out his wrench. "It's moving! The beastie's still living!"

"Mine, too!" another calls, and they all began to back away. The looks on their faces ask the same question I have: How can something so full of holes be alive?

"Get out of there!" I shout, finally understanding. The Dræu are coming back to life. I tap in Vienne. "Eyes on multiple targets in the maze. Take out the Dræu that regenerate."

"Negative, chief," she responds. "Too many friendlies in the line of fire. I can't get a clear shot. Get the miners out."

"Will do." I shout into the maze. "Everybody out! You're in the line of fire!"

Easier said than done. The cables the miners rappelled down aren't attached to cranes. They have to climb out. Too many miners in the hole. Too long to get them all out.

"Jenkins," I say. "We need you on deck for backup."

"I'm going in," Jenkins says, recognizing the problem as soon as I do. He's about to jump into the mix when a reviving Dræu reaches up from the ground and grabs a miner by the ankle. Instinctively the miner swings his heavy wrench at its head, smashing the base of the skull.

"Tch," he says. "Would y'look at that."

The other miners gather around him. They nudge the Dræu with the toes of their boots. One kicks it in the ribs. Then rolls it over. A huff of air escapes its lungs, and the eyes roll back into its head.

"It's dead," the miner says.

"It is. A knock with a wrench is all it took."

They get the idea quickly, and the real slaughter begins.

"Chief?" Vienne says.

"Stand down," I tell my davos. All men have a breaking point, and this is mine. "Turn your backs. All of you. Let them finish but don't become part of it. Ebi, abandon your station. We're going to need another short-range gunner in the maze."

A few minutes later a cheer goes up. The container full of slaughtered Dræu, its doors sealed and locked, is lifted out of the maze and then dropped into the gorge. The miners climb up the cables one by one, their overalls blotted with blood. They start singing. I look into Fuse's face and see the same expression that must be on my face, a mix of horror and shock.

"Know what they reminded me of?" Fuse says.

"The Dræu when they've got fresh meat?"

"Yeah."

"One difference between us and the Dræu," I say.

"What's that?"

"Our bellies are still empty."

"That's a mighty thin line, chief."

"It's the thinnest lines that define us, soldier."

"Oy, that's very wise. D'you make that up on a lark?"

"No, I say, "I stole it from my father." Turning to Áine's crane, I signal her to drop the container across the bridge. Time for the second batch.

Ebi comes running across the top of the maze. "Ebi reporting, chief."

"Stay close," I tell her. "Don't fire until I give the signal."

Mimi pipes in, "A mass of signatures gathering at the bridge."

"Battle stations, Regulators," I say through the vid. "Here they come again."

Áine lowers the container, and the rest of the Dræu roar across the bridge, intent on reaching their comrades. When they are past, she raises the box again, trapping them.

They're screaming for blood as they rush like a flood toward the gate. "Open it!" I order. The Dræu stream inside, blind with bloodlust, too berserker with rage to stop their charge. Their eyes are mad, and they're frothing at the mouth, their faces wild and terrible to see. It's insane, insane.

But I'm counting on their strength being their weakness.

This time there is no need to use Jenkins as bait.

"Close the gate?" Fuse asks.

"Wait," I say. "I want to make sure we've got them all. I don't want us to go through this more times than we have to."

"Got it."

"Mimi," I say, "scan the perimeter for signatures."

"Yes, cowboy," she says. "Wait. I am picking up a unique signature on the far side of the bridge and closing fast. It is—"

"The queen!" Vienne yells through the link.

I turn as a power sled emerges from the tunnel, its turbines blazing. Two Dræu ride with the queen, one of them driving and the other manning the gun. She straddles the jump seat, the mortar launcher on her shoulder and two bandoliers of ammo draped across her chest.

"She's going to jump it," I say.

Ebi scoffs. "Impossible."

The sled hits the end of the bridge and goes airborne. The front of the craft lifts, the heavy engines tilting its approach angles upward. It lands hard but with several meters to spare. The rear end fishtails, flinging the gunner from his post. As he tries to stand, Vienne takes him out with one kill shot.

The queen maintains her balance perfectly, firing a mortar at Áine's crane. The shell hits the thick plexus window, cracking it. Then it falls onto the hood, where it detonates.

"Áine!" I yell above the din, though I know she can't hear me.

Fuse starts toward her. I check him with a halt sign. At the same time the driver steers toward the opening and the Dræu that wait inside.

"Drop the gate!" I shout. "Don't let the power sled in!"

Too late. The gate falls a second after the sled skids inside. Seeing their queen, the Dræu roar louder. The driver, obeying a silent command, guns the engine and heads toward the back of the maze.

"Drop the rest of the containers!" I yell.

Boxes one and two fall into place perfectly, trapping most of the Dræu. But as the crane dropping number three swings into action, the queen fires another mortar. It strikes the boom.

The cable snaps and the box swings free, crashing into the back wall and knocking it down. The driver sees his opening. He drives the sled between two fallen containers and disappears from the maze.

"Where is she going?" Ebi asks.

I know exactly where she's going—the treasure. "Fuse, you're in command of the maze. Drop another back wall now. Take these rooters out. I'll get the queen. Vienne—" I start to say and then reconsider. Her wounded foot will slow us down. "Ebi, you're coming with me."

Seconds later Ebi and I are running along the top of the maze, headed toward the Cross. Behind us, the shooting begins. So that was her plan all along, I think. Distract us with mad rushes, then go for the treasure when our hands are full. Simple but brilliant. And it shows that she doesn't care about the Dræu. They're a means to an end, a toy to be played with until it's outlived its use. I know how they feel.

"Mimi, where is the queen?"

"Signatures are stationary. They are fifty meters ahead."

In the Cross. Ebi and I sprint down the tops of the cargo boxes. For an instant I pause, taking it all in, feeling the rush of . . . something. Old memories? Déjà vu? At battle school, I commanded my own acolyte davos, and my first skirmish was against Eceni. She won that time. She won every time we matched up. But this is a real battle, not a student exercise. When we reach the edge of the maze, I signal Ebi to halt. We drop low, and both of us scan the Cross for targets. That's when Ebi shoots me in the back of the head.

The force of the blow knocks me forward, and I fall to hands and knees. Roll to my back.

"Permission to fire now, *chief?*" Ebi says.

"Mimi," I say, my head a hive of noise. There is no answer. "Mimi?"

"My name is not Mimi," Ebi says, pointing the barrel of her armalite at my head. "It is Bramimonde, Jacob Stringfellow, from the proud House of Bramimonde that men like your father destroyed."

"No." I try to rise, but my thoughts are full of bees. The symbiarmor is sluggish. Where is Mimi?

"Oh yes." Stomping my chest, she drives me hard onto the top of the cargo box. "But the queen is going to change that. When she finds the treasure, she's going to return the Orthocracy to power, and I will be able to realize my true destiny." She spits in my face. "The added benefit will be killing you. Remember when you disgraced our home with your presence, *dalit*? I said I would repay you one day, and that moment is now."

CHAPTER 35

Hell's Cross, Outpost Fisher Four
ANNOS MARTIS 238. 4. 0. 00:00

"Not on my watch," Mimi says through the static.

Reflectively, my hand shoots out and grabs Ebi by the wrist. A numbing shock of electricity shoots into her symbiarmor. Her eyes roll back into her head, and a small moan escapes her lips before a burst of bullets leaves her gun, striking me in the chest. They bounce off, leaving me unharmed, as I hear a second noise—the crack of a single shot—and Ebi falls backward and topples off the cargo box.

"Who shot her?" I say.

"Three guesses," Mimi answers.

"Vienne."

"Fast work for a wee little brain."

And I look across the line of cargo boxes, up on the minaret, where she stands holding her Armalite, scoring the barrel with a combat knife. "Thanks," I tell her via aural vid.

"My job," she says. Then uses the zip line to reach the ground, absorbing the landing with her good leg but coming up limping. "I never did like that girl."

"Could've fooled me." I get to my feet.

"I often do," she says. "It's really not that difficult." Limping, she joins me, and we move to the courtyard. The queen has deserted the sled, leaving it parked in the open and still manned by the Dræu.

"Where is she?" I say aloud.

"Chief," Vienne says, looking through her scope. "I have lock on the targets. Permission to fire?"

"Wait. I want to take them both out at the same time."

"Affirmative," she says. "I have both targets locked."

"Both?" This, I want to see. "Fire at wi—" *Twip!* One bullet leaves her rifle. Two Dræu fell.

"How did you do that?" I say in awe.

"Large-caliber ammunition and two targets willing to keep the bases of their skulls in the same line of fire."

"Don't tell Jenkins. He'll have to take out three just to prove he's better than you. Come on, let's flush out the queen."

We jog slowly to the sled to examine Vienne's shots. Both are clean kills, right through the base of the skulls. "Mimi," I say as we disable the chain gun, then move away from the sled. "Where is the queen?"

I scan the chigoe holes while waiting for an answer. So many places to hide in the Cross. She could be anywhere.

"Cannot pinpoint her location. The signal is erratic. I—cowboy!"

Foosh!

A mortar shell slams into my stomach, blowing me off my feet. I land hard, dazed, eyes full of static.

Vienne? I think, gasping for breath. Where's Vienne? Then I see her, safe, near the sled.

Foosh!

A second rocket! It slams into the bishop's statue. Chunks of marble rain down, and I cover my face as the bishop's decapitated head slams into my forearms, then bounces away, rolling across the tiles.

Luckily, I, unlike the statue, am still in one piece.

"Look," Mimi says, "'a shattered visage lies.'"

"Keats?"

"Shelley."

"I always get them confus—"

Eceni isn't finished. A third rocket shoots from the launcher. For an instant I'm relieved because it looks like a misfire that flits impotently toward the high ceiling of the cave. Then it hits, and a cloud of black dust explodes into the air. With the squeal of grinding metal, the container wedged in the hole breaks free. Above me, the ceiling cracks open. The shipping container that Mimi expertly placed for me earlier slips from its hole and comes crashing down.

"You should move," Mimi says.

But I don't. I lie there watching it fall, mesmerized by the way the metal rectangular box rights itself as it falls, the floor of the container on a collision course with my skull.

"Durango!" Vienne dives across the tiled flooring as the container falls. She slams into me. Her momentum should knock me out of the way, but my suit absorbs the blow, and we huddle together in an awkward embrace.

"Go!" Mimi shocks me, and I start to move, but too late.

Silently, Vienne aims her weapon at the bottom of the container, and one, two blast shells leave her armalite. I grab her, pull her to my chest, and brace for impact.

CHAPTER 36

Hell's Cross, Outpost Fisher Four
ANNOS MARTIS 238. 4. 0. 00:00

The container slams into the ground. Its floor, already blasted apart by the explosive shells, shatters completely when it strikes my back, trapping us inside. Its weight slams me onto Vienne, who is balled up beneath me.

My armor handles the impact. My ears, however, can't deal with the sound, and for a few seconds I'm stunned. Until Mimi decides to zap me again.

"Move it, Regulator!" she barks into my brain, sounding like my old chief.

"Vienne?" I shrug off the wreckage. Roll her onto her back. Check to make sure she's okay, but it's pitch-black inside, and the air is saturated with dust.

"Her vitals are good," Mimi says. "She's just unconscious."

Just unconscious, I think. Then Vienne moans, and I know it's true. The queen. Where is she? Does she know we survived? Is she coming in for the kill?

I peer outside between the twisted doors of the container.

Eceni is as beautiful as the day I met her Offworld, and I might have been smitten by her again, if she weren't a homicidal maniac who just dropped a shipping container on my head. While I'm checking Vienne's pulse, the queen bounds across the courtyard to the statue. She leaps onto the dais, throws an arm around the bishop's crumbling waist, and does a series of high cancan kicks while humming the tune "ta-ra-ra boom-de-ay."

"Come out, come out, wherever you are, Jacob," she says, singsong. "I know you're not dead, Jake. Ja-ak-ey."

"Vienne," I whisper, and shake her gently. She lets out a quiet moan. Okay, I think, Vienne needs time to recover, so I need a diversion.

As quietly as possible I extricate myself and crawl over to the damaged door. Eceni is still dancing around the statue, oblivious to my movement. I slip through the narrow gap, my muscles screaming, my head full of static, looking for something to use to draw the queen away from Vienne.

The power sled! It's parked a few meters away. Covered in debris, but the engine's still idling. Lucky me.

"Only you could say *lucky me*," Mimi says, "after a structure the size of a small house lands on you."

"The eternal optimist." I slide onto the seat and grab the handlebars. I goose the sled and roar toward the queen. She turns at the sound of the revving engine and brings the launcher to bear.

Before she can fire, I whip the sled into a fishtail, which

slams the rear end into her legs. The force blows her back six meters, and I jump off, sending the sled crashing into a column nearby. The fuel tank ruptures, and I can smell petrol in the air, even as I kick the launcher out of her hand. She blocks my next three punches with counter blows to my wrists.

"You're quick," I say.

"You say the nicest things." She lands a darting front kick to my chest, then follows with a succession of blows that I struggle to block. The last kick brings her in for a punch to my throat. I dodge it and pull her shoulder down, ready to use a hip throw. But she's ahead of me, and her foot comes up behind her back and smacks me in the face, knocking my helmet off.

For a half second I'm dazed. She makes me pay with a roundhouse to the gut that knocks me on my butt, and I do a backward roll to recover.

She fires the helmet at my head. I catch it easy like a ball and shove it back on.

"Bring it," I motion her forward, goading.

"Darling, you have no idea of how much *it* I have."

We each throw three punches—right, left, right—simultaneously, blocking so that the flurry ends with our arms intertwined, the hard bones of our knuckles centimeters from each other's noses. Then she leans forward and kisses me on the lips, pushing her tongue into my mouth.

I bite down. Hard.

"Ow!" She yanks back, wincing. "You bad, bad boy!"

Though our arms are still tangled, she throws a hook kick to my temple. The force of it snaps my head to the side, and I hear bones pop in my neck. She lands punches to my right clavicle as I fall against the side of the shipping container.

Eceni moves in for the kill. "Oh Jakey. I can't wait to get my hands on you."

"Stop!" Vienne bursts out of the container, kicking the door open as Eceni steps in front of it.

Boom! The force slams Eceni on her back several meters away. Her butt leaves a trail in the dust like a snowplow, and I grin.

"Forgot about me, bitch?" Vienne steps out into the light. "Keep your hands off him."

"Thanks for the save," I say as I rise to my feet.

"Just returning the favor, chief."

I hear the telltale click of Vienne's armalite. Then see a RPG streak across the Cross. Eceni hears it, too, and as the grenade reaches her, she spins to her feet with inhuman speed and brings up her launcher. It smacks the warhead mid-flight and diverts its course upward. The shell flies straight up into the pitch dark.

An instant later I hear a muffled boom. The queen waltzes a few yards away as rubble from the blast plasters the stone floor. A smile breaks across Eceni's painted ruby lips. "Soldier girl, you shot my pet Regulator."

"Your *pet* deserved a worse death than I gave her."

"Not that she didn't deserve it, I suppose," the queen says. A smile curls the corners of her mouth. She shakes the dirt from her dress. "Look what you have done. Do you have any idea how difficult it is to get real silk on Mars? No, I suppose you wouldn't, not a girl who sleeps in symbiarmor."

Vienne tries to launch another RPG. Click. The chamber is empty.

"Oops," the queen says. "You are out of grenades. Didn't you keep count?"

"I don't need grenades to take care of you."

In that same instant the queen sprints to a column. Leaps high into the air. Bounds from the column to a second one, then to the arcade. Before Vienne can move, the queen attacks, striking with a series of cobra-quick kicks that knock the armalite from her grasp. Vienne stumbles, her wounded heel throwing her off balance.

I catch her. Pull her out of harm's way. The queen misses, and she curses as she lands on the balls of her feet. Vienne tries to charge, but I won't let go. Instead, I lock arms with her.

Vienne looks down at our hands, then into my eyes, and something passes between us. Or rather falls, like a curtain cut loose from its hanging rod. Her knees buckle—it's the wound, I think.

"You're injured. You can't beat her alone," I say. "Together?"

"Together."

Eceni screams. She launches a flying kick, her mouth bent down like twisted metal. We duck, hands still locked, and she flies above us. With a clang, she hits the container, then executes a perfect two-step walkover and flips off the side, turning in midair so that her kick is aimed at the base of Vienne's skull.

"No!" I shout, and swing Vienne out of the way. My forearm blocks her kick and gives us time to recover.

Vienne looks at me. I know what she wants.

Planting my feet, I swing her around like a ball on the end of a tether, and she throws a kick at Eceni's head. As easily as nodding, the queen ducks, then throws a roundhouse kick. We block it with our locked arms, and I let go long enough to lift Vienne into a *grand jeté*, our combined mass swinging her around so fast, the queen can't dodge.

The heel of Vienne's boot catches Eceni in the jaw, and I hear bone crunch. But the queen doesn't go down. Instead, she comes up spitting blood, eyes wild and full of rage.

I swing Vienne around my back and into my arms, and we both slam into Eceni, knocking her against the shipping container. She shakes her head, dazed, and we go in for the kill. Using me for balance, Vienne runs along the side of the container and hits Eceni with a succession of front kicks to the face, the side of the head, and the base of the skull.

Eceni falls backward and stumbles away. "Blood! All over my dre—"

Vienne launches herself, a human missile. She goes vertical, her body laid out like a board. Strikes the queen in the midsection. Her head driving into the solar plexus. Her arms wrapping around Eceni like a vise. Momentum carries them to a mound of debris, and Vienne twists so that her weight hammers the queen's gut.

"Oof!" The queen's tailbone cracks, and she sags as all the air leaves her body, a piece of broken rebar impaling her gut. Her eyes gloss over.

Vienne looks at the queen's fallen body. I stare at Vienne, the flames from the fires burning around us reflected in her eyes. Finally she looks at me.

"You're okay?" I ask.

"Yes, chief."

"It's *chief* now? You called me Durango before."

"Before when?"

"When you blew holes in the bottom of the shipping container."

"That was different."

"Different how?"

For a second I think I see a mist in her eyes. "You're not going to do something stupid, are you?" she says.

"Like what?"

"Like this." Vienne pulls me close and kisses me. Her lips are warm, and I feel that heat spread to my cheeks.

"Cowboy," Mimi says. "I hate to interrupt, but—"

"How sweet," the queen says as she stands. "Two lovers

snuggling over the woman they *almost* killed. Tsk. And you call the Draeu animals."

Her dress is a matted mess of blood and guanite, and her neck is bent at an odd angle. Blood seeps from a wound where the rebar impaled her. But she places a hand on the pipe and pulls hard.

"Missed me, missed me," the queen sings. "Now you have to kiss me." She screams, and my stomach lurches.

"How?" Vienne says.

"Nanosyms," I say. "She must still have some in her bloodstream."

"Millions of them, actually. Doing their best to keep me alive." The queen waves the pipe at us. "Lucky for me the Dræu aren't here to see this. They get so hard to control when there's blood in the air."

I open up with my own armalite. Bullets spray the court-yard, and the queen drops to the floor beneath the line of fire.

"The head!" Vienne yells. "Aim for the back of the head. It's your only chance!"

I chase the queen with a line of bullets, but Eceni ducks behind the rubble, the bullets missing her by centimeters. I pop the empty clip, then jam another into place and step out into the open to make the kill shot.

The queen is gone.

Shimatta! I say under my breath. Stupid move.

"Where is the target?" Vienne says. "I've no visual."

"Wait," I tell Vienne. "Mimi?" I scan the perimeter for the queen. "She can't just disappear into thin air, right?"

The queen cackles. Her laughter echoes across the hall. I twist my head back and forth, trying to locate the sound. Then my eye catches a flash of movement, the queen tossing something small and shimmering.

"Grenade!" I scream.

It lands with a quiet squeak.

Next to us.

The light-mass grenade expands impossibly fast, and balls of light shoot through the air as Vienne and I are blown back and slammed into the wall. Vienne slides down, her head lolling to the side, eyes closed. I slide down, too, my body twitching and jerking like it's been shocked, the symbiarmor like lead skin.

I try to call to Vienne, but it comes out garbled. "Mimi? Mimi!" No answer.

"Now, if you'll excuse me," Eceni says, skipping toward me. "I'm going to collect the treasure and be on my merry way."

"There's no treasure," I growl, lifting my head. "You *vitun iso* psychopath."

Eceni leans down, her face inches away from mine. "You've failed, Jake, and according to your precious Tenets, you're supposed to kill yourself." She pulls a shiv out of a boot. "Feel free to use my knife to do the Rites on yourself. And because you mean so much to me, if I come back and find you dead, I'll make sure the Dræu don't eat your corpse."

"Don't do me any favors."

She blows a kiss. "Farewell, Great Chief Stringfellow. I wish it had ended differently for us."

"You *jumalauta* liar!"

She grins. "That's true. I am lying. I've been waiting to see you dead since the day you dumped me." Then she dances away toward the tunnels, pausing as she passes to plant a kick in Vienne's side. "Oh, too bad. Looks like you're alone again, lover boy."

"*Cào nǐ zǔzōng shíbā dài!*" I roar.

"Thank you," she calls back as she jogs away. "But I have no ancestors." Then disappears.

"Mimi?" I say, moving slowly, my body feeling as empty and lifeless as a drained battery.

"Happy Birthday!" she shouts in my head.

Do what? "Mimi!"

"Happy New Year! Auld lang syne!"

Oh *kuso*! Her functions are fubared. The light-mass grenade must have scrambled her functions. Not now. Not when we need her. "Mimi! Perform reboot sequence on my mark. Three, two, one."

My synthetic eye goes black, and I hear a quiet ping. I crawl over to Vienne. I don't need Mimi to tell me she's alive. Her chest is rising and falling as she breathes. Lightly patting her cheeks, I try to wake her. I keep trying for a few minutes, without success, until Mimi comes online again.

"Oh, my aching head," Mimi says. "What was in that stuff anyway?"

"Pay attention, Mimi. Can you reboot Vienne's suit?"

"Make contact, and I'll see what I can come up with."

Cradling Vienne's head in my lap, I place a gloved hand at the base of her skull. For a few seconds nothing happens. Then a spark leaps from my suit and spreads over her symbiarmor. She tenses, the armor going rigid, and her eyes flutter open.

"Wake up, Regulator," I say. "It's up to us to finish this job."

CHAPTER 37

Hell's Cross, Outpost Fisher Four
ANNOS MARTIS 238. 4. 0. 00:00

We follow the path that Maeve showed me. We reach the cliff, and I find myself staring into the blank air that held me hostage. It should be easier, facing the same fear that you had conquered. But fears are like thirst. No matter how many times you quench them, they always return. This time, though, I can't afford to crawl like a worm to the rappelling rope. I have to grab it and slide fast. So that's what I do, anger and adrenaline fueling my engine.

Before Vienne can beat me to it, I grab a handful of cord and swing out over the ledge—all false bravado, but I have to do it for her. My feet hit the wall, and I push out again, belaying the rope between my hands, then swing out, and the arc carries me into the mouth of the small tunnel again.

"Get up, get up, get up," I cajole myself. When I'm on my feet, I hear the sound of Vienne's descent and make sure I'm there to catch her.

"Good work, cowboy," Mimi says.

Once we're free of the landing area, I pick up the queen's trail. It leads to the holding pens.

"Mimi," I ask, "locate Eceni."

"Located. Fifty meters ahead on your current bearing."

"Before we go any farther." I grab hold of Vienne. "There's some intel you need." So I debrief her about the chigoe.

Vienne takes it all in, then answers the best way she knows how. "I don't give a fig about Big Daddies or diamonds. All I want is that woman's head on a pike."

"Well," I say. "Okay then."

Vienne takes the point. We crouch low and move at a deliberate pace, keeping our weapons trained ahead. When we reach the pens, Vienne stops and points at the vault door. It hangs ajar, the hinges scored and melted. Black, sooty streaks stain the metal, caused by C-42 explosives.

Vienne covers me while I move in a zigzag pattern to the opening, then flatten myself against the wall, weapon ready. I look inside the anteroom on the other side of the vault door. All clear.

Crouching low, we creep around the corner. It's pitch dark, but we don't dare strike a light. That leaves nothing to do but wait until she shows her face.

Breathe. Calm. Calm.

"Mimi? Can you get a lock on her location?"

"Ten meters. Bearing indeterminate. The chigoes are creating interference."

Think. Where is she? There has to be a light source somewhere.

I remember the low ebb of fluorescence from the tanks that hold the chigoes. I blink. There, in the next chamber, I see a flicker of something. There's a rattle and hum, and the overhead lights in the chamber ahead come on, followed by the crash of breaking glass. I wave Vienne forward, and we move together to the edge of the antechamber, our backs pressed against the smooth stone wall.

Eceni is trashing the chamber. One tank lies shattered on the ground, a dozen chigoes scrambling toward the shadows to escape. She stomps around, trying to pound them with her boots, chasing them deeper beneath the equipment shelf, one chigoe tucked under her arm. The chigoe's shell is thick and ridged, the shape of an oval. Its back is covered with patches of black eggs.

It's a female chigoe. She's found the queen.

"Where are they?" Eceni takes the chigoe queen in both hands and shakes her like a petulant child. "Where are the Big Daddies? Why are there only babies?"

I stand up. "Why don't you pick on somebody your own size?"

Eceni sighs and turns slowly toward me. "Jakey. You found me. How unlucky for you. I was just about to take my treasure and go home."

"I'm not so sure about that." Vienne follows me into the chamber and circles back until she's standing in front of the largest tank of chigoes.

"Sorry to disappoint you," I say. "These aren't babies. They're as full grown as they're ever going to get."

Eceni lifts the queen so that it shields her. "Don't lie to me!" she screams. "Where are the Big Daddies? Tell me, and I'll let you live."

"Too bad we're not feeling so generous." Vienne opens fire.

"No!" I shout, too late to stop her.

The bullets rip through Eceni. The force of impact drives her back, and she crumples to one knee. She shakes her shoulders, and the healing begins. The open wounds start to close, the bleeding stops, and within a few seconds, it's as if she was never shot.

"My god," Vienne says. "What kind of devil are you?"

"The human kind," she says. "Surprise! My turn."

The gun is small, and the plasma ball is only the size of a marble. But it's still white hot, and when Vienne dodges the shot, it sears the tanks behind her. "Damn!" Vienne roars, and drops to the ground, dragging her foot.

"I missed?" the queen says, inspecting the plasma gun. "These things are so unreliable."

I take two steps toward Vienne before the chigoe tank begins to make a high-pitched sound. Cracks spread across the glass, and in the next breath, the tank bursts. A cubic ton of nutrient bath pours out on Vienne, sweeping her across the floor.

"Chief!" she calls, and reaches out, the slimy liquid covering her body.

"Hang on!" I yell, and try to crawl toward her.

Then I freeze—the chigoes! They're free!

Cào nǐ zǔzōng shíbā dài!

Dozens and dozens of drones skitter from the broken tanks, their legs clacking, mandibles working, as they pile atop one another, chittering and confused. A few reach Vienne, but they skitter away quickly, repulsed by her warm flesh.

I dive across the floor. Grab Vienne and try to get us both to our feet, but my boots only slip on the floor.

"Shoot her!" Vienne yells.

I pull her close. "It won't do any good."

"Try!" Her face goes white. Her teeth chatter. "I'm c-cold."

"Mimi? What's happening?"

"She's going into shock again, cowboy."

"What's the matter, Jake? Can't get up?" Eceni holds the chigoe queen above her head. Looks at Vienne. "Tell me where the Big Daddies are, or I'll smash your little honey's skull to pieces."

"What's so important," I ask as I try to shift my weight to shield Vienne, "about being queen of Mars? It's a crappy planet, as planets go. You remember Earth, right? That's a planet worth being queen of."

"Oh, shut up," she says. "I know what you're doing. Distract and delay. So predictable. That's why you're a terrible leader. Everything by the Tenets. Too bad for you, I read the book. Memorized it, in fact."

Keep talking, I tell myself. Get closer to her. "What happened to you, Eceni? Top of the class. Destined for a generalship, maybe even CEO one day. The best of the best of us. Now, you're chopping people up and talking world domination."

"Not the girl you loved, right?"

"Don't flatter yourself." I move away from Vienne. Inch closer to Eceni. And I know that what I felt for Eceni wasn't even close to love.

"Tell that to the CorpComs, Jake. They were the ones who did this to me. Secret Operation MUSE."

The chigoes' distress keening gets louder and more high-pitched. The noise grows in my ears, and I shake my head.

"They say ninety-nine of our best of the best. You'll be the new Paladins, God's warriors. We'll just take some of the nanosyms from your suits and inject them into your bloodstream. Add a little gene manipulation, and voila! Instant regeneration. A soldier who can't be killed. Except they didn't count on the side effects. Want to know about the side effects, Chief Durango Jake Jacob Stringfellow?"

My god, I think. What did they do to you? What did they do to me? "Tell me."

"Brain lesions to start. Psychotic breaks. Fugues. Self-mutilation. Insatiable hunger. And then, madness. Only one subject was deemed a success—me."

"And the others?"

"You call them the Dræu."

"What?" It can't be. My father helped make the Dræu? No. The madness, the rage, the cannibalism, the way they seemed to come in waves, even when so many had been killed. I bury my head in my hands. Dear God, Father, how could you?

"You know what else?" she says, her eyes flashing. "The CEO who ordered this little experiment? Oh Jake. I can tell by the look on your face, you already know his name."

Yes, I do. "My father."

"Ding, ding. You win the prize. And I am a prize, aren't I?"

"Eceni, I want to help you—"

"So you see, Mars remade me this way," Eceni says. "It seems fair that I get to remake Mars the way I see fit. Now, for the last time, give me the Big Daddies."

I can do it. I can tell her that the chigoe are native to Mars, that they will reproduce. That the Big Daddies can be remade using their DNA. Or I can find a way to set them loose so that she can't lay her hands on them, ever again. But what if they run wild? What if Maeve is right that they have enough intelligence to become a threat? Jacob Stringfellow, the man who started the chigoe plague.

Just like my father.

You are less the man I thought you were. I'm damned if I do. *It is the thinnest lines that define us.* The miners are damned if I don't. *I am less the Regulator for serving under you.* The miners hired me to protect them from the Dræu. I gave them my word. Made a vow. I will keep my word. As a Regulator. As a man.

"Joke's on you," I say. "There aren't any Big Daddies left, and these chigoe are as big as they'll ever get."

"Liar!" Eceni screams, and raises the chigoe queen high over her head.

Now! I fling the knife.

Eceni swings the queen into the blade's path. The razored tip plunges into the soft, fleshy covering of the shell, sinking a few centimeters deep. The chigoe screams, a sound like grinding metal, and wraps itself around Eceni's face. It rips the flesh open with its ridged legs and then, from a set of glands on her belly, douses Eceni's body with rancid purple mucus.

I know that smell—the same scent pheromones once used to guide the Big Daddies to dig.

And kill.

Eceni throws the queen across the chamber. "Look at me! Look at this, this—"

The drones roar in unison. The sound is so loud, I clap both hands over my ears and bend low to the ground as the other tanks shatter, glass flying, nutrient bath exploding like a ruptured dam. Diving across the floor, I grab Vienne and hang on as we're swept against the wall.

Hundreds of drones erupt from the tanks, a wall of screaming chigoes climbing over each other to get to their queen. They swarm Eceni, who is still clawing at the mucus on her face. They pour up her body, legs and shells clacking, oozing, oozing, oozing, dissolving her flesh the same way they can dissolve stone.

Within seconds, she is jelly. I catch a flash of her bare skull before the tower of drones topples.

"Let's get out of here," I say to Vienne, though she can't hear me. I grab her hand. "Before they decide to eat us, too."

Using the rack of a fallen tank for leverage, I push my way across the chamber, carefully dragging Vienne behind me. I find a dry patch where I can stand, then gently pull her out of the nutrient bath, thankful that the liquid is drying quickly.

I lift her into my arms. Carry her out. Behind me, the chigoe drones make a humming sound, the noise of contentment. As if they've finished enjoying a good meal. I set Vienne down on the ground and begin checking her vitals. Her boot is soaked with blood, and she's freezing. I pull her close, trying to warm her.

"Mimi, how is—"

"Still in mild shock but stable. You need to get her to the infirmary."

"Can you tell the armor to heat up her body or something? She—"

Then I hear a chattering noise that makes my blood turn

cold—the unmistakable sound of claws on stone. I'm frozen with fear, my brain seizing up from panic. My feet kick at the ground, trying to move my body away, but it's like being in the beanstalk elevator again—I can't move.

The chigoe queen slips out of the antechamber. She's followed by the mass drones, and slowly, excruciatingly, they surround us.

"You're having a panic attack. Breathe, cowboy!" Mimi implores me, but it's no use. I can't.

They click their mandibles in unison. But they don't scream. The queen scuttles forward so that she's standing at my feet. The knife that I threw is still embedded in her shell, and she raises herself on all eight legs, so that she reaches my knee.

She inclines her shell, and I reach down to pull the knife out. The queen chatters. She sinks low to the ground, and all around the circle, the other chigoes do the same.

Not knowing what else to do, I touch my two middle fingers to my forehead and bow. They hum with delight, and the queen scuttles away, the drones following her in single file as they disappear into a dark tunnel.

Exhausted, I fall back on the ground, panting to catch my breath. I'm still shaking.

"Mimi," I ask. "Was this the right thing to do?"

"Right or wrong, you have no choice now," she says. "But if we're making moral judgments, then yes, you did the right thing."

"I didn't know you were programmed for moral judgments," I say, lifting Vienne into my arms.

"I wasn't," she says. "But I *am* capable of adaptive self-programming. Just like you."

"Thanks," I say because I can't think of anything else, and what would be the point? She can already read my mind and knows what lives within my heart.

CHAPTER ∞

Near Outpost Tharsis Two, Tharsis Plain
ANNOS MARTIS 238. 7. 13. 11:59

The road ahead unwinds like a coil of wire toward Olympus Mons and its cousins, a family of volcanoes thousands of kilometers from Hell's Cross. As the sign for a petrol station rises into view, I cut the power on the snowmobile and drift into one of the pumping islands. All the station's signs are written in the bishop's Latin, with prices crossed out. In front and behind us is a pock-marked landscape formed by volcanic lava flow. The sky is dark, the clouds low, swift, and angry, and I wonder if this was what the Earthers saw when they first settled the planet.

My snowmobile, like me, is caked with dust, and when Vienne slides off the seat and beats the soil out of her miners coveralls, the stiff wind makes us look like a rolling dirt devil. She unstraps her helmet and shakes out her hair.

"You ought to keep that on," I say. "Might be bounty hunters hereabouts, and there's a price on your pretty head, after all."

"If there are bounty hunters in this godforsaken wilderness, they should worry about me, not the other way around." She walks past the station clerk, a swaybacked old woman dressed in a tattered blue CorpCom jumpsuit.

"Mimi?"

"I read only three biosignatures, cowboy."

Silently, I nod. That's what I thought. It's better to be safe, though, when you're a wanted man.

"This way to the latrine?" Vienne says, too loudly. It seems innocent enough. In reality, she's sizing the woman up, a hand near the armalite she has strapped underneath her jacket. Despite what she says, the bounty on our heads— a gift from Dame Bramimonde, who swore charges of murder against us—makes her cautious.

The clerk nods. "You're a long way from home, miner."

Vienne barely glances at the woman as she passes.

"Pumps need to be hand-cranked, mud puppy." The old woman pushes me aside and starts pumping the fuel into the tank. "Won't nothing electronic work out here. Satellites and dust see to that. Hope you got coin on—oh." She sees that my hand is missing a finger.

I'm thankful to have both the miners' payment and the missing half of the Dame's fee, which the miners decided the Dame owed me and lifted from her purse before she left. Of course, it only inspired the Dame to add grand theft to her charges against us.

I hand her coin in payment and display my hand like it's

nothing to be ashamed of. "Lost it to a Manchester when I was a kid. Thanks for the help with the pump."

"Funny things, them Manchesters. Most times, they take off a man's whole arm. Never seen a snowmobile with wheels before."

"It's a custom job." Spiner did it for us when we left Fisher Four. It was a going-away gift from the miners and Fuse and Jenkins, who decided to remain at Hell's Cross and leave military service behind. Though I couldn't blame them for staying, we miss their company. Well, I do. Can't say the same for Vienne.

"Where you two headed?"

"Outpost Tharsis Two. Know it?"

Fuel spills out of the tank. The clerk curses and shuts off the pump.

"I'll take that as a yes."

"You got a death wish, son? Most of Tharsis Two is controlled by Mr. Lyme's men, and what ain't is full of angry spirits."

I know all about Mr. Lyme. It's the reason I'm looking for the outpost. "What do you mean, angry spirits?"

The old woman lowers her voice. "Men killed by unseen forces. Meat stripped clear down to the bones. Folk used to say it was the Dræu, but they ain't been in these parts for half a year. And the Dræu always left marks, if you know what I mean."

"That I do." I think of the rumors we've heard the past

couple of weeks as we've traveled north from the mines—unexplained deaths, usually blamed on the Dræu or other boogeymen. The possibility that it might be the chigoe turns my stomach. "Still, that's where the work is. Tharsis Two."

"Hope you're getting paid a fair wage, then," she says.

While she's cleaning up the last of the spill, Vienne returns. She slides onto the seat behind me and lets her head, for a moment, rest on my back.

"All set?" I ask her.

"Affirmative," she says, and I can almost hear her smile. "All systems copacetic."

The old woman grabs my forearm. "If I can't change your mind, then may god let your death be a beautiful one." She holds up a hand. The pinkie is missing. She makes the sign of the Regulator and bows. "One eye. One hand."

"One heart," Vienne says as she puts on her helmet.

"We're not Regulators," I say. "Not anymore."

"Once a Regulator, always a Regulator, son." She shakes her head. "Watch yourselves out there. Watch the road, too. There's a fresh hell of trouble waiting at the end of it."

"That's funny." I gun the engine. "There was hell at the beginning of it, too."

With a nod to the old woman, I point the snowmobile toward the towering image of Olympus Mons, which is now my guiding star. As we accelerate, the foothills streak by, a vast volcanic plain filling up our horizon.

"'Boundless and bare," Mimi says, "the lone and level sands stretch far away.'"

"Wordsworth?"

"Shelley," she says. "I've told you that a thousand times."

"One hundred seventeen times, to be precise," I say, flipping down my visor and leaning over the handlebars. "But who's counting?"

Acknowledgments

Many heartfelt thanks to those folks who read and critiqued the early drafts of *Black Hole Sun*: Patti Holden, Denise Ousley, Steve Exum, Julie Prince, Shannon Caster, Lindsay Eland, Lauren Whitney, and Jean Reidy.

To all the bookmakers at Greenwillow: Martha, Tim, Paul, Michelle, Barbara, Lois, Steve, Sylvie, and Virginia. And to Emilie, Laura, and Patty in HarperCollins Children's school and library marketing.

To my fabulous agent, Rosemary Stimola.

Finally, to Deb, Justin, Caroline, and Delaney, for not letting me get the big head.